# Titus of Pompeii

Ken Frazier

# DEDICATION

I would like to thank artists Billy Tackett and Kevin Stephenson for their contributions to the cover art and maps, respectively. Also Brenda Stephenson and my fellow authors, Charles Carfagno Jr. and Carla Christopher, for great editorial suggestions. Thanks also to the staff at Waid Books. Finally, I would like to thank my wife, Leigh, for indulging my creative side, and for putting up with so many nights on the computer.

.

# Table of Contents

*Cast of Characters:*

Vibiana – dead woman and prostitute
Titus – blacksmith
Livia – wife of Titus
Gallus – deceased father of Titus
Gallianus – brother of Titus (away with legions in Brittania)
Aule – fishmonger and friend
Gordianus – customer of blacksmith
Loreius – city Prefect of Pompeii
Crispus – friend and Pompeii guard twin
Palindus – see Tarquinus; Mithran exile in Egypt
Primus – Pompeii guard and twin of Crispus
Septimus - Officer of guard of Pompeii
Portius – older soldier of the guard, senior to Primus and Crispus
Blandus – former Mithran prisoner from Herculaneum
Pentius – young soldier of the guard at Marina gate
Scaevolus – the Mithran from Herculaneum
Silvanus – high priest of temple of Venus
Tacitus - Priest of Isis
Tarquinus-alias for Palindus, a Mithran who had the medallion
Zahret - Bearded merchant of Alexandria, boyfriend of Vibiana
Marcus – messenger boy
Dorian – high priest of temple of Isis
Dania – infant daughter of Titus and Livia
Alycia – barmaid and friend of Titus
Cassia – Livia's mother
Lucius Batallius – patrician citizen of Herculaneum, duovir and art collector
Aerulius – son of Palindus and a friend of Scaevolus
Marius – Livia's father

Leto – Livia's brother

Antonio Menando – Equestrian neighbor of Titus, husband of Helena

Helena Menando – Equestrian neighbor of Titus, wife of Antonio

Claudius Antonius Aquilinus - patrician citizen living in Aequana

Aelia – wife of Claudius and resident of Aequana

# MAP OF POMPEII

1) Marina Gate
2) Temple of Jupiter
3) Temple of Apollo
4) Forum
5) Public Administration Building
6) Prefects Office
7) Temple of Vesta
8) Market
9) Temple of Venus
10) Grainery
11) Forum Plaza
12) Shrine to Augustus
13) Herculaneum Gate

14) Castellum Gate
15) Temple of Isis
16) Lupanare
17) Stabiane Bathhouse
18) Teatro Grande
19) Stabia Gate
20) Aquila Neighborhood
21) Blacksmith Shop
22) Amphitheatre
23) Nocera Gate
24) Nola Gate
25) Samo Gate
26) Entrance Plaza

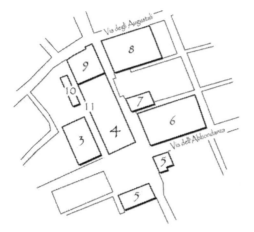

## MAGNIFIED AREA - POMPEII FORUM

3  Temple of Apollo
4  Forum
5  Public Administration Buildings
6  Prefects Office
7  Temple of Vesta
8  Market
9  Temple of Venus
10  Grainery
11  Forum Plaza

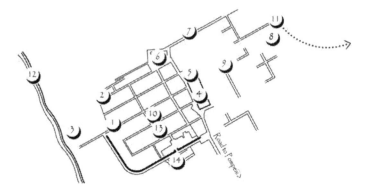

# MAP OF HERCULANEUM

1. House of Lucius
2. Library House
3. Beach
4. Forum
5. Temple of Augustus
6. Theatre
7. House of Scaevolus
8. House of Blandus
9. House of Marius/Cassia
10. Bathhouse
11. Trailhead to Mt Vesuvius Caves
12. Marina
13. Merchant's Shop
14. Palaestra

## Prologue

As I pounded the bronze piece in front of me smooth with several strokes of my mallet, my thoughts drifted to my brother. I had not seen him in over four years. Gallianus had joined the ranks of the Roman legion as soon as he was of age and left Pompeii for the glories of conquest and adventure late in Nero's reign. He had only been back twice since then. As my wife often reminds me, our blacksmith shop was most successful when the Roman legions were back in the province, in between their campaigns into the north and far west. During a brief period almost a decade ago, the legions were more concerned with events in and around the capital. The prospect of civil war loomed then. I was able to refit several cavalry officers with leather and tack for their horses. Our furnace was kept busy with fashioning and fixing pieces of bronze armor for the ferentarii and triarii of the legion elite. There are still soldiers here in Pompeii of course. They man the towers, ramparts and ballistrae which surround and protect our town, and provide the city magistrate with a security force he can use to maintain order and control. The city is surrounded by thick walls, with arched gates at six locations where outsiders may enter the city.

The guards of the wall that stay year round in Pompeii should not be confused with the powerful Praetorian Guard of the capital who guard the emperor. The soldiers who man Pompeii's ramparts are nothing like those troops, or the seasoned soldiers of Vespasian's legions. Several of the Pompeii guards are friends of mine and have no more military training than I. Others are too young, too old or just lazy, and are little more than the magistrate's personal bodyguard and errand boys. I think they would fare poorly in combat against the highly trained Roman legions who fight constantly in distant lands, against the uncivilized tribes of the north and west. I wondered how a blacksmith like myself would survive in wars with the Brigantes or Picts of Brittania. I doubted I would last through my first battle.

The protective walls and ramparts around our city were built and manned originally to help hold off the pirates who used to plunder port cities along the coast in decades and centuries past. These raids are a distant memory kept by only the very oldest in our town. Through the might of Rome and its powerful armies dating to the time of the great Julius and Tiberius almost a century ago, these shores have been largely free of invading armies. Our greatest turmoil has come from politics within the capital city itself. After Nero died, several generals vied for control of the empire. That was a frightening time to be in the provinces. Power struggles between factions of competing armies of Rome led to the year of four emperors. Roman legions loyal to one or the other of their generals burnt many towns to the north and east, including the temple of Jupiter in Rome itself.

My brother was lucky to have missed most of the civil war, as he had just the year before joined the Legio III Augusta under the great general Marcus Antonius Primus. He was stationed at the fortress of Aquinicum along the Danube river in Pannonia when the early battles broke out. The Pannonian troops  fortunately declared their loyalty to Vespasian. Of course, Vespasian was victorious and eventually became the unchallenged ruler of all that is Roman, but he was once Legate of the Legion. In the past he led the soldiers in Judeah, and in his younger days was general in Brittania. While the armies of

Galba, Otho and Vitellius ravaged each other following Nero's fall almost a decade ago, the troops of Primus joined those of Mucianus, and under Vespasian's banner ultimately defeated Vitellius and his German legions at the battle of Bedriacum. My brother, who is now a member of the triarii, was injured in that battle. He healed in due time and eventually rejoined the Legion in the west. Vespasian just died this summer. He was succeeded as emperor by his son, Titus.

I was actually named after Titus Flavius Vespasian, the former emperor, not the current one. My uncle fought with him about thirty-five years ago in the wilds of Brittania and always boasted to my father of the general's fine qualities and bravery in battle. My father Galleus therefore named me Titus in his honor, not knowing my namesake and his son of the same moniker would both become emperor of Rome and all of its provinces! My uncle's stories were what convinced my brother to join the legion in the first place. Vespasian was a much better ruler than most of his predecessors. There have been no civil wars in a decade. Nero, Caligula and Tiberius were all trouble for our citizens and taxed us heavily. Vespasian was a man of the people. After the battle of Bedriacum, Vespasian was proclaimed emperor by the senate. After that, parts of the Legio III dispersed, some going back to Judeah, Pannonia or Dalmatia. Gallianus returned to Pompeii and stayed for a time to mend his broken bones. Many other soldiers also came to Rome and the southern provinces in the lull after the civil wars. I profited briefly from the soldier's need for metalsmith and leather work. Equipment needed mending, dents needed straightening and some soldiers (especially the rare centurions around) had enough silver denariis to buy some new gear. I made several belts for the soldiers at that time, the cinculum militaire style, with their many leather pteruges hanging in front.   Eventually, Gallianus and his companions left for Brittania and joined the Legio XX Augusta under the famous general Agricola. I am glad that Gallianus was able to stay with my father at that time, for Galleus died only a few years later. Gallianus has been back home only once in almost a decade, when the legions were briefly recalled to Rome. It is said the Legio XX Augusta are fighting the Brigante barbarians in the north of Brittania at present, but we seldom get news of their exploits.  I envy Gallianus, for he has seen much of the world in his travels, and has battled enemies in Gaul and Germania. Because of his courage and valor, I am sure he will eventually be made centurion. I hope he can one day return to Pompeii.

I finally quit daydreaming about soldiers, brothers and war, and my thoughts returned to the job in front of me. I was crafting the four bronze horns that make up raised points on the typical Roman saddle.  Two larger ones go in front, and the two smaller horns are in the back of the saddle, with two layers of stretched leather formed over the top.  I finished pounding the curved boot shaped piece of bronze over the rounded granite boulder with my large hammer. The metal was taking shape nicely and would complement the bronze buckles and fine leather straps I had already fashioned for this tack. The rich client who had commissioned the saddle was picky. I was taking extra time to do it right, but this would bring a nice income for my family once I was finished. My concentration was broken again by the appearance of a boy at the front door of the shop who was staring intently at me as I finished hammering.

# Titus of Pompeii

## Chapter 1: The Egyptian Villa

The cryptic message from Vibiana was delivered by one of the many young street peasants found in the Lupinare district of Pompeii. He was no more than seven, and was probably a child of one of the poorer prostitutes—most likely a slave. His face was dirty, as were his clothes, and he wore no sandals on his little feet.

"The lady said to come to her house as soon as you can. It is urgent, and bring your hammer and other tools." he said.

I handed him a copper coin, and then he flew off down the vicolo dell Efebo (Avenue of Cadets) toward the more familiar alleyways of his own neighborhood. It took some time to file the sharp points of metal off of the edges of the curved pieces and to polish them with pumice, but I eventually reached a good stopping point. After close examination of my handiwork, I was finally satisfied and I tidied up around my workspace and placed my tools in my traveling satchel.

Our family blacksmith shop has been a fixture in the southern neighborhoods of Pompeii for almost fifty years. It faces the Via di Castricio (Boulevard of the Geldings) and is just a throw of a stone from the giant villa of the Menando family. The shop sits in front of our two story villa at the corner of Castricio and Efebo. It is a nice location, halfway between the giant amphitheater with its adjacent grand palaestra to the northeast, and the quadriportico and adjacent two outdoor theatres towards the marina side to the southwest. The shop has two large wooden doors which open to a small marble floored portico and enclosed working area with a dirt floor. The shop backs up to a small open terrace with a nice sunny garden, and is bordered by our living quarters. We used to live up stairs, but moved into the larger bedroom and kitchen downstairs after father died. The baby now shelters in the small upstairs bedroom. The proximity to the Stabia gate provides easy access for farmers outside of town to our workshop and also allows those from the marina in our natural harbor a quick detour around town to gain access to our store. From the Stabia gate it is only an hour's carriage ride to the village of Stabia to the south.

Inside the shop, the space is tight with the central furnace and bellows taking up the center of the room and two large dunking tanks on either side. Leather straps, cutting shears, clamps, smoothing stones and other leather and metal working tools are strewn about or hang from a series of wooden hooks attached to the wall. My favorite mallet (actually a large bevel hammer) usually sits prominently on the wall shelf to the back, but it has already been placed in my satchel for use at Vibiana's. There are two small benches that allow a place for both my wife to work the bellows while I pound and form the metal, and a bench to work the leather. Everybody wonders how my skinny wife can work the bellows. She is quite proud of her ability to utilize her arms and legs simultaneously, and get just the right amount of air to the fire and coals, but her method is pretty unorthodox. She has mastered this technique, but her aptitude as bellows master was gained through practice and necessity rather than by any driving desire for professional competence. I had to tear her away from her other interests and hobbies, as we have no other hands to help us in the shop. My brother never wanted to follow the family legacy and couldn't wait to join the legion instead of apprenticing with the paterfamilias as a blacksmith. Although we are property owners, and members of the Pompeii middle class, we cannot afford to own slaves like the patrician or equestrian classes of our town, who comprise the elite. Many middle class men also own a few slaves, but I can barely afford to feed my wife and child. She has to do all of the cooking and cleaning as well as help in our blacksmith shop.

There are many slaves in this city and most work daily in the shops and markets, or as domestic servants in the homes. In fact, almost a fourth of our inhabitants are of the slave class, and many more work in the olive groves in the surrounding countryside for the landowners. Some of these are of foreign birth, from the distant shores across the Mediterranean seas and some from far beyond the ancient towns of Greece in the great plains of the East. Many of the men have been captured in campaigns of the army in Germania and Gaul by the legions. However, most have lived in Pompeii for their entire lives and have been born into the slave class, or were transported here as children after being bought in the slave markets of Rome. In any case, they are primarily in service to the high-born who govern, own and otherwise dominate most of the actions and directions in Pompeii. It is only the lucky (and more well to-do) in the Plebian class who has slaves to cook, care for children or work in the craft shops and markets for their owners. So Livia is stuck with working in the shop daily, manning the bellows, crafting artful designs on leather and enticing street side customers in the front door. All the while, she has to nurse and care for our infant daughter. I hope someday to afford enough wealth to provide her with a domestic servant of our own to do the home chores.

Less than two hours after the visit from the little peasant boy, I finally shuttered the large wooden doors to the shop, went through the small terrace and into the dwelling chambers of our villa. I kissed my wife goodbye (despite her somewhat suspicious glances in my direction) and headed down the cobblestone pavement toward the entertainment quarter. It is only a short fifteen minute walk to Vibiana's place, but I wanted to get there before dark as I was feeling the first pangs of evening's hunger. I can't understand why Vibiana didn't just come to the shop herself if she needed work done around her house. She has money. Besides, I'm a craftsman, not a handyman, I reflected. As I entered the evening air, it still felt warm and dry. The weather in late summer can be stifling, but the last few days had been beautiful, with some welcome rain during the day and a nice breeze off of the Mediterranean Sea to cool the mid day's heat. It would be a couple of months before frost would come with the cold night air. I love Pompeii this time of year, when the fruits are ripe, the vegetables are plentiful in the markets, and the mountain's shadow casts long and imposing to the northwest.

Walking down the two lane Via dell' Abbondanza (avenue of Abundance--this is one of the main thoroughfares in Pompeii), I was hit by the putrid stench of the house waste washing down the gutters by the walk. Crap mixed with urine mixed with rotting vegetation even the neighborhood dogs won't eat. I am used to this stench, having lived here all of my life, but it can be overpowering at certain times of the day (first thing in the morning comes to mind!). As more people use the faucets and watering troughs along the sides of the main road, and as the day progresses, the overflow of water helps push the mess down into the flowing sewer canal and out of the city. In some parts of Pompeii, like near the stables, this smell is masked by the somewhat more pleasing aroma of horse dung. As I was thinking to myself that I much prefer the latter, I welcomed the sight of a two horse cart working its way toward me down the via. I recognize the driver as Aule the fishmonger. We wave simultaneously, and he smiled broadly. He must be bringing today's catch up from the marina boats. Aule is from an old Campanian family that has been netting fish for centuries in these waters. I was thinking to myself that the fish in his cart did not smell much better than the street, but as he drew near, the foul odor of street sewage was replaced by the scent of the two horses. Horse sweat reminds me of the country. I sometimes like getting outside of the town walls, where the air is fragrant with flowers, grasses and olive trees, instead of the barrage of smells from poop and garbage. There are downsides to city life.

"How are your beautiful wife and the new baby?" He asked. "Tell her she can come live with me if she ever tires of roasting around your smithy's bellows!"

I told him it beats reeking of dead fish, then added that I am out visiting a friend and wish him well. He stopped long enough to water his team at the street side trough beside me on the sidewalk. I also paused for a minute to admire his two bay mares. I go to his stables every six to eight weeks to trim their hooves. They are of the Hobby type of horse, common to this area. They have a wonderful ambling gate, pacing as they go, with the right and left legs alternating in parallel. People say these types of horses were brought by the Etruscans long ago from the East and were bred from the mighty warrior horses of the Persians.

Aule's horses were led to the fountain where they drank

readily from the trough in turn. After a long draft water, one mare pinned her ears and nipped at the other's neck for maneuvering the cart so that only the second could get to the water. Aule yelled something unintelligible and slapped the mare on the side with his switch. Soon we were both on our way, and the old fisherman continued down the Via dell Abbondanza northeastward toward the stables and his villa. I continued in a more southwestwardly direction past the palatial villa on my left. I worked inside that marvelous house at one time. It belonged to one of the city elders. I remember the beautiful fresco of a harpist which covered one wall of the main gallery. I marveled at its opulence, and remembered my father had installed the original pipe work in that mansion. The grounds alone took up almost the entire city block and each room held magnificent mosaics throughout.

Light was beginning to wane as I crossed the Via Stabiana and rounded the corner past the Stabiana neighborhood bathhouse and spa. This reminded me I needed to bathe tomorrow or the next day. Like most of our town residents, I try to clean up at least two or three times per week, and the baths are great for getting the sand and grime off. It is also a great time to catch up on all of the news from other people and is one of the most popular places to eat and to be entertained. Before the birth of our daughter, my wife could spend several hours there with her girlfriends and neighbors. We are blessed that our local magistrate provides this service for free to everyone in town—even the slaves. There are bathhouses in virtually every neighborhood. They have both cold and heated areas, and even steam rooms, provided by a

set of stout men working the fires underneath the floors of the pools. I helped place some of the underlying pipe work before the great mosaics were applied to the floors and walls, but the actual designs for the waterworks were implemented by the best architects in Rome. The building has a marble façade from top to bottom, with benches to sit and chat. One of the things about being a blacksmith is the number of different types of things I get to do. Naturally, I work with leather, copper and bronze, as well as a few other hard metals. I prefer to make tack and saddlery for horses, but I'll fashion any item that my clients need. I have made harnesses and reins for many of the carts which move merchandise back and forth upon the vias and vicolos of Pompeii. I have fashioned everything from bits to bridles. Unfortunately, most people in our city can't afford a horse, and so I don't have the chance to work on tack as often as other projects. In fact, I spend more time building and fashioning metal pipes in houses for the city's rich. These pipes weave their way through many of the walls of the houses in Pompeii and provide our citizens and more well-heeled plebeians with fresh water. That is how I was able to work on the spa pools in the Stabiane bathhouse. The pipes are made from Plumbum taken all of the way from mines in Britannia, and have to be formed and welded together to make the necessary connections for water to flow from the larger terra cotta pipes coming from the aqueducts. Terra Cotta is formed by the masons of the city, and so I work with them regularly. The pipes are drawn from a great fornix nearby that arises from the canal and regional aqueduct coming out of the mountains to the west and south. They drain into channels going below the houses into the surrounding street and the sewage combines with rain runoff, trough and fountain overflow and run into the gutters lining the streets of our great city, eventually flowing out into the countryside. It is a marvelous system of sanitation and this bit of Roman engineering marvel keeps the residents healthy. Before there were aqueducts and plumbing, we had many plagues and constant dysentery in our cities.

I learned to plumb from my father. He worked his entire life in my grandfather's blacksmith shop, but he hated animals, and preferred to work alongside other masons in building the homes and shops of the city. When he spent time working metal for some of the grand mansions owned by Roman senators in the capital city, he apprenticed in the process of tube making, and brought these plumbing techniques back to Pompeii. Until he died several years ago in one of the great plagues, he was the best of the city's craftsmen in forming the pipes out of the pliable metal, and flaming the ends together with small bits of resin. The pipes get even stronger with age and use, as the center builds up with a white lime coating, and even now years later, his pipes never leak! Most of the best houses in the city have used his talented services, and it is still a source of pride in our community to boast of "Gallus' plumbum in their villa"! I am not particularly gifted at working with Plumbum, at least never to my father's satisfaction, but I understand the trade and have made enough coin from pipe working to keep my grandfather's shop in business and to support my wife and family. Every decade or so, the pipe work needs to be cleaned out so the water continues to flow. That means I have steady work.

As I finally passed the last of the tall marble columns lining the Stabiane bathhouse, I was startled out of my daydreaming by a clear voice.

"TITUS! TITUS!"

It was Gordianus, who is one of my clients, and not the person I really wanted to be talking to at that moment. He approached from across the street and blocked my further progress along the walk.

"Where is my saddle?  Why aren't you working on them?  You know they are late.  I should have used a more reliable smithy.  You are not the craftsman your grandfather was...."

He seemed to be swaying slightly while he rambled on, which made his thick frame wiggle under his tunic.  I snickered and wondered if he was breaking into the family wine cask again.

He snorted, belched loudly and said he was "...off for a steambath and a rubdown."  "I want you to have my order ready by the week's end."

His manservant followed a few pedes behind, carrying linens and a basket filled with who knows what.  The slave shot me a knowing glance and rolled his eyes.  I had been working on Gordianus' damned tack for the past several days, but due to his large fat frame, it was taking longer than expected to complete.  In any case, we needed the money and he was an important person in Pompeii with influential friends who may be future clients.  After I apologized profusely, nodded in assurance at his demands and boasted about the fine embellishments I was working to add to the piece, he seemed placated and stumbled on to the spa with his servant.

Once finally clear of Gordianus the bore, I reached another intersection, where there was a clear view of Vesuvius in the distance, and the pink and white rooftops of Herculaneum at its western base.  The sun was just setting in the west, so the last light of day cast a hue of pink and violet over the cloud tops which perennially ring the dome of the great mountain.  I have never climbed to the peak of Vesuvius, but Gallianus has. He said from its summit you can see all of the way to Rome and across the sea. He said that the view is beautiful, but the journey to reach it is treacherous. He tells of a steep and jagged trail, with foul vapors, and believes the rim is haunted by spirits. Those lands were once the dominion of Hercules, who first conquered the demons on the slopes of the mountain. Gallianus (little Galleus, named for my father) claimed to climb the slopes of Vesuvius only as proof of his bravery and aptitude for the legion, but he swore to me that he won't ever go back. I have been to Herculaneum in the shadow of the mountain several times—the first as a small boy with my grandfather to meet some distant relatives, and later when I met my future wife. I have done metalwork there many times in the past few years in the grand palaces lining the beach. We visit there often, as it is only a half day's journey. My wife's family still lives there, and her father and brother fish the shores of the clear Mediterranean waters. She says she still misses its wonderful beach with its inviting surf, and the cool rains that come from the mountain. As I made the final turn to my destination, these reflections made me yearn for a country walk. I reminded myself that I needed to leave our city's walls and venture out into the countryside more often. The healers say the fresh air helps clean the body and rid it of disease. I wondered if a jaunt in the country could help with the feeling of melancholy and impending dread that I have held these past few weeks.

I finally reached the veranda where Vibiana lived and worked, just off of the main avenue of via Lupanare (Boulevard of Brothels) near the corner of vicolo dell Balcone Pensile (street of the hanging balcony). It is a nice villa, with a pleasant terrace, a few olive trees and potted plants in abundance.

There is a small shallow reflection pool in the center of

the terrace, with green marble mosaic tile lining the bottom. As I made my way along the stone path to the living quarters, I noted that the surroundings seemed strangely quiet, given that it might be considered "working hours" around here. At the opening of the portico, I came to the door, which was surrounded and covered by a small white limestone colonnade. Just to the right of the door, I examined a beautiful painted fresco on one wall, in ochre, gray and blue paint. Careful examination of the subject matter made me blush slightly. The female partner was barely clothed and appeared to be in the throngs of ecstasy as she straddled her heavily muscled, erect lover. His expression brought a wash of past images and pleasurable memories flooding through my head. Wow, I thought, that is some successful storefront advertising. I mulled over the intent of placing this image in the foyer of her business, and wondered what I could add to the shop front wall to make people think about blacksmith work. Somehow, I didn't think a picture of a horse would have the same effect.

Unlike most of the other working girls in the entertainment quarter, Vibiana is an effete prostitute, who caters to the upper classes. She is quite beautiful, and her light colored hair is unusual for women in Pompeii. She came from a plebeian family who struggled to keep everyone fed. In her mid- teens, due to impressive beauty and striking blonde hair, she garnered the favor of an older magistrate. She eventually became his concubine and was set up in her own villa. This afforded her money, prestige and influence unheard of for most girls of her age. After his passing, she had acquired enough money from her lover by her twenties to own her own property, and her "business" apartment now even boasted a soft bed and linen fabrics! Most of the poorer prostitutes in the quarter kept busy entertaining the steady stream of sailors and merchants who ventured into town from our busy port. Hard beds, cold walls and dark rooms— a steady line of men in and out the door. Not Vibiana; she maintains a clientele of patrician dignitaries from Rome and Ostia. Rumors have swirled for years that she has even been visited by a senator. I have known her since we were young, and we have remained steadfast friends, in spite of our different circles and largely separate lives. As we both share light colored hair, we were often confused for siblings in our youth, though I do not believe we are related. I have never known her bed, although in my early adulthood I spent many wine-filled evenings farther down the Via Lupanare with the poorer girls. It was a rite of passage in Pompeii for young local men to gain worldly experiences in that quarter. "Follow the phallus" was the standard joke among the teens of my youth. This euphemism described the penis-shaped beacon, carved as signs on the walls of nearby street corners, allowing directional navigation to Pompeii's most notorious attractions.

The penis-shaped street signs were an aid to wandering drunken sailors (who often lacked knowledge of the local layout or even of the language) and were a boon to the local economy. Similar reliefs of grape clusters advertised the route to the wine bars in the adjacent sections of town. With the coming of the baby, I no longer have the interest nor extra money to waste on such frivolities. I don't miss the Lupanare. I come home to Livia every night and can't afford the complications that come with outside trysts anyway. I am not expressly forbidden from venturing there, but my Liv has the temper of Juno and the battle reflexes of Mars, when it comes to sharing my affections with the slave girls of Lupanare. I would have to tender my bruises for weeks afterward, and would likely be sleeping upstairs with my daughter for several days.

I called out to Vibiana through her doorway. When I received no reply after two attempts, I looked in the window on the left, adjacent to the door. The apartment appeared to be in a mess. I hadn't visited for a few months, but it didn't appear to have been cleaned in at least that time, as things were thrown all over the floor. That struck me as unusual, as I always considered her a very neat person. More importantly, her parlor is her place of business, where she meets the gentlemen she has as her clients. Something about this did not seem right. I entered the doorway and looked around. No, this was definitely wrong. There were pillows on the floor shredded open, and small objects scattered everywhere. Several amphora were broken in the hallway and their oil was leaking out into puddles across the marble of the floor. I moved from the foyer into the bedroom, and suddenly froze in fear. The bed was in shambles and a dark red spot, several digitii across, stained the linens. I called out again for Vibiana and looked all over the room and under the linens of the bed in a futile (and stupid) attempt to find her unconscious body. I was now really confused, and I wondered again why she wanted to have me here. I also questioned why she asked to bring along my tools? Did she hire some other mason to fix a problem around the house and he ended up trashing the place? I glanced down at the cloth bag in my left hand and noted a few clamps, pliers and the large hammer. I should have come earlier.

"Why was the house ransacked?" I wondered. One of her clients must have wanted to hurt or rob her! I looked again at the blood spot on the bed linens, with a matching red spot on an adjacent pillow and some blood on the floor. Not a huge amount of blood. "She is probably fine," I assured myself. "But where is she? Did she run away in fear? Did she go to the magistrate to protest? And when?"

I just received the message from the little boy only a little over two hours or so ago. I cursed myself for not dropping everything and coming as soon as I heard from the child. But the peasant boy didn't say anything about the house being torn up or that Vibiana was hurt. I walked through the house again and noticed that many of the scattered and broken objects on the floor were Egyptian amulets. I picked up a light blue carved soapstone object by my feet. It was the figure of a male god or a pharaoh with a typical Egyptian headdress and a short thin chin beard. The arms were crossed with two crook staffs in each arm. The legs had been broken off and were lying nearby. Near it on the floor, there was also a much larger figurine painted in gold, red and black. I recognized this as Isis, the Egyptian goddess of life. There was another similar and even more ornate jeweled statue of Isis on the other side of the room that sat in pieces. I saw candles and scarab beetles made of fine lapis lazuli also littered on the floor. It was then that I noticed a few more drops of blood in a linear trail moving towards the door. I bent down and touched the still wet, but congealed substance and tasted the tip of my finger with my tongue. Salty, bitter, yes it was blood. I examined an alcove on one wall, which was empty, but for a single candle laying sideways on its base and a small candle holder beside it. On the back wall of the alcove was a beautiful fresco of a person with a shaved head.

I recognized it as another picture of Isis, but an unusual representation. This was the Isis as manly deity, and it was painted with incredible skill by one of the finest of Pompeii's artisans. This only further confirmed that the house belonged to a devoted follower of the Egyptian goddess. I recalled that Vibiana had venerated the Egyptian gods and goddesses and was a follower of the temple. Until that moment, however, I hadn't really understood the depth of Vibiana's religious beliefs. Many locals frequently worship at the Temple of Isis in Pompeii, but I have never seen this many religious objects in anyone's house, and especially of this quality (and cost). Vibiana must have spent most of her income and a good portion of the old magistrate's fortune on furnishing this studio.

Although Venus is the patron of Pompeii, and there is a very large temple dedicated to her in the center of town (at the northwest entrance to the large central courtyard), there are multiple deities that are worshipped in Pompeii. There are hundreds of devotees of Apollo and Jupiter, and temples here are dedicated to both, but neither is as grand as the temple to our beloved Venus. There is a statue of Venus adorning the central square and the one in the temple of Venus is fashioned of the finest bronze. A surrounding marble and travertine sanctuary in the temple is both impressive and imposing in its splendor. Gold, silver and alabaster are found throughout the inner sanctum and the large painted bronze goddess at center of the cella is breathtaking. The temple of Apollo, which is situated on the southwest corner of the forum plaza, is also an impressive site, surrounded by beautiful travertine columns and an equally large statue of the god in the center of its dais. The temple of Jupiter is a little larger than the one dedicated to Apollo (as it should be), and is located just inside the city walls adjacent to the Marina gate on the west side of the city. The statue of Jupiter there is a little larger than the one of Venus and is also outlined in gold relief, but it is not as elaborately painted as the statue of our city's patroness.

There is also a cult of Hercules in Pompeii, due to our proximity to Herculaneum. Many of Hercules' famous deeds were performed in the area surrounding Vesuvius, although it is said that his twelve great labors were performed in Greece before coming to the shores and lands near Rome. The herculean cult followers don't venerate their demigod in a temple, but there are shrines to his image in shops and houses all over the city and a wonderful marble fountain sits in the forum with a beautiful statue of his image grappling the lion. There are also a variety of other smaller cults. Of these, probably the most visible is the one dedicated to Isis, with a temple that is both elaborate and richly decorated, but somewhat smaller in size than those of the Roman gods. The temple sits a few blocks to the northwest of the forum. Religious ceremonies in honor of the Egyptian goddess are performed at sunrise and around mid-day, highlighted by chanting and incense. Animal sacrifices are performed by the priests during special festivals during which many local women dance and sing in front of the temple. In fact, one of the Isis festivals of resurrection just concluded a couple of weeks ago. We have many festivals this time of year, when the summer harvest is underway and fruits and vegetables are plentiful.

I have seen many private shrines to the Egyptian gods in the houses of Pompeii, when I have been called to install or fix the plumbing. I even remember seeing a large painting of Isis and some wonderful carved figurines in the great villa of Loreius, our current town magistrate. However, none of these private shrines, that I ever recall, have matched the splendor and scope of Vibiana's house. The number of the figurines and Egyptian amulets lying about the floor simply amazed me. I noted figures dedicated to Horus, Anubis the dog god, and a short round funny figure that I recognized as Bes. I am not very familiar with the Egyptian gods, though I understand that they are quite powerful. Isis and Horus have some kind of connection to resurrection and the afterlife, but I don't remember the stories. I thought to myself perhaps if I attended more of the festivals, I would have become more familiar with the other gods, and would then have understood better what I was seeing in this room.

I was still feeling confused and many thoughts about Egyptian magic, gods, and the meaning of amulets were racing through my head at once as I decided to leave Vibiana's apartment. As I moved toward the portico, I noticed a strange leather object near the door. I reached down and picked it up and discovered it was a scabbard, but one I had never seen before. As a blacksmith and worker of leather, I am familiar with a whole variety of these implements which sheath knives. I have seen both hard and soft cases, as well as ornate, bejeweled scabbards, and the simple functional varieties that are used commonly by the fisherman to house the blades with which they clean their fish. This scabbard consisted of thick dark leather, and had a large figure of a bull in bronze along its length, with two prominent bronze horns protruding beyond the leather. It also contained strange ornate swirling markings on its surface, and had small gemstones embedded in the leather and unusual writing on its back surface. This was an extremely expensive piece of leather crafted by a talented artisan. Although I cannot read Greek or Roman script like the scholars in Rome, I recognized that the markings were not of the alphabet. Nor were they Egyptian hieroglyphics. Instead, the scrollwork was of a language or design that was foreign. The scabbard also appeared to house a large knife, and was therefore not something I would have expected Vibiana to own. When I turned the leather over, I noticed that the straps were torn on the back side. I tried to make sense of the objects and ramshackle surroundings, but as these events were circling in my brain, all I really felt was light headed. I was intent on leaving, but for some reason that I couldn't readily explain, I decided to bring the scabbard with me and threw it in my satchel. I would regret that decision later. I was relieved when I finally exited the portico and entered the night's air. The sun had completely set in the west, and the quiet of twilight had settled on Pompeii.

As I moved through the small terrace and rounded the corner to the gate of Vibiana's property, I noticed the young boy hiding behind a corner of the vestibule. Only half of his upper body was visible, and he had a concerned look on his face. When I came up to him, he tried to flee, but I was able to grab his arm and he settled in front of me.

"What is your name?" I asked. "Come on boy; tell me, what is your name?"

"Marcus, he said, my name is Marcus."

"Where is the mistress Vibiana?" I asked. "Where is the lady who gave you the message to send to me?"

"She's gone. I think she went with the scary man," he said.

"What man?" I asked in desperation.

"The dark headed man in the tunic. He was yelling at her in the room."

This revelation frightened me even more than seeing the condition of her apartment. "Marcus, tell me exactly what you saw".

He began, "I ran back to the villa to tell the woman that I delivered the message like she wanted, and I hoped she would give me another copper coin. But there was a man yelling and things crashing inside. He scared me with his loud voice, and I hid out here by the terrace. There were a lot of loud noises coming from the bedroom and screams. I saw the dark man come out on to the porch in front and I ran down the street because I thought he saw me. He might have gone back inside with the woman. He scared me. I don't know what happened after that. I was afraid, so I stayed in that alley down there for a long time, but when I saw you coming towards the house, I hid here by the terrace again. Then you came out of her house and grabbed me and hurt my arm."

I realized I was still clamping down on his wrist very hard, and I released. "I apologize Marcus, I didn't mean to hurt or scare you," I told him. "I only want to find Vibiana. How long ago did you see the man with her?"

He said the man was here when he came back from my shop, which could have been no more than a few hours ago, and the man was gone now.

"Did you see which way the lady or the man went when they left?" I asked, and the little boy just shrugged. I gave him a small coin from my satchel and he scurried off down the street. I didn't know what had happened to Vibiana or who the man was, but I had a bad feeling of foreboding that things were going to get ugly. I was right.

I moved off the Via dell Lupanare and turned on to the Vicolo dell Balcone pensile towards the central plaza. I needed a glass of wine to calm my nerves. The bar was near the grainery across the plaza of the forum, and it was a little out of the way. In fact, it was in the opposite direction of my house. It was a comfortable spot and they served food and wine of high quality. I was friends with one of the waitresses there. If Vibiana had gone this way, maybe I could catch up to her and get the story about the man and her mess of a house. I was sure that Livia wouldn't mind me taking a while to get home based on the circumstances. I figured a slight detour to the bar was justified, especially once she heard of the weird events of the trip over here. As I walked, I had the weirdest sensation that I was being watched or followed, but every time I turned around I saw nothing. The vicolos were still quiet at this early hour of the evening. I glanced back and forth again and saw no one on either side of the street.

As I crossed into the area of the forum, I looked around briefly for Vibiana but did not see her or hardly anyone else. Everyone was probably at home preparing their evening meal, the coena, at this time of the evening. The forum is the central hub of our town and is beautiful. A large rectangular open plaza is bordered on the west by a long tall building which stores grain for the city, and adjacent to it sits the temple of Apollo. Across from the temple to the north is the somewhat smaller temple of Vespa, with its famous virgin attendants. To the southeast are the public administration buildings where the council elders conduct the business of the city. Just to the left of the temple of Vespa as you look from the center of the forum plaza is the Macella with its vegetable and fruit stands, and where the butcher provides meat for the residents as well as sacrificial animals for the temples. Most importantly, and most impressively, is the temple which sits across one end of the forum as you look toward the mountain. This is the grand temple, and is dedicated to our goddess Venus.

I entered the forum from the north side on Via degli Augustali, passing through the great marble arch and shrine dedicated to the famous long lived Roman emperor. I considered how Caesar Augustus had brought glory to the empire, and expanded our borders to the edge of the world. It was hard to imagine how a blacksmith could ever hope to take part in such monumental events.

I walked along the quiet passage with the market on my left and the tall imposing grand temple of Venus on my right.

## CHAPTER 2: MURDER IN THE TEMPLE

As I entered the forum near the entrance to the temple, I heard a loud scream. This was not a scream of fright or even one of distress, but rather the howl of someone in pain who was trying to call out to the very gods in Olympus. It sounded like the wail of an animal, and if anyone else would have been nearby in the forum they would surely have turned and noticed. Thinking it could have been Vibiana, I took off towards the sound to my right with a renewed sense of urgency and sped across the grass and into the area in front of the temple of Venus. I ran up the steps and heard some sobbing coming from inside of the delubrum in the vestibule of the temple. I am not sure what possessed me to take matters into my own hands. I didn't even know for sure if the screamer was someone I knew. But I thought I recognized that voice, that high pitch wail, and there was a great chance that it was Vibiana. I am not a particularly brave man, and I am certainly no soldier, but I was worried for my friend. I raced up the last of the sixteen limestone steps of the temple façade to the entrance. I hurried past the marble columns into the entranceway. There in the hallway leading to the sanctuary, was the body of a woman. She was laying prone on the tile, clothed in a pale white linen dress, and her blonde hair obscured her face. I knew in an instant that it was Vibiana and I ran to her. As I approached, I noticed that there was a huge pool of blood surrounding her midsection. Her gown was painted with blood and her pale face appeared bruised. Blood matted some of the hair on the top of her head. I knelt down and lifted her head and shoulders to me.

"Vibiana, can you hear me, are you okay? I asked. Her eyes fluttered for an instant and she looked dreamily into my eyes.

"Titus." She muttered, and then she said, "It's bad."

I quieted her and examined the rip in her gown. It was worse than either of us could have imagined. There was a deep gash from her navel to just under her ribcage. It was a deep penetrating wound and her insides were poking out.

She looked up at me and gasped, "The Mithran, in Herculaneum, the medallion. Save us."

With that, her expression became pained and bits of blood came out of her mouth. She gurgled then gasped several deep breaths.

"It hurts." she said again, then her head fell from my hands, and her eyes rolled back in her head.

I could not keep the tears from welling up in my eyes as I held her limp body in my arms. I did not love her as a husband. But I did feel for her as if she were my own family, and cared for her almost as much as my brother. I had known her most of my life. I examined the huge bruise across her eye and forehead, and the huge red stain that colored her abdomen. I instinctively reached down to stop the bleeding on her stomach and hold her intestines inside her abdomen. After a few short moments, her eyes closed and her chest stopped heaving. The red stain above her waist now covered the entire front of her gown and much of the surrounding marble floor. I looked again at the penetrating stomach wound, and thought it resembled those from battle, even from a sword. I was sitting there holding her, and wondering who could possibly do this to such a kind woman, when I heard another scream.

I looked up from my lifeless friend's body in time to see two people staring in horror at me from across the room. They had just come up the steps of the temple to my right from the plaza. One was a man dressed in dark robes and carrying a small oil lamp and the other was a woman in a long flowing white robe holding a basket full of fruit, which she abruptly dropped. These were the high priest of the temple of Venus, and one of the vestal attendants of the temple of Vesta nearby. They were likely sharing offerings. The priest was someone who I knew, but I had only seen the woman once or twice. I was not a frequent visitor to either of the temples, but I had done some very personal and confidential work for the priest about five years ago in the sanctuary. Because of my "repairs", there had been a renewed interest in the temple and the priests had grown prosperous in the ensuing years with the increased attendance. I thought he still held me in high regard.

I said, "Thank Jupiter, you are here, Silvanus, go get help please. Vibiana needs a healer. She is mortally wounded!"

However, to my surprise neither person did as I asked and instead the woman ran towards me yelling, "Murderer, killer, defiler!"

The horrified priest just stood transfixed, muttering something to himself and fumbling with his gown with his free hand. He stared blankly at me. After a few moments he said something about going to the magistrate and hurried off in the opposite direction before I had a chance to explain myself. The robed woman approached me.

"You killed her" the attendant said accusingly, then added, "and in the temple. You have defiled and disgraced this holy place. Venus will have her vengeance."

I did not know what to do. A vestal virgin was a very important person in our society and one of only six of her position in the city. She had taken a vow of chastity in honor of the goddess Vesta, and her word carried the power of a priest or governmental official.

I kept saying, "Please go get help. We may yet save her", but I knew that it was already too late. Vibiana's face was ashen, and she lay in my arms unmoving. The amount of blood oozing from her abdominal wound was beyond what any person's body could withstand losing. As the attendant kept yelling loudly at me from a few pedes away, a crowd was beginning to form from passersby in the central plaza that eyed me suspiciously from the steps of the temple. They weren't coming in closer; probably for fear that I would try to kill them too. I heard a man say "get him", and another threw a stone that narrowly missed my head.

I kept hearing "She's bleeding, she's cut! He must have beaten her!"

I did not know what to do. From the front entryway, I left Vibiana's body on the marble and retreated away from the slowly approaching mob and farther into the temple toward the inner sanctum. I noticed the partial outline of a man hiding behind a column in one corner.

"This could be the killer", I thought to myself. "He is still here!"

If I could catch him, I could show the gathering crowd who the real murderer was. I quickly made my way towards the column at the back of the cella of the temple. As I ran toward him, he moved backwards away from the base of the column and off into the shadows. I could not see well in the darkness of the temple, so I pursued him slowly along the side colonade that lined the left side of the inner sanctum of the temple. I could no longer see him. This part of the temple lacked natural light and was backlit only with the light of candles that surrounded the sanctuary. Long shadows pervaded the space. The large draped bronze statue of Venus to my right looked eerily luminescent in this light, and the shining, candlelit golden dolphins and gigantic alabaster clam shell at her feet made the surroundings seem even more surreal. I stopped for almost a minute to listen and see if I could hear where he went. Nothing.

I moved slowly to the back of the altar and as I turned around the corner of the last ionic column, I was tackled from behind. While I was wondering how he could have maneuvered behind me, I suddenly felt the cold hard impact of a blunt fist across my left cheek. This left me momentarily stunned, but I was able to roll away from him and cover my face and protect from another blow as I maneuvered my body away from him on the ground. I was kicked in the ribs and immediately got to my hands and knees and turned toward the attacker as quickly as I could. I knew instinctively that another blow was coming, and put up my left arm just in time to block another punch to the face. I got to my feet and circled to my right and evaluated my attacker. Medium height and build with a dark beard. Another undercut blow came from below, but all he met were my crossed forearms. I grabbed his wrist with my left hand, twisted his elbow inward, and spun him away from me in an arm lock. I planted my left foot and sprung back at the man who was now facing slightly away from me. The force of my weight caught him completely off guard. We both tumbled together into the space behind another column. His head hit the travertine floor with a thud, and I thought that might have finished him. No, this man was in good shape and no stranger to fighting. We both stood up, but still intertwined and I could smell the perfumed oil emanating from his skin. He said something in a language I didn't understand, or at least with a heavy accent, and tried to hit me again with his right fist. My left arm came up and easily blocked this strike as he was too close to really get much leverage. My right hand jabbed him heavily in the stomach, and I followed with a left to his chin. Again he uttered something in a foreign tongue and backed up. I was thankful I spent so many hours of my youth sparring with my older brother. I was a pretty good fighter, but I was having trouble seeing out of my left eye and my cheek hurt. I was beginning to think I might get the upper hand, when he bull rushed me. I landed on my back and the wind was knocked out of my lungs. He was lying astride me and his dark beard and heavy breath smelled of wine and fish. My knee came up squarely between his two legs and did some damage to the underlying sensitive parts. He howled again and rolled off, but once he was up, he kicked me squarely in the side of the head before I could get to my knees. I called him a goat's mother and quickly got back up to my feet, but the original blow to the head left me a little groggy.

I said out loud, "Murderer, I will not stop until you are down or dead. Vibiana will be avenged."

He looked at me strangely then and put his hands down. In this brief respite when there was a lull in the fight, a sudden burst of light entered the sanctuary. I heard a door slam shut as the darkness returned. I looked to my right to see if there were more attackers coming, or if the mob of people out front were now coming for me and this man. When I turned back toward him, I saw the bearded man fleeing into the shadows behind the statue of Venus, and retreat through the same side exit of the temple where the door had just closed. He reopened the door, and headed out into the street before I could gain my senses and follow. I was dizzy from the beating I had taken and my damaged ribs made it difficult to breathe.

It was several long seconds before I got my wind and my head had cleared enough to pursue the bearded man. I kept shaking my head to think clearly, but all I could see was a blurry ten cubit tall statue of Venus to my right, and the dark outline of a huge marble altar to its left. My head hurt, but I knew I had to get out of there and find the bearded man again. I heard more yelling coming from the front of the temple. I finally got to my feet and stumbled toward the side door. I reached it, pushed it open and almost fell onto the steps in the night air. By this time, the light was almost gone and the stars were just beginning to appear. I looked both directions up and down the passage on the north side of the temple, but there was no sign of the bearded man. On my right, people were running towards the front of the temple from all over the plaza and their voices made up a panic-stricken cacophony. I had no idea what to do or where to go, but I didn't think staying here with the mob was a very good idea. Instead, I went northwest through the great arch of Augustus and down the Via degli Augustali back toward Lupanare. I crossed the Via Stabiana with as much stealth as possible and into the Aquila neighborhood a few blocks northwest of our shop. All the way back, I was ducking in and out of small alleyways and terraces in between the shops and houses of this business quarter to keep from being seen. I was innocent, but apparently the crowd of people around the temple didn't think so. If they caught up to me, I did not think I would be given a chance to explain the circumstances, much less prove my innocence. I could go directly to the magistrate and make him understand. I could plead my case and he could send the city soldiers out and find the bearded man. The bearded man, who was he? Why did he hit me? He must be the killer. Most likely a foreigner, here from one of the ships in port. He had an accent and spoke strange words during our fight. And he had a beard. As I stealthily worked my way towards my home, I considered the bearded man and his origin.

Beards are not common among the citizenry of Pompeii. We find them brutish, as they are more often typical of sailors from the south or uncivilized barbarians in the north. The Gaulic and Germanic men all wear beards, and they live in huts and caves and wallow in the dirt like jackals. It is said they even eat their own dead. Pompeian's follow the convention in Rome and in ancient Greece. Cultured gentlemen keep their faces clean of hair, not like the animals in the forest. The great athletes of our day and the mighty gladiators shave their faces, and indeed, their entire bodies. They say even the great Alexander did not allow his generals to wear facial hair, and Gallianus told me that he heard Julius Caesar had his hairs individually plucked from his face. While these days some men actually burn their hair off with hot coals, most of us use the razor which is sharpened with water and a wetstone. Some men in Pompeii have their servants shave them, but those of us without slaves usually go to the tonsor. He has a shop over on vicolo del Efebo near mine and uses a very sharp iron novacila to shave around the mouth, chin and neck. Beforehand, he applies steamed wet towels to our face to make the hair easier to cut and afterward he soothes the skin with more wet towels. He then layers on the spider web and vinegar paste which makes the little cuts heal. The novacila gets really close and only costs most people a single bronze coin. I was thinking a shave, warm towel bath and spiderweb paste would feel really great right now on my bruised cheekbones. I get my shaves for free since the tonsor has to bring the implements to me to rework the blade every two months. The iron that it is made from is a wonderful metal, but difficult to work with. I have two tools made of iron that I use to bend or cut other metals. My bevel hammer is made of iron and that is why I prize it so highly. Iron is not as expensive as tin (for which we make bronze), but it is equally as rare and harder to obtain. All of these thoughts were rambling through my brain as I made my way home.

I was beginning to wish I was a swordsmith instead of a blacksmith. I could have really used a weapon at that moment to protect myself from any future attacks by the foreign bearded man. I have frequently imagined myself as a great arms-smith, able to forge the greatest of swords and small blades for the imperial army. In point of fact, I have rarely ever made a gladius for anyone except my brother, and never for any other of the Roman soldiers. It is difficult for one of my stature as a plebeian to obtain sufficient metal starting material to build a sword. Most of the legion's bronze gladius blades and shields are obtained via smiths in the great armories of the Roman republic in the capital city, not from unknown blacksmiths in the southern provinces. I can forge copper and tin into bronze, but the base metals are expensive to buy, and must be shipped from the old Etruscan quarries to the north. Gallianus received the only sword I ever constructed as a going away gift. I hope it has served him well.  There certainly was no time to fashion another sword now, even if I had the bronze to construct it with. Then it hit me. My tools were in my satchel, and included one rather large iron hammer.

"Goat's testicles!" I shouted, because at that moment I realized I did not have my tool satchel with me. I must have left it in the temple beside Vibiana. Perhaps I dropped it when I was attacked by the bearded man. This was a problem on multiple levels. The tools in that satchel were my livelihood. I used them every day in my work, and I can't afford to replace them. The hammer, in particular, is essential for almost everything I do. I thought again of the iron mallet. I could have used that to protect myself from the bearded man. Actually, during the fight I didn't have time to reach for the bevel hammer. I only had time to react. But I could sure use it if and when he comes back or we meet up again. I could wield it like Apollo and fend off anyone, even with a sword. A blow from the iron head of the mallet might even bash through a centurion's helm, and a blow to the body would easily break limbs. I briefly considered going back into the temple and retrieving my hammer and other tools, but the thought of the mob seriously frightened me. They would undoubtedly stone me to death before I ever reached the vestibule.

"Oh goat's mother!"

It occurred to me that, even worse, they will find my tools lying next to Vibiana and that will just lead them right back to me. There is only one other blacksmith in Pompeii and he doesn't have a tool satchel like that. I was contemplating my options, when I finally reached the entrance to my house and shop. There was no time to waste. I needed to tell Livia what had happened and between us decide what to do.

## CHAPTER 3: EXPLANATION TO LIVIA

I took the side entrance from vicolo dell Efebo to avoid going through the shop doors, which were latched. I entered the front door of the house from the terrace behind the shop. Livia had just breastfed our daughter Dania upstairs and was re-entering the downstairs living quarters to place her on a pillow on the floor. She was about to say something about my tardiness when she noticed my black eye and the blood on my tunic.

"What in Jupiter's name happened to you?" she said and hurried over to hug me.

I smothered her with my arms and told her that I was in trouble and to listen very closely. I told her about the condition of Vibiana's apartment and then about what had happened to her in the temple.

"I answered her summons and went to her villa. It looked like there was a great struggle. Things were smashed all over the floor. Lots of religious objects, things from Egypt. I didn't know what to do or where to go. I headed for the forum. That's where I found her, laying there, flayed open like a slaughtered calf, bleeding on the marble of the temple vestibule. She died in my arms."

"Oh, great goddess," she exclaimed, "The poor woman. She didn't deserve that, no matter how much I didn't like her." She paused and then said, "And the killer defiled the temple! It is highly forbidden to draw human blood on sacred ground."

"And now they think I killed her!"

"Why would they think that? You were her friend. And who are 'they'?"

"Silvanus, and a priestess of Vesta. They saw me holding her and just assumed it was me that killed her."

"Nonsense. Silvanus is your friend."

"Friend or not, he couldn't keep the crowd of people from coming after me."

"You said you saw Egyptian objects scattered all over the floor of her villa? I wonder if that had something to do with her death." Livia looked down at the floor and a wave of recognition flashed over her face.

Livia then explained that Vibiana was a devotee of the Egyptian religion of the pharaohs, and that it was known widely that she kept in her possession objects of great beauty and religious importance from that foreign land.

"Maybe someone was after some of her Egyptian objects." She offered.

I wondered why they would have broken them or left so many on the floor, but I didn't say this out loud.

"Vibiana was a favorite of the priests of Isis, and she took part in some of their ceremonies, which is pretty unusual for a woman, especially one of her calling." She continued, "People say she contributed money and other valuables to the temple of Isis, things that she obtained from traders coming from Egypt. She danced in the last festival for the Egyptian temple, and was adorned head to toe in gold and jewels during one of the processions by the temple of Isis. She saw me there and waved at me, but you know how I've always felt about her, so I didn't wave back."

I frowned at her, but she shook her head and said, "I don't like you being so close to a woman in her profession."

I reminded her that we were longtime friends, and I didn't care what she did for money.

"For her to take part in the procession and especially lead the dancers, means she was held in high regard by the Egyptian high priests. You would have known that if you ever attended any of these festivals."

I asked Livia why she attended the procession of resurrection, since she wasn't a follower of the Egyptian goddess.

Livia answered, "You know me, I don't follow any specific religion. I prefer to curry favor with all of the gods. Plus, the ceremonies are beautiful, especially the Egyptian ones, and I love to dance and sing."

I nodded my head in acknowledgment, and then rubbed my sore jaw. In truth, I'm not very religious, and I don't attend any ceremonies for any gods. My experience with many of the priests is that they are cheap conjurers playing to the crowd. Most of the offerings to the temples end up in their living quarters or in their bellies. I believe in the gods, but I have never seen one or ever met anyone else who has. I watch Apollo's flying chariot hoist the sun across the sky every day, and I recognize the ancient forms that make up the lights in the night sky. I have heard all of the stories of the great heroes of the legend days of the ancients, when Hercules, Achilles and Perseus acted in great deeds on behalf of the gods, but those days are long past. It is said that the Oracle at Delphi in Greece still communicates with the Olympian Gods, and we have prophets in our streets who also talk to some of the gods, but the gods do not talk to me. As a blacksmith, I identify most with Vulcan above all others, as he is the craftsman for the other gods. Vulcan built palaces and other beautiful and luxurious things for all of Olympus. He made the thunderbolts for Zeus to throw during storms, the chains that bound Prometheus and invincible armor for great heroes of old. I wish he could craft a sword and armor for me now. I occasionally pray to Vulcan for knowledge and strength, and given the current circumstances, I am thinking I should be praying to him now.

Livia told me that after the end of the procession and ceremony two weeks ago, Vibiana came over to her and asked if she could commission some work from me. She said she had something interesting for me to work on.

"She seemed a little too interested in you for my liking, so I told her you were very busy with other work and that you would get back to her later. I guess I forgot to tell you that she wanted to see you and talk to you."

"Livia, that was over two weeks ago!" I protested.

"I know, I'm sorry, really sorry, but I get so jealous with her. She is so beautiful, or was so beautiful, and I know how fond of her you were."

I only nodded.

"You know, when she talked to me, she seemed excited, but not scared of anything. If she had seemed concerned or worried, I'm sure I would have told you right away." She paused to reposition our baby, and then added, "By the way, you haven't told me yet how you got hurt."

I then told Livia about the bearded man and our fight.

"After the crowd started gathering, I got scared that they would stone me to death so I left Vibiana there on the floor and hurried into the back of the temple. No one would listen to my explanation. They all thought I killed her. As I retreated back towards the sanctuary I saw a man spying on me from behind the columns. I tried to sneak up on him because I was sure he was the killer. Somehow he got behind me and surprised me. We fought for several minutes there at the back of the temple, and he smacked me pretty hard in the head. He left before I could catch him."

She listened intently to every detail, and put down our daughter to hug me. After she thought for a few more minutes, Liva looked at me earnestly and asked, "Why didn't he stab you too?" I asked her why she asked that.

"You said the bearded man stabbed Vibiana" Livia said. "I just wondered why he didn't stab you with his knife or sword, when he had just cut her open with his blade." "There wasn't any sword or knife lying with her body, was there?" she asked.

I answered that there was no blade by Vibiana, and pondered her question again for a second. It did seem strange. "He tackled me from behind near a column in the sanctuary, but I never saw a weapon." I then explained, "Actually, I never saw him stab Vibiana, but the wound on her abdomen was made by a sharp blade." In fact, I had never seen the bearded man with Vibiana at all, but it seemed obvious to me that he must have killed her just a minute before I arrived. "Maybe it fell from his hand when he wrestled me to the ground," I said, but that didn't seem likely either, as I never felt or heard a knife fall, and he never tried to pick it up.

Livia went on, "and if he wanted to kill her, why didn't he do it in her villa. You said there was blood there, but only a small amount. Why would he take her all of the way to the temple and kill her. And how could he carry her there without anyone seeing him?"

That was something I hadn't considered until she mentioned it. I too thought it strange that the killer would take her from her villa to the temple. "She must have escaped him after a struggle at her villa."

"Maybe they fought and struggled at her house and he was only planning to abduct her, not kill her. But she woke up and ran into the temple and he stabbed her in desperation." That scenario made some sense to me, and might explain the small amount of blood at her house and then the big slashing wound in her stomach when I found her.

Livia was not convinced of the validity of that theory, but she didn't have any better ideas of her own. "And you never recognized the bearded man you fought, as a friend of Vibiana's or anyone you know?"

I said I'd never seen him before, but that it could have been a client or a boyfriend, as I never really cared to talk to her about her lovers. "I wonder who else would want to kill a woman of her profession, if it wasn't a client or a lover?" I asked, and she reflected on that.

"This is a huge mystery, Titus." she said, and hugged me again. "I'm worried for you. It sounds like the people at the temple probably still think it was you who killed her. We need to let the magistrate know what really happened." Then her brow furrowed again and she asked, "Why was she in the temple of Venus in the first place? She was a follower of the Egyptian gods, not of the Olympians."

"Maybe the killer brought her there to desecrate the temple." I said.

Livia shook her head in disagreement. "We already discounted that idea. He would not, and could not, bring or carry her there without being seen, so she must have gone there on her own."

Livia added, "Besides, if he wanted to desecrate the temple he would have taken her all the way back to the holy inner sanctum to the cella, not kill her in the outer vestibule."

She paused a moment and then paced around the room thinking, before starting again. "The Temple of Venus is pretty close to her villa", she said, "and the temple of Isis is farther away. If she was running away from the killer, she might have wanted to go to her own place of worship and the priests she knows, for protection, but maybe she could only reach the Temple of Venus and tried to take refuge there." Livia was definitely good at explaining things. She has such an analytical mind.

I said, "In that case, she may have been too hurt or too frightened to reach the Isis temple. It is in a completely different direction from the Temple of Venus."

Livia liked that idea better. "Exactly. I think she was trying to hide from the killer or just seek someone to help, but he caught her before she found protection."

Then I remembered the scabbard, and told her about finding it in Vibiana's room and the weird symbols all over it. "I have never seen workmanship like that. I'll bet the knife it held was equally impressive." Then I remembered that that same knife may have been responsible for Vibiana's death and my enthusiasm drained away into revulsion.

"That sounds like the scabbard of a ceremonial dagger, Titus, and those aren't very common." "Some of the priests use daggers like that for ritual sacrifices to the gods."

"So you think the murderer is a priest?" I asked in confusion.

"No, I'm sure he is not a priest, but the killer may have taken it from a priest or a temple. I doubt that Vibiana would have owned a dagger like that." She then paused and said, "Although, if it was an Egyptian relic, she might have possessed it for religious reasons. Maybe that is what the killer was after...he wanted to steal that dagger from her."

I explained how the straps on the back of the scabbard were torn off and the blade was missing when I found it at her place. I asked Livia why she thought he had left it in the villa and only taken the blade.

"He was probably in a rush to follow her if she was escaping." Livia then suggested that it must have come off of the man's belt in a struggle with Vibiana. I told Liv that the bearded man wasn't very big and Vibiana could have put up a good fight, but then I remembered how hard a fight he had given me, and questioned that logic.

"Do you think she could have run all the way to the temple after being stabbed like that in her house?" Livia asked.

"She couldn't have traveled more than a few pedes with that huge wound. Her innards were showing, just like a sheep at slaughter." I said in disgust. I was happy that Liv was helping me understand all of this. Even though she was born into a fishing family, and was only a blacksmith's wife, she is much smarter than I will ever be. She's always had a knack for solving problems.

"What we need to do is think of a motive for this man, why he would want to kill her. There are lots of reasons for someone to kill."

"Which one fits here?" I wondered.

Livia said that as large as the slashing wound sounded, she was not cut by the man by accident, so we could rule that out. "He meant to kill her with the force of that wound." She continued, "You've already mentioned that he could be a client or even her boyfriend or lover. Love gone wrong is always a possible motive."

"Vibiana was a very beautiful woman. If she had a boyfriend, perhaps he became jealous of one or more of the men who came to call on her. In his passion and rage, he could have meant to hurt her. He chased her down and killed her with the lust of a jilted lover." Livia was nodding as she said this.

I did not know if Vibiana had a steady lover or not, but with her line of work, there was certainly plenty of opportunity for jealousy. That might explain the fight at her villa and the brutality of her attack in the temple.

"If this was a jealous lover, he should be easy to find. We can ask about any bearded men who frequented her bed. However, we should explore all possibilities if we are to clear your name. Let's see, what are other reasons to kill someone?" she asked.

I said "War, but I'm pretty sure that's not it either."

Liv chastised me for not taking our conversation seriously and not helping, then said, "Well, it could be for money. Vibiana had plenty and the house sounded like it was ransacked."

I explained that many of the amulets were broken, even ones that looked really expensive, but that didn't mean it wasn't robbery. There could have been many valuable objects missing from her villa.

"But then why kill her in the temple?" Livia asked. "If the murderer meant to rob her, he needed only take what was in the household after she escaped to the temple. Why follow her?"

"Because she knew him." I answered. "She would tell everyone that he had stolen from her and go to the magistrate who would have him arrested and prosecuted in the field of gladiators. The murderer knew the only way to get away with the crime was to kill the only witness." I was very proud of myself for coming up with the potential plot and helping to figure this all out, but Livia again was unimpressed with my theory.

"If that is true, the murderer sure took great risk in being seen by killing her in a public place like the Temple of Venus. It still doesn't make sense to me." countered Livia.

We spent several minutes considering the merits of each motive and decided that robbery or jealousy were both likely possibilities, and if we were ever to find the killer we would have to chase down those probabilities to find the suspect. That seemed an insurmountable task, even in a city as small as Pompeii, and especially if everyone still thought I was the killer. Pompeii was known for relatively swift, but not necessarily accurate, justice, and thus we had little time to waste in our quest to find the truth.

"You said she mumbled something to you as she lay dying?"

I told her it was something about Mithros and saving a medallion. Recognition instantly swept across her face, and she grabbed my hand excitedly.

"I have never heard of anyone named Mithros, but I think I understand the bit about the medallion!" said Livia. "During the festival last week, she was wearing a large, fabulous golden amulet around her neck shaped like the sun, but with a huge light brown jeweled stone at its center. I remember eyeing it when Vibiana came over to me. She was very proud of it." Livia then explained that one of the revelers at the festival had said the golden necklace was magical and had great healing powers, as it was said to have once belonged to the Egyptian goddess herself. "I have no idea where she obtained it or if it belonged to the temple," said Livia, but the priests of Isis claimed it would bring great prosperity to Pompeii and their temple." "Everyone at the festival was talking about that magic necklace and where it came from." She said. "I'm surprised you haven't heard about it before."

I hadn't heard anything about any necklace, but after thinking about Vibiana's last words, I offered, "Well, the bearded man must be named Mithros and he must have stolen it from her."

Then Livia asked, "Was the bearded man carrying anything when he fought you? You said he had no knife. Did he carry an amulet or was he wearing it?"

I tried to remember the details of the fight, and finally said, "No, he didn't have anything and if he was wearing it I would have felt it when we wrestled."

"So what did he do with it, if he had just taken it from her, and if he only wanted an amulet, why did he stick around the temple after he stabbed her and wait for you?"

"Perhaps he was hiding from the priests" I offered, but then countered, "but there wasn't anyone else in that part of the temple to hide from. Silvanus and the attendant only showed up in the front foyer afterwards, when I was there." I then wondered again why he did stay there and watch me from behind the columns. The more we thought about the events of the night, the crazier everything sounded.

"We still need to consider any other possible reasons for her murder. Are there any other motives you can think of?" asked Livia.

I said, "Well, people kill people for feuds or vendettas, but I can't think of anyone who holds anything against Vibiana like that."

"No, I agree," said Livia, "so that leaves the possibility of a man named Mithros who could be a jealous lover or jaded client, the possible theft of an amulet, or something to do with Egyptian magic as clues to why she was killed."

I suddenly remembered something else Vibiana said, and told Livia, "Vibiana mumbled something about Herculaneum". She said "Mithros is from Herculaneum." No wait, I think she said, "Mithrim medallion from Herculaneum, save Isis."

Livia looked intently at me and a deep frown came to her face. "Mithran. Did she say Mithran from Herculaneum?" she asked.

I said, "Yes that was it. Mithran from Herculaneum, save us the medallion." "Why, do you know a man named Mithran from your hometown?" I asked.

"Oh great Jupiter," she replied, "That's not a person, that's a religion. The Mithrans are a cult that has roots in Herculaneum. They were largely pushed out when I was a child because of their outlandish beliefs and their tendency towards brutality."

Livia proceeded to tell me what she knew about the strange cult from her childhood. "The Mithrans were a group that came to Herculaneum before I was born. They were mostly plebeians and masons, but they were all men and I'm told they were secretive people. They eventually took over the entire town, but mostly by illegal means. I remember when I was a little girl, we were all scared to leave our houses at one time and my father could not tend his fishing nets. When a young girl disappeared in Herculaneum, the disappearances were blamed on the Mithrans. There were lots of rumors about secret ceremonies and human sacrifice. People in the city sent word to the senators in Rome to help Herculaneum rid itself of the Mithran scourge. There were beatings and killings of some citizens, but I was too young to understand who or why. Many soldiers were sent from officials in Rome to hunt down all of their followers, and those that didn't escape were either executed or imprisoned. I have not heard any news of them in years and thought them all dead or converted to other religions. If they have returned and are responsible for Vibiana's murder, then there is trouble for Pompeii."

I had lots of questions about the Mithrans and why they would want to steal a medallion or kill a prostitute who had never done anything but make people happy. "How do you think Vibiana got mixed up with some kind of secret cult of murdering criminals?"

Livia was about to answer when our discussion was abruptly cut short by violent banging and loud footsteps outside. The pounding on the portico adjacent to the shop and the yells coming from the terrace could only mean one thing. I had been identified and already accused by the city elders of murder. They had sent the Pompeii guards to collect me, and my punishment would be swift and final, once taken to the dungeons. If found guilty, which almost always was the case, I would likely be tied to a stake in the center of the amphitheatre and either burned alive after being covered in oil, stoned to death by a mob, or whipped until bloody, then quartered. If I was really lucky, I might be given the slim chance to fight to the death in a gladiatorial bout with another prisoner, but I didn't think there were any other prisoners left in the dungeons after several recent public executions. Instead, I would have the unenviable alternative of fighting one of the gladiators from the training academy in the northern most of the city. As professional fighters in tremendous shape, they are trained killers and would hack through me as quickly as a piece of butcher's meat. They were more dangerous than legion soldiers. I shuddered when I thought of these various options. I had a brief notion that I might be able to run upstairs, step out onto the loggia, jump from the balcony to the ground of the terrace below, and run away to my freedom. Perhaps I could then go find the bearded man and make him confess to the magistrate that he was a Mithran and a killer. But about that time, three uniformed soldiers came from the terrace and burst through the front door into our living quarters. Livia screamed and ran for our infant daughter, but she was slapped in the face by the nearest of the three, a large dark haired man with a prominent beaked nose and who was the most elaborately dressed. He was wearing the helmet of an officer with large red feathered plumes and a bronze breastplate that cost more than my house. I did not know him personally, but had seen him around the walls occasionally barking out orders and had also seen him accompany the magistrate on official occasions in the town center. I easily recognized the other two guards. They were the twins, Primus and Crispus, who I had grown up with in Pompeii. They had played in the courtyard when my house was my father's, and had learned to swordfight with my brother Gallianus as children. In fact, the small scar on the chin of Crispus was put there by Gallianus, when their fencing bouts got a little heated one day. That scar was about the only way we could tell the two apart when the twins were younger. They both have very curly black hair that resembles a sheep and thin faces with strong builds. As they have gotten older, it has been much easier to tell one from another, as Primus has much harder features and seldom smiles. He has dark creases and lines on his face, whereas Crispus is much more light hearted with softer features and a constant laugh and smile. Except Crispus was not smiling now. He wore a very pained expression and was helping Livia up off of the floor.

"I'm sorry we have to do this, Titus." He said, as he hoisted Livia to her feet and helped her over to our infant daughter's pillow. "We're here on the orders of Loreius; he wants us to take you back to the forum."

"That's enough Crispus", said the officer and he immediately put his big beaked nose right in my face. "Titus of Pompeii, you are charged with killing the lady Vibiana and defiling the temple of Venus with innocent blood. You will be taken to the Prefect's office for sentencing and execution."

"But I'm innocent," was all I got out before Primus batted the left side of my head so hard I fell to my knees. Damn, that was the same side of my head I had already been hit on tonight. Figures. Crispus muttered something to his twin brother and shoved him, which made me smile. I never liked Primus much. He was always the cruel one and took advantage of Crispus and me whenever possible when we were young. Thankfully, we always had Gallianus to protect us, who was older, stronger and bigger than Primus and kept him in his place throughout our early teen years. I always wondered why Crispus became a guard of the wall with his brother, but I suppose it is true that brothers, especially twins, like to stick together no matter what. The officer shouted to Primus to bind my arms and legs. I held out my hands while Crispus and Primus tied my wrists and legs with a thin tan rope. While they worked on my hands, I was staring at Crispus head, which did not have a helmet on like the other two.

He noticed my gaze and said casually that "It gets too damn hot and sweaty in the summer, so I never wear it unless

I'm around Loreius or the other city elders." Despite the circumstances, he made me smile again, with his gentle and care-free demeanor.

## Chapter 4: Bound for the Magistrate

Unlike Crispus, Primus seemed to delight in applying the rope hobbles to my ankles and forcibly tying my wrists. I was hauled down the Via del Abbondanza to meet my fate, towards the forum and the magistrate's administrative building. Primus gave me several shoves in the middle of the back, which caused me to fall down on more than one occasion. Thanks to Crispus, I made it back up to my feet and never landed directly on my face. People were coming out of the shops and villas and looking at me in consternation as we walked. We moved through the arches on the south, across the large open square of the forum representing the town center, and continued past the Macella and across the lawn toward the large imposing steps of the marble administrative building on the southeast side. We reached the end of the forum grounds, just past the temple of Vesta and turned to walk up the steps into the Prefect's building. A servant I knew from the wine bar, Alycia, came running up to me and asked if it was true that I had killed someone. I told her I was innocent and reminded her that Vibiana was my friend, but I was hustled along by the three soldiers before we could finish our conversation. Alycia shouted back that she would pray to the gods for me, but I wasn't sure anything was going to help me now. The large public building holding the Prefect office had few windows but some beautiful relief along the top cornice below the roof. The design consisted of mounted horsemen engaged in battle. I guess I never really noticed that before, but then I don't remember ever being inside this building except to pay my yearly taxes. I was taken up the steps, through the entry hall to a small side room on the right of a large main chamber. Inside, the room was lit with two oil lamps and a man barely older than I with closely cropped hair and a stern face sat prone on a bench. He wore the regal white toga of an important citizen and it was adorned with a purple sash consistent with one of his high stature and bearing.

"Ah, Septimus. Finally, I thought you were going to make me wait all night!" he grumbled and sat up.

The soldier bowed and stated simply, "We have retrieved Titus the blacksmith for you, Prefect."

"I have had another idea while you were delayed, Septimus, and hence I have another task for you." He then grinned broadly and whispered something into the officer's ear.

Septimus looked puzzled, but bowed again and said, "Yes, Prefect, I will go now and attend to the woman. These two will be posted here in case Titus decides to cause trouble." He pointed at the two other guards.

I tried to explain that I was bound in rope and unarmed, but Primus slapped me again before I could finish. Crispus was frowning, but not at Primus, and probably only because he forgot to wear his helmet in the presence of the local magistrate. He kept fumbling with his hair. When Septimus had mentioned a woman, I thought he meant Vibiana, and wondered if she had survived her wounds after all.

Unfortunately, those hopes were dashed quickly. Loreius the magistrate had taken over the job of justice keeper in Pompeii, when Vibiana's former lover and patron had died of old age. The position was called praefectus urbi in the local tongue, but it was a lucrative and powerful job. In addition to acting as judge in all matters, the City Prefect sat on the town council with other elders and was responsible for collecting all taxes in the province (much of which was then sent to Rome). He made laws and enforced them, and provided for all city services including the soldiery, which protected the walls. Loreius was from a very powerful patrician family in Rome and had been appointed by a senator to the position. He was the chief member of the Pompeii ruling council, and his word carried more weight than any of the other town elders. It was a position he relished. I had never liked him, but I respected and feared him, as a simple wave of his hand was enough to send a man to his death. I needed to be polite, contrite and convincing if I was to entertain any hope of surviving this ordeal. I hoped he would listen to and accept my version of events, but I held no illusion that the proceedings would be fair.

"So," said Loreius in a self-important tone, "these are the facts. You bludgeoned Vibiana the prostitute with your blacksmith hammer, and then stabbed her in a blind jealous rage in the Temple of Venus." You were identified at the scene by the Priest, Silvanus, and your blacksmith tools were found laying beside the victim with blood on the satchel with which they were carried. The sheath of the blade you stabbed her with was also in the satchel."

I stopped him, and said, "I found that scabbard in Vibiana's house. It belongs to the killer!"

"You admit to stealing a knife from her villa."

I said "No, I do not. I only took the scabbard because I thought it might be a clue to her whereabouts. She wasn't in her home when I arrived."

"Well, you certainly found her. You were seen fleeing the scene of the crime with blood all over you. You are not only a murderer, Titus, son of Galleus; you are a very stupid one. I can't believe I allowed such a dangerous man in my villa to work on the water pipes."

I shouted back at him, "But I didn't kill her, she was my friend!"

"Hush!" He said as he waved me off. "Quit talking such nonsense. This is an easy case for a Prefect, and one that I am afraid can only end one way -- in your death in the amphitheatre. Fortunately for the people of Pompeii, we have another holiday festival coming up tomorrow to venerate our patron and goddess Venus, and your execution will be fitting entertainment."

"Wait, please wait and just listen. I have known Vibiana most of my life. We were dear friends. She sent a messenger to me to come to her house tonight. When I got there the house was ransacked. I was going home and found her in the temple bleeding, but still alive."

"How do you expect me to believe such a ridiculous story? Where is this mystery messenger? We know the house is a mess, as we have been there. Neighbors say they saw you there too, so you probably were there to steal all of her magic amulets from Egypt! You even stole her knife and scabbard! And how is it that you came to arrive at the temple if not to slay her? It is not even on the way to your house from the prostitute's villa! You are a liar as well as a murderer and a thief, and not a good one."

I exclaimed, "I have no amulets or anything else from the temple of Isis, and I did find the house in shambles. I was on my way to the wine bar to try and think things through. It was not me who killed her, it was the bearded man. He's a Mithran."

"So you say that the messenger was the bearded man named Marathon?" He asked.

"No, I replied, the messenger was a small boy from the streets of the entertainment quarter named Marcos."

"Nonsense," he said again, "little boys don't have beards, even in the Lupanare. First you say his name was Marathon, now it's Marcos."

"You're not listening to me," I replied again, just before Primus slugged me in the shoulder.

"Besides, he said, you have Vibiana's blood all over you."

"That is because I tried to help her."

He responded quickly, "You helped her die, and you admit you were there with Vibiana when she was slain."

"No, I arrived just after she was stabbed by the bearded Mithran man."

Loreius shook his head again and said, "This is getting us nowhere. No one else has said anything about any bearded man or accomplice named Marthos. They saw you and you alone beside Vibiana as she lay dying" he said as he wandered around the room pondering the events.

"I think he hit her and knocked her out and then took her to the temple and stabbed her. I hear these Mithrans are ruthless."

Loreius was becoming more and more agitated with me. "Listen Titus, you do not make any sense. Why would he bludgeon her in one location and then bother to carry her far away and then stab her later somewhere else?"

I thought for a second and then said, "Maybe it was because she woke up and screamed. He was taking her to the temple for some reason and she must have been unconscious then awakened there. That was why I went to the temple tonight. I heard her screaming as I was crossing the courtyard of the forum to the bar and went to check it out."

"You concoct such wild stories, young man." "But you do seem earnest in your defense, however silly the story. Perhaps you are just insane."

He continued, "There are only two reasons for killing someone, jealousy and thievery, and in your case I am afraid it is both. Yes, I think you are obviously insane."

I said, "I am not jealous of Vibiana, I have never even slept with her, and I am completely faithful to my wife. I have not stolen anything. You can search my house."

"Oh, we will search your house," he said,"and everything in your house and shop will be confiscated and turned over to the state." "And as for your wife, she should be coming along any minute."

I stared at him blankly for a minute to understand what he meant. "My wife. Why is my wife coming?" I asked. "She was nowhere near Vibiana and did not witness the events."

Loreius went on for several minutes explaining his version of the night's events and the various motivations which would cause a crazy person like me to kill the woman they loved. I wasn't listening and didn't really answer him. I was praying to the gods that Livia had escaped the house with my daughter before Septimus had reached the villa.

At length, Loreius looked out the portal of his office. "What could be keeping the soldier and his prisoner?"

Almost on cue, my wife was dragged, still yelling and

cussing, across the front entrance to the administration building and into the Prefect's office by the officer of the guard who had earlier arrested me. I began to cry out and strain at my ropes. I asked again what Livia was doing there.

"She is an accomplice," said the magistrate.

"I have it on good authority that she was seen talking to Vibiana two weeks ago at the festival of Isis, and it was noticed she was frowning at Vibiana all the while. It is known that you have had close connections with the deceased woman for years. If you did not kill the lady Vibiana in a jealous fit, then she must have killed her. It was surely out of jealousy, based on the fact that you were having an affair with the prostitute."

"We were not having any affair. My wife is innocent. Please let her go. She wasn't even present at the temple when Vibiana was killed. You can't keep her. It isn't right."

Loreius shook his head, and said, "Then you must confess. My hands are tied in this matter. You and your wife accomplice will die tomorrow in the amphitheatre."

I was desperate at this point and implored, "I'll say whatever you want, just let her go. If agreeing to your demands frees her, it will be worth it."

Loreius smiled broadly and pounded his fist on the small table in front of him. "See what I told you, Septimus, I can always get them to confess in short order. It is simple human nature! I didn't even have to have you torture them for a confession."

He grinned with a cold satisfied expression and then looked directly at me. "I always find the killer and prosecute them. That is why I am the Prefect. We have had three murders in our city in my time in this important post. The husband who strangled his wife when he found her sleeping with the neighbor, I caught him easily. Then there were the two foreign sailors who were fighting in the bar. One stabbed the other with a gladius. We used his own sword to behead him in the grand theatre. It was an awesome spectacle." "And now you."

At this point, my wife was sobbing uncontrollably and Crispus looked like he was about to vomit. Primus was listening with awe and admiration at Loreius as he went on. Loreius looked at the both of us and then reminded us of one of the central tenets of Roman law.

"*Dura lex sed lex*" he said, "The law is harsh but it is the law." He then looked to Primus and said, "Take them to the dungeons of the amphitheatre and we will put them on the docket tomorrow as a main event. Stoning I should think, as I'm feeling beneficent this evening".

Livia was moaning, "My baby, my dear baby Dania," and then she looked to the heavens and prayed, "Please Great Goddess, save our family."

Loreius bent toward her and whispered, "My dear, your husband is obviously guilty and you are better off dead than to live as the widow of an insane murderer." "Besides, two executions are better theater than just one, if only for sheer crowd appeal."

I screamed again that he was about to condemn an innocent couple to their death, but Loreius only shook his head and said, "Not in my eyes, and I am the only lawgiver here. Only a miracle intervention by one of the great Gods of Olympus would save you now. Unfortunately for you, because you defiled the temple of our beloved patroness Venus, I don't believe you will garner any favor with her or any of the other Gods today."

"Wait!" I said, as an idea suddenly occurred to me. "Before you have us both killed, let me prove my innocence in the temple. I will publicly plead for Venus' forgiveness at the procession tomorrow and the great goddess might grant Pompeii favor for your mercifulness."

"No," he said again, "I have all of the proof I need. And you are just stalling to postpone your execution."

"It is a festival day tomorrow and there will be a ceremonial offering at the temple for the holiday. Allow Venus in her wisdom and power to show everyone I am not guilty of this crime. I am certain of a miracle. The goddess will not let this injustice happen and will reap vengeance on the perpetrators if more innocent blood is spilled. And when retribution from the gods comes, you will be the one responsible and a target of their wrath. Instead, If you allow me to beg for justice from the goddess, and a miracle does occur, the whole town will rejoice and you will be responsible, but this time on the right side of justice." I continued, "If I am guilty in the eyes of the gods, and there is no miracle, you have at least attempted to placate the goddess and cleanse the temple with a plea for justice. I will go readily to my death in the amphitheatre later in the afternoon, and my wife will go with me to my death."

Livia screamed at me and shouted "what are you saying?" "Why would I volunteer to kill both of us when we are both innocent of any crime? What will become of our baby daughter?" She started sobbing again, and bent down to her knees praying silently.

With that, I looked directly at Livia and said slowly and loudly, "I am sure that Silvanus, the high priest of the temple, would welcome the opportunity to have another miracle occur in his presence. The goddess has demonstrated her magnificent splendor before in the temple of Pompeii. She will show her mercy again and intervene to protect an innocent family."

Loreius laughed to himself, and said, "Titus, I admire your devotion to the goddess, but just because we had a miracle occur in the temple five years ago, doesn't mean it will ever happen again, and certainly not on your behalf."

Livia suddenly stopped crying, pulled her head up, wiped her nose with her arm, and peered directly into my eyes. A sudden look of understanding came over her. "Let the priest pray for the truth," she said, "and make an offering of food and fire." She crawled over to Lorieus on her knees and became prostrate before the magistrate. She begged that if he would agree to this, she would be compliant and accept their fate as one dictated by the gods. She also offered to give him our entire savings in tribute (which wasn't really very much, but she embellished the amount of the bribe).

"We will have your riches in either case" he said as he pondered our request. Finally, he stated, "It is against my better judgment, but it should be very entertaining to see the pained look on your faces when there is no divine intervention tomorrow during the ceremony, and besides, it should increase attendance at the stoning afterwards." He laughed at his own wisdom and clapped his hands on his knees, pleased with his generosity.

Livia then pleaded with Loreius for one last favor to allow her to go back home to get her affairs in order and especially to find a place for our infant daughter to live and grow up after her parents are gone.

"I can't exactly let a felon go walking around Pompeii unguarded," he said, adding "even a woman."

It was at that moment when Crispus stepped up and said, "I'll guard her, your lordship. I won't let her out of my sight until tomorrow morning when I'll join you at the temple." Primus was about to interject, when Crispus gave him a stern look that would stop a snake from striking.

Primus then just shrugged his shoulders and said, "Prefect, I'll take Titus here down to the ergastulum beneath the grand amphitheatre and make sure he is comfortable tonight". He gave me a smile that actually gave me the chills.

The officer named Septimus clicked his heels together and asked Loreius if there were any other orders, then told the men that they knew what to do and to go do it. He warned Crispus again not to let Livia out of his sight, and cautioned him not to fall asleep on duty tonight. And then he told Crispus to find his helmet. With that, we separated and my plan, if you could call it that, was put in motion.

As I was hustled through the city streets toward the dungeons of the giant amphitheatre in the northeast corner of Pompeii, I was trying to formulate what needed to be done. I wondered how or if I was to survive the next day. I think Primus must have felt a little sorry for me, because at least he was not tripping me every block, as he had on the way to the magistrate's office. However, he said nothing for the twenty minutes or so that it took to reach my captive cell. I had some idea of what Livia was planning to do, but I did not know the specifics since our plans were made without verbal communication. I hoped that she understood what I had tried

to impart to her by innuendo. I was hoping she could ensure our baby's safety and somehow make her way to Silvanus in the temple before the ceremony tomorrow. I didn't know if she could persuade him or not, but it was the only salvation for our family. It is a very long walk to the amphitheatre from the forum, over a millarium in distance and on the very northeastern boundary of the city. I hadn't eaten anything since the early morning, and combined with the bumps on my head; I was dizzy and needed some sleep. But I needed to consider what could happen the next morning, and what our options were to be if things played out as I hoped. If things went badly, it meant there would be no more worries tomorrow night for either of us. I walked along the road and thought of the Via Appia during the Spartacus revolution over a century ago. The conspirators were all crucified on posts for long distances on each side of the road as a deterrent to future rebels. I hoped Livia and I wouldn't end up as similar road signs. As we approached the large amphitheatre from the Via dell' Abbondanza, I could see its great outline to our right. It is not as large or as grand as the new fantastic coliseum that Vespasian has built in central Rome, but it has been here for many years and provided our people with much entertainment. We have gladiatorial combat at least twice monthly and battle re-enactments with large numbers of participants. The gladiator's barracks are very near our shop, so I have known several of them personally. During festivals, there are always some gruesome but thrilling and dangerous events to watch.

They have even brought in elephants and lions from far distant lands, but it pales in comparison to the tales relating to the magnificent staged events from the new coliseum in Rome. Livia has never enjoyed these spectacles, with her weakness for blood. I was thinking at that moment that she may have been right and it might not be as entertaining from the other side of the gallery. Tomorrow, I was to be the entertainment for the crowd, and I was petrified of that prospect, especially since my wife would also be the subject of torture. I could only hope that our plan would be successful.

Primus and I walked past the huge palace of the Prefect on our right, with its massive outer wall and inner courtyard, and finally reached the vineyards at the far corners of Pompeii. We turned the corner to the right, and faced the large imposing marble pillars and arches which made up the amphitheatre. We entered the front gate, passing under the many statues of heroes lining the upper colonnades, and after walking some distance around the outer circle, we descended a series of steps which took us to the catacombs of the ergastulum below. It was very dark and the hallway was not lit. I almost tripped and fell several times on the steps, thanks to the hobbles on my legs and poor visibility. It smelled stale and putrid. At the bottom of the steps, we went through a small corridor to the right. There was a small oil lamp which was lit on a ledge next to a small door.

Primus grinned and said, "See Titus, we have had your quarters all prepared for you. The lamp is already in place. Stay warm!"

Primus escorted me into a small cell, which had a dirt floor, no window, and no bench or seat that I could see. The ergastulum was the area where slaves were confined and punished. It was also used as a holding area for prisoners condemned to be crucified in the arena above or before they were placed into gladiatorial battles. It was little more than a pit in the ground.

Primus gave me a shove, then said, "Good night, old friend."

He shut the door, leaving me in total blackness. I was hoping that he would bring the lamp in with us, but it stayed out in the corridor. I was a little chilled from the night air, and my whole body hurt. My head was still swimming and I was hungry. But I was still alive, and if circumstances worked out, I might be alive tomorrow. I fell asleep within minutes, but awoke shivering in the early morning hours. It was late summer, but this cell was below ground and the air was cool, dark and heavy, and I had no wrap to cover my bare flesh. I was huddled in one corner with my bound wrists draped over my hunched up legs. The rope gave me some nice red burns on the skin of both ankles and wrists and the chilled night air of the dungeon wasn't helping. I made my way to my feet and urinated in the corner of the room. I was glad I was not going to be imprisoned here for very long. With no sewage, the room would begin to smell terribly in a few days. It didn't smell that great now. Romans did not believe in prisons and most visitors to the ergastulum stayed here only a few days before they were crucified or sent to slaughter amongst the gladiators.

I had a lot of time to contemplate before the light of dawn arrived. I sat in a corner and tried to make sense of the events of the previous day. I was not a murderer, but I was to be treated as one, and my family forever shamed. Through no fault of my own, I would be responsible for my wife's death and the orphaning of a baby girl. I had only confessed to the Prefect to protect my wife, and he had used that pressure to trick me. His only intention was to trap me, and he cared only for the spectacle of death in the arena, not for truth or justice. He was going to use Livia's crucifixion as theatre. I cried when I thought of Dania's prospects. She would likely end up as a slave, and probably as someone's cook or maid. She might even end up as one of the plebian prostitutes in the Lupanare. My baby girl deserved more than that. The shop would be taken by the Prefect and likely given to one of his friends or family. The business that had been built up over 3 generations was going to be dismantled in only a blink of time. My grandfather and father would be forever seeking vengeance on me in the afterlife. Although I had followed in their footsteps and maintained the family business, I could never seem to garner their praise while they still lived. I could hear my father's voice ringing in my ears now, about my poor choices and my propensity for continually taking the 'easy' road. And now this. I think the only correct decision he ever considered I made was when I married Livia. He died shortly after that. What a contrast to my brother Gallianus. His life was one of valor and glory. I had always looked up to him, and even though he chose to forego the family business, my father had always fawned over him. Galleus was intensely proud of his son's achievements on the battlefield and believed that Gallianus would bring renown to our family and raise our position in Roman society. Unless I did something, those plans were going to be shattered on the amphitheatre grounds tomorrow. I shivered again when I thought of what would become of Livia and Dania. I had hatched a plan, but I had no way of knowing if Livia had completely understood and there were no guarantees that it had much more than a sliver of a chance to succeed. I felt more and more hopeless as the night progressed. I needed my brother's courage. I sat in the corner huddled like a beggar and tried to stay warm, but it was impossible to sleep. My thoughts kept running back to my death and the various ways in which it was possible that it would be enacted. If I had a sword, I considered the possibility that I would fall on it, but realized I was probably too cowardly to go out that way. Somehow I would need to borrow my brother's courage and ability to think and react during a time of crisis. Whatever happened, I needed to save my wife and child.

If I survived, and that was unlikely, then I needed to go find the bearded man and clear my family's name. It would be great to bring justice to Vibiana's killer, but it was more important to remove the stain of guilt from the family.

I tried to think of what could happen if my plan worked. We had the slimmest of chances of escape. Then what? I thought of what I liked to do before I was caught up in this mess. I liked to be around horses, although I couldn't ride them very well. I had never owned a horse, so it was rare that I had the opportunity to mount one and go for a gallop. My friend Aule had horses. He rode them occasionally, but more often just used them to haul his cart. I tried to imagine the smell of horses. It wasn't very difficult in this dungeon. My thoughts drifted to other pastimes. I was especially fond of taking my wife and daughter for walks, especially outside of the city walls. The sights and smells of the Campania countryside were wonderful. In fact, I decided I loved doing just about anything with my wife and child. That was my favorite thing in life and all that I cared for. I really hoped that I could see them again. Unfortunately, those thoughts brought me again to despair. I decided I needed to keep my mind busy by focusing on the plan. I was going to have to give the speech of my life to save my family and business. I wasn't an orator, but I needed to know exactly what to say and to be as convincing as possible in order to garner the favor of the crowd. I needed public opinion on my side. I silently went through my speech over and over in my head, refining it as I went. After hours of rehearsal, I finally fell asleep.

## Chapter 5: The Miracle in the Temple

Shortly after sunrise, I heard Primus fumbling with the wooden latch to the door of my cell. It opened wide.

"On your feet, Titus, we are taking you back to the square."

We had a long walk through the city back to the forum, and it gave me time to think about what I was to say to the people of Pompeii.

Even though it was early in the morning and Apollo's sun chariot had barely risen above the horizon, there were hundreds of people in the plaza of the forum. I could taste blood, dirt and grass in my mouth from sleeping on the ground of the cell. I must have looked like a Cyclops, with my matted blonde hair, black eye and dirty tunic, and everyone was staring. There were some cat calls and obscenities thrown in my direction, but I think most people were just curious. We made our way through the crowd towards the steps of the temple of Venus. The seven virgins from the temple of Vesta were clothed in beautiful white gowns, and had wreaths in their hair. Although they worshiped in a different temple, they were always present at events like this, and provided legitimacy to the proceedings. There were three robed priests present, but I couldn't tell from where I was if Silvanus was one of them or not. I did not see Livia anywhere, and most of my friends and clients from Pompeii appeared to be lying low and not taking an active part in the ceremony. After a series of chants and dances by the attendants, one of the priests spoke and explained the meaning of the festival today. It was in remembrance of the emergence of Venus from the ocean, and the bringing of mortal love into the world. I was becoming impatient with the proceedings, and feeling extremely anxious at my wife's lack of appearance, when I saw her being brought into the vestibule of the temple. I was then escorted to her location and we were moved together from the main chamber into the back of the temple in the cella facing the large, tall bronze statue of the goddess. The statue's painted features were beautiful and the white flowing robe and blue eyes were set off by a gold crown and the golden dolphin statues that supported the weight of her legs. Next to her was a wooden square platform and podium behind which Silvanus was standing, and adjacent to the podium was a large granite bowl, which held wood timbers and charcoal, which had been set afire just as everyone entered the sanctuary. Just in front and slightly to left of the large granite fire pit was a flat table-like alter, in which a small black and white goat had been sacrificed. The goat's neck was cut evenly severing the jugular vein and associated arteries, and there was a trail of blood streaming down one side of the white marble alter.

Silvanus spoke to the crowd massing in the main chamber behind us in a loud booming voice. "What say you, Titus of Pompeii? Do you confess your desecrations on the temple of our great goddess, and beg her forgiveness for your transgressions? And do you also beg forgiveness for the complacency of your wife and partner, Livia? Rise and speak!"

I had practiced this speech in my head all morning in the grand theatre catacombs, but my throat still crackled when it came out and I stuttered. "Oh great Venus, goddess and protector of Pompeii, hear my plea for justice. I have been wrongly accused. You are all powerful and all knowing. You saw that I came to your temple only to help Vibiana, when I heard her screaming. I shed none of her blood, and I only wish vengeance on those who took her life from her and defiled your place of worship. I beg your mercy, and I beg for a sign to the people of Pompeii that I speak only the truth. I beg for a miracle to show everyone that there is an evil growing in our city. There is a murderer free to kill and who goes unpunished. I also beg mercy for Livia, who has done nothing wrong, but for the crime of loving and supporting her husband when threatened with death. I ask for you, oh Great Venus, to show us a miracle in the name of Love!"

It wasn't everything I needed to say, and it certainly wouldn't convince anyone of my innocence, but it was enough to cause a loud murmur to go through the crowd of spectators behind us.

Silvanus, said, "Very well, Titus, you have pled your case to the gods of Olympus. They know whether you are true and just or a murderer and a liar." He looked around as if something was about to happen and the crowd was hushed.

For a full minute it was terribly quiet, and I began to wonder if I had made a terrible mistake.

Silvanus suddenly spoke, "Time is past. There is no divine intervention. You have failed to show contrition for your crimes, and you have failed to confess to the goddess of your guilt. Let her vengeance be swift, and be carried out by our Prefect on behalf of the citizens of Pompeii. These two shall be sacrificed to the glory of the gods in the theatre this afternoon."

Silvanus then bowed low to the magistrate who was watching from the corner of the dais. I looked at Silvanus with alarm, but he did not return my gaze. I was scared, and actually shocked at the words that Silvanus had spoken. He seemed nervous and was definitely rushing the ceremony. I wondered if Loreius had told him to allow only a short minute for a miracle to occur. He seemed to already have considered us guilty. Silvanus was a firsthand observer to my presence near Vibiana at her death, so he might have already made up his mind that her murder was by my hand. Livia grasped my fingers tightly with her left bound hand, and had her eyes clinched closed as if she were waiting to be flogged.

The crowd was a mix of people yelling various things, including "they are both guilty," "Goddess, save them", "stone them now" and everything in between.

All of the town elders were huddled in a group to one corner of the temple, observing everything as it occurred. Loreius was right. This was great spectacle, but I didn't appreciate being the main event, and I was quickly losing faith that anything was going to happen to save us.

Loreius walked up to us, and placed his hand over our heads, and said finally, "The goddess has not, and will not intervene. She knows, as we all do, these two are murderers and deserve their punishment. We will see them executed in the arena!"

Some of the crowd cheered and the smiling magistrate strolled leisurely through the crowd towards the others on the council. He shook some of their hands and then headed towards the front steps of the temple and out to the plaza of the forum. He was enjoying his popularity and several people were engaging him in conversation or patting him on the back. I was crestfallen. I had failed, and my family was to be destroyed. The blacksmith shop of my father and grandfather would be dismantled and sold off for the good of the town council, and our family legacy would rest with my brother fighting wars in foreign lands. I wished again that Gallianus was here to save me, as he so often did when we were young.

Primus and Crispus were about to escort us out of the building when someone from the crowd shouted, "Look! Look at the Goddess! "

Another said, "Oh great Venus, it has happened again."

"A miracle, a miracle again in Pompeii."

All eyes immediately went to the head of the huge bronze statue of Venus just to our left. There, very faintly at first, and then more pronounced, were bright red tears welling up in the white marble eyes of the flesh colored, painted face of the statue. Red droplets, then streams of blood dripped down from the eyes of Venus, into the giant scalloped clam shell at her feet. Several women screamed and there were many people falling to their knees and praying before the goddess.

"A miracle. A miracle again in the temple." They kept saying.

"It is justice. They are innocent. The goddess is telling us so, said an old man. I instantly recognized him as Aule the fishmonger, and he looked directly at us.

"Yes, free them, they are innocent" said a woman to his left.

Shocked voices were speaking all over the temple. For his part, Silvanus looked terrified and was walking briskly toward the columns on the right and to the door I had exited only the night before. All seven of the vestal attendants were down on their hands and knees with their heads bowed low before the statue of Venus. Primus put his middle digit into the clam shell and tasted his red, wet fingertip.

He exclaimed loudly, "It is blood, Oh goddess, it is blood and it is warm!", and a new wave of oohs and ahhs went over the mass of people behind us.

Aule said again, "Free them. The goddess knows. Free them!"

The magistrate and the soldier named Septimus came back into the temple in all of the confusion and Loreius stared at the bleeding statue with a bewildered look on his face. He tried to quiet the crowd down with arm movements and shouts of "Easy. Quiet. This can be explained." He said, "Silvanus can tell us that this doesn't necessarily mean these two are innocent. It might mean that Venus agrees they are guilty."

"No, the gods have spoken, they are innocent!" yelled a woman I recognized as Alycia the slave girl from the bar.

There were arguments going on back and forth between people of different factions with Aule and Alycia leading the chorus for our release. Septimus ran off to get more guards to try and contain the mob, and Loreius was surrounded by men and women trying to ask him what to do and how to understand the miracle that had just happened.

Of course, this event was no more miraculous than the event of the crying statue of Venus that had occurred in the very same temple five years earlier. That miracle had been engineered by a young priest named Silvanus with the help of the town blacksmith/plumber who was able to run a small lead line through the back of the statue to two small pin-sized holes in the corners of the eyes of Venus. A bronze statue of ten cubits in height is not solid. The bronze is wrapped around a wooden lattice frame. It is therefore relatively straightforward for a metalsmith to place the tubing through the floor into the statue base and run it up to the eyes. The ingenious part of this conjurer's trick involves how the blood is pumped into the eyelids on cue. The tube runs from the floor into the wooden platform under the podium, and into a nippled tube on top of a copper pot inside the platform. The pot is filled to a specific line with the goat's blood that is used for the early morning sacrifice, before anyone arrives for the altar ceremony. Another nippled tube on the opposite side of the copper pot is connected by another lead tube to the base of the granite fire pit. As soon as the fire is lit, the air inside the granite bowl and the connected square chamber just below it, heats up.

After several minutes, the superheated air from the glowing coals and flaming timbers pushes hot air into the copper pot and this forces the blood up the attached tube and eventually to fall from the eyes. The design for this actually came from a papyrus Silvanus had received from another priest that said it was taken from the library in Alexandria. Similar apparati have been designed by the great philosopher Archimedes of Syracuse, and other plumbers, including my father, have utilized like systems for "miracles" in temples all across the Roman world. However, it is a sacred trade secret among priests and those of my profession, and other than Silvanus, another priest from his temple, and Livia, no one was in on the secret of the original miracle of tears. The townspeople rejoiced in their original miracle, and now it had happened again.

When Livia met my eyes, last night, I knew she would

try to contact Silvanus and to get him to rig the system again. I assumed that he would be okay with another miracle, as it might help boost attendance again. I sat smugly next to Livia, who still had her eyes closed and was clenching my right hand, but there were a lot of things that could still go wrong.

"Where was Silvanus?"

Finally, the din had quieted, and Loreius came before both of us and glared down into my eyes. "I am not sure how or why this miracle occurred," he said to everyone in the temple, "but I will find out. In the meantime, we will postpone the executions until our great priests and scholars can contemplate the meaning of this great message." He leaned over me and whispered, "And I think you will still be executed as early as tomorrow." With that, he raised his hand and said, "Take them away, guards."

There then arose a series of shouts and cries from the crowd about misplaced justice, but the magistrate would hear nothing more.

Crispus said again, "I'm sorry, Titus", and then when Primus was out of earshot, he added, "I really thought this would work."

So, I thought to myself, Livia had let Crispus in on our plan and secret. I was okay with that. He could be trusted, but I hoped he didn't share it with his twin brother and I told him so.

"Don't worry," he said, "When Primus tasted the blood of the goddess, he became a believer. He is now firmly on your side."

I wasn't so sure.

Word had spread quickly. There was still dancing and singing and lots of rejoicing in the forum plaza and the crowds were everywhere. Even those who were not devotees of Venus had joined the festivities in the forum. Crowds were gathering everywhere and the entrance of the temple was clogged with throngs of people who wanted to witness the second miracle of the tears. Primus had indeed decided that he might have been wrong about me and was contemplating his cruelty to me the previous night. Therefore our progress was very slow as we headed down the steps and away from the temple.

As the twins sauntered leisurely among the mass of people in the forum grounds, Livia came close to me and whispered, "It was a good plan. I thought it would work."

I nodded, and said, "I was beginning to think you were unable to convince Silvanus to help us."

"He is afraid of Loreius and would not agree to it, even when I reminded him of his debt to you."

I looked puzzled until she continued in a hushed voice, "It was Crispus. He sensed Silvanus fears and threatened to go directly to Loreius and tell him of the trickery from five years ago. He said the people of Pompeii would then demand that he join the two of us at the executioner's pike. He was very convincing, and Silvanus finally relented and agreed to take part. He was still terrified of the prospect of Loreius finding out, but he followed the higher path. I am proud of Crispus and of Silvanus, even if it only bought us another day together."

Primus was trying to clear the crowd in front of us, while Crispus held each of our arms and helped us walk slowly.

"Where is our baby Dania?" I asked.

"She is with Aule's wife, who has promised to watch over her. They are feeding her goats milk."

I whispered to her that that brought me some comfort.

Livia said in a hushed voice, "When Crispus and I arrived home last night, I told him the whole story that you related to me. I had to tell him about the secret of the miracle of the tears or he never would have let me go to the temple. We carried Dania over to Aule's and told them of the events. We did not divulge our intended plan to them, but hurried off to the temple. We were fortunate to find Silvanus still there at that late hour. He was readying the temple for the festival. When he heard what we wanted, he refused again and again until Crispus finally convinced him with threats. He was still worried that someone would question the same miracle happening twice and that an investigation by the magistrate would result in his arrest. Crispus settled his mind somewhat last night by telling him to remove the podium pot at his earliest opportunity and to fill the holes in the eyelids with candle wax. I am sure as soon as he comes out from hiding, he will arrange to cover his tracks just so."

Crispus heard part of this and smiled at me.

Livia abruptly stopped talking when she saw the magistrate walking briskly toward the both of us, a scowl still on his face. When Primus saw the Prefect approaching, he also moved back over closer to us, and we remained silent.

"Primus, I told you to take these two to the dungeons of the amphitheatre!" barked Loreius.

"Yes, Prefect, but the crowd has impeded our progress." said the soldier with his head bowed low.

Loreius only grumbled then said, "I think your delay is instead due to the sloth and incompetence of you and your stupid brother."

"Yes, Prefect," they both said in unison, then each took an arm and the four of us were about to walk through the crowd with greater intent when our progress was again delayed.

## CHAPTER 6: THE TEMPLE OF ISIS

The fake miracle hadn't worked as I planned, but at least we weren't dead yet. As we began to be escorted out of the forum by the two twins, a miracle did happen, however. The ground began to shake violently and those nearby had to catch their balance for fear of falling over. The earthquake only lasted for several seconds, but it was enough to scare anyone in the vicinity. There were more screams and shouts and all at once when it stopped things got eerily quiet. Faces from everywhere stared at Livia and me, and then back at the Prefect. Loreius now had a horrified look on his face.

Aule came running up to him again and said, "Prefect, please, there can be no doubt. The gods are angry. We must let the blacksmith and his wife go free. Don't take them back to the dungeon. Please don't execute them. The goddess will punish us! The gods have already intervened twice. They are trying to tell us of their innocence?"

I was too astonished by the earthquake to think things through carefully. I said a silent prayer to Vulcan, Jupiter and Venus and thanked them for any part they played in what was happening. We have had earthquakes before. We even had one a few months back, and the town was severely damaged in an earthquake seventeen years ago, but they are still uncommon. Even I was beginning to believe in divine providence. Maybe the gods were on my side after all.

The magistrate did not know what to do. He noticed everyone around him was staring at him and then again at the two of us. The twins refused to move, and Primus looked absolutely miserable. I think he feared he would be struck by Jupiter's thunderbolt. Someone else asked the Prefect what he intended but he was so perplexed he just stood there unmoving. Just as he was about to say something else, which may or may not have meant that we were to go free, the gods intervened for the third time. Surely this was another miracle and one that could not have been better timed.

From across the wide expanse, a small balding older man, clad in robes and sandals, came running and yelling for the Prefect. "Your Excellency, Your lordship. Stop. Wait. Please." He was out of breath and struggling to talk and inhale at the same time. Both twin soldiers turned simultaneously to examine the man and gauge his intentions.

"There has been an incident at the Temple of Isis. (He paused to breathe). We need a healer as soon as possible. (another pause as he bent over.) You must see to it."

"An incident?" Loreius said, "What kind of incident. What do you need a healer for?"

"There has been an assault. One man is wounded and our brother Tacitus is dead, I fear."

"Again. It has happened again!" They have defiled another temple!" said the magistrate. Then he paused and looked at both Livia and I with a puzzled look on his face. "What is your name? When did this happen?" he asked again of the priest.

"Just now, Prefect. (deep breath). This morning.

(deeper breath). My name is Dorian and I am high priest of the temple of Isis."

"Did you see what happened?"

"Not exactly, Prefect. But it involved a man with a large knife, and there is a stranger lying next to Tacitus with a deep chest wound." He exhaled heavily and took in another deep breath. "And they have stolen some objects from the temple."

"They?" asked the magistrate, "there was more than one?"

"One got away. I don't know why the bigger man stabbed the bearded one, but they were fighting."

I looked at the priest and said excitedly, "That's him, that's the bearded Mithran that attacked me."

More and more people were gathering around to hear what the new excitement was about. Loreius noticed the attention, and then reflected for a moment on what the squat priest had said. He looked again at Livia and I and an expression of realization flooded his face.

After a moment of staring into many expectant faces among the gathering crowd around him, he said, "Ah yes. It was Marathon, the bearded man, who attacked both temples and killed Vibiana. I knew it all along. That is why I sent Titus here to plead his case with the goddess and allow this divine miracle to occur. The meaning of the messages by the goddess is conclusive. Venus has provided us with the answer. Justice will prevail."

He then looked around and paused, waiting for agreement, but there was still general confusion, given his complete reversal in tone from only minutes before. I think everyone was trying to get over the shock of the earthquake and did not have time to process what he was saying.

"We will capture this Marathos and his accomplice."

Slowly it sank in. Everyone around was beginning to shake their head in acknowledgment and understanding. Lorieus was now getting more confidence and gathering more bystanders to listen to him speak. I considered correcting him about the name of the Mithran, but one look from Livia and I thought better of it.

Loreius said, "We must go to the temple directly. Lead us there, priest." He looked around and asked, "Where is Septimus?"

After hearing the officer was still rounding up more guards of the wall for riot control, he scowled again and said, "There is no riot. There is only celebration here. We have just witnessed another miracle. Do I have to do everything in this town?"

He turned toward an elder to his left and said, "Clarion, gather some of the rest of the council and join us at the temple of Isis as soon as you may." He looked at Crispus and said, "You two soldiers come with me."

"What about us?" I asked.

He looked annoyed with me and said, "The goddess has saved you. You are free, of course." He thought for another few seconds and said, "However, I still have questions of you about this Marathos man. You come with us too."

We headed towards the north of the grand temple. It was several blocks to the temple of Isis from the forum, first past the large market on the right, then under the arch of Augustus and then past some beautiful houses and shops. It took several minutes walking to reach the temple of the Egyptian goddess, and the lack of food in over a day had made me weak. I stumbled along the cobblestone vicolo, and had trouble keeping up with the forced march of the magistrate.

Fortunately, Crispus and Primus had freed us from our bonds, so we didn't have to hobble along with bound ankles. It felt good to finally get the hemp ropes off of my wrists. The skin on my legs and arms was deep red where the fibers had dug into the flesh. As we walked, I gazed up to see the looming haze of Mt. Vesuvius visible in front of us in the distance, just catching the late morning light. Cloud tops obscured the dome, as they usually did. I thought of Herculaneum, the city in its shadow below, and wondered whether the Mithrans were gathering there to reap havoc on the community, as they had in the past. When we finally reached the temple of Isis, there was quite a commotion going on. A healer was busy trying to wrap bandages over the neck of a priest, but judging by the blood on the linens, it looked pretty bad and the wounded man was not moving. Resting against a column along one wall was the bearded man, in the same gray tunic he wore last night. He was holding a linen to his shoulder and seemed to be bleeding severely. He looked quite pale and in great pain. He also had a slash wound on his leg and a cut on his forehead. I only glared at him when he looked up at me. A group consisting of Dorian the priest, Loreius, Crispus, Primus, Livia and I, all approached the bearded man together. He looked at each of us in turn.

He finally looked back at me, smiled, and said, "I thought you would come. I'm sorry about last night."

"So," said Loreius, "Mithros, the murderer, you are sorry for killing the prostitute Vibiana?"

"No, I am sorry for hitting this man in the temple. And yet again, your lordship, you have implicated the wrong man. I did not kill Vibiana."

"Hah, so you say." was all that Loreius could manage but he was obviously flustered by the bearded man's challenge.

"She was the love of my life, and had she lived, we would have been happy together in the land of the pharaohs." he said in a thick accent. "And my name is not Mithros, it is Zahret of Alexandria."

I interrupted and explained to the magistrate that he was a Mithran, and that was his religion, not his name. Loreius only glared at me, and I immediately shut up. Livia then whispered to me to be quiet and listen.

"I do not know what you have heard, Prefect, but this man is correct about one thing. The killer was indeed a Mithran, but he and I are opposing forces in this matter. Neither the blacksmith nor I harmed the lady Vibiana. The Mithran is to blame."

Loreius looked at the bearded man incredulously. I wanted to argue that this was the man I fought in the temple, but Livia quieted me again.

Both of the twins had their swords drawn and pointed at the wounded man. The bearded man coughed heavily and finally spoke again before lowering his head to his chest. "Sadly, it does not matter now."

"I fear that I will bleed to death by night's end. I have lost my love and I am responsible for her death, though it was not by my hand and instead due to my own folly. I will follow her to the west shore of the Nile and the glory of the afterlife. We are of the faithful of the great Gods of Egypt, and will be judged at our end by the scales of Osiris." He paused long enough for a healer to hand him a fresh bandage and to clean the wound on his leg. "If I tell you the story, maybe you can reap justice on the mad dog who killed my Vibiana, and who has pierced my chest with his bewitched dagger."

Loreius was intrigued to hear more, and bent in closer to listen. The Egyptian man coughed up some more blood and closed his eyes, then looked at the soldiers and asked for some water. "See to it," said Loreius, and Primus left for a nearby fountain.

"I am the captain of a small merchant ship, which trades the sea ports between Egypt and the lands of Rome and Greece. It happened that I came about five years ago to come into the port of Pompeii, and visited the city to have some wine and rest. In a wine bar on one side of the forum, near the Marina gate, I looked upon the loveliest woman I had ever met, with golden hair and dark eyes. I inquired about her, and eventually found her house in the Lupinare. After introducing myself, I stayed the night in her bedroom as a client. I was enchanted from the first. I returned frequently to Pompeii when I was on this coast and spent much time with her. As we shared a passion for the Egyptian gods, I often told her of the stories I had learned from my homeland about the great gods and goddesses of our lands, the histories of the great pharaohs, and their many exploits. I brought her the finest ornaments and protective amulets from our land on my visits back here. I frequented the bazaars in Alexandria for presents for her, and brought lavish gifts back to my love each time I returned from Egypt. Her villa became a shrine to the gods, and held very great and wondrous objects from the lands of the pharaohs. She welcomed my return every few months and I would spend many days with her before returning to the sea. Our trysts changed over time. Eventually I became much more than her rich client or even her friend and patron. We fell in love and were planning to settle back in my home in Alexandria as life partners. I required but a few final trading forays in the east to establish my fortune to sustain us for the remainder of our lives. He coughed again several times and winced in pain. Blood was continuing to ooze from his chest wound.

"This has nothing to do with the murders, Zahret, please get to that!" exclaimed Loreius, who was afraid the bearded man would die before telling him about the killer.

"I'm coming to that," said the bearded man. "On my last trip to Alexandria, about eight weeks ago, I was approached by a foreigner at the Alexandria docks. He said his name was Tarquinus of Herculaneum, and he offered to trade an impressive bronze, gold and onyx medallion for transport back to his home city. He said he had lived in Egypt for many years, but was dying and wanted to return to be buried in the necropolis next to the town of his forefathers." He paused and drank from a wooden bowl of water that Primus had brought from the fountain. "Thank you soldier." He said to Primus, and relaxed a little.

The priest then interjected, "That is the magical medallion of Isis. The other man ransacked the temple looking for it and slashed Tacitus' throat, when he refused to hand it over."

Dorian then looked over at the other priest who was being carried away by two other men. Everyone gazed at the bald priest named Dorian, and then toward the spot where Tacitus had been tended to. He had apparently died and was being wrapped in linens and prepared for his burial. The woman healer had given up on Tacitus and was coming over to again tend to the bearded man's wounds.

Zahret waved her off, and said, "I am past the point of your help, healer."

The woman looked disappointed, but waited a short way off near a large column in case she was needed further.

"Please continue, Zahret." said Loreius, "especially about this magic Egyptian medallion."

It was plain that the magistrate was patently interested in this part of the story. No doubt he would like to collect this artifact and bring it back to Pompeii and discover its secrets.

"Actually, the medallion was not Egyptian. I think it was made in the Far East," said Zahret. Everyone looked confused, and he went on, "I told Tarquinus that I was a tradesman, and my little vessel did not take passengers, but he was persistent and persuasive. He said the medallion held many secrets and that its possessor could gain great riches. He said it was a gift to the pharaohs from Isis, hoping that I would want to purchase it. Shopkeepers where he had attempted to pawn it told him of my interest in these types of ornaments and ancient amulets of the pharaohs. However, I knew immediately that the medallion was not Egyptian. Unlike Tarquinus, I am able to read the ancient script of the pharaohs. There was scrollwork and symbols on the medallion, but I think they were of Persian origin, and there were no hieroglyphs that I could recognize."

Loreius then interrupted, "But you decided to purchase it anyway, even though it was not genuine."

"Yes, I did. You see, I could see that it was made of gold and was very old. I think its worth was much greater than a ticketed journey across the Mediterranean. I eventually accepted the offer and brought the man on board my ship. But I never trusted him. He kept an eye on the hold where I kept the medallion at all times, and I think he meant to steal it back for his own purposes once we arrived in the port of Pompeii. Fortunately, at least for me, he never made it. His heart gave out on the voyage over here. When he was at death's door and his soul was ready for its journey to the afterlife, he told me to take the medallion to Herculaneum and find any remaining followers of Mithra. He said they would pay handsomely for the medallion and it would be worth my while. He died before I could get any more information out of him, and I buried him at sea." He winced again deeply in pain and stopped for a minute before going on.

"It took a few weeks to reach Pompeii, as I had other ports of call to stop at on my voyage. Once I arrived here, I was planning to leave soon after and inquire in Herculaneum about the medallion. But when I showed it to Vibiana, she coveted its beauty and power. I could not refuse my love, so I presented it to her immediately as a gift without further thought. When she showed it to your priests here and told them it had been given to me as a "medallion of Isis" with mysteries of great magic and power, the priests of the Egyptian gods allowed her to wear it in the procession at the ceremony of resurrection two weeks ago."

"Vibiana wore the medallion at the festival for all to see, hung by a simple leather strap laced through two holes in the back of the golden piece. The two holes represented the eyes of a bull etched into the back of the metal of the medallion. She told me she knew a blacksmith and planned to have a great elaborate matching chain made for the piece to replace the leather strap. That was when there was the first hint of trouble. Rumors spread wildly about the medallion and its power after its debut in public, and word must have reached the Mithrans in Herculaneum that their missing medallion had finally returned. Several days later, I left for Herculaneum to see about the medallion's history. While I was away for a few days last week, a man visited Vibiana wanting to buy the medallion. He offered her many bronze and silver coins, but she feared the looks of the man and told him only that she would consider his offer. He asked to see it, but she did not trust him and even though it was in her villa at that time, she told him that she was having it made into a necklace and didn't have it in her possession. He then changed tactics and told her he admired her great beauty and would like to spend the night with her as a client. However, again she was suspect, and told him she had another client coming directly and declined his offer. He left without the medallion, but she became frightened and unfortunately I was not yet there to protect her."

"When was this visit?" asked the magistrate.

"It is now five days since."

Everyone reflected on this, and wondered what had taken place in the ensuing days between then and the murders.

# CHAPTER 7: THE MITHRANS

"As I said, I had taken a three day journey to Herculaneum to inquire further about the medallion and its origins. I had no knowledge of these Mithrans, so naively I asked about them everywhere I went. I discovered they were a religion, albeit a misguided and evil one. Everyone I met told me to end my quest and go home, and that the Mithrans were no longer living in that city. I could tell they were still reluctant to speak each time I mentioned the cult, and more than once I was dismissed by people who no longer wanted to answer my questions. I became more and more intrigued by this cult and their relationship to the medallion. After several discussions around bars and restaurants, I had heard all sorts of wild stories and rumors of their exploits."

The bearded man tried to get up, but struggled. Crispus was able to keep him from falling with a hand under his arm, but after a few seconds of straining, the man slumped back down and rested against the column to his back. The Prefect looked over at me with some concern. He wanted to hear the story but he was afraid the man was going to pass out before we could get more information.

Crispus again bent down and wiped the man's brow. Zahret looked up at the soldier with an expression of thanks, and then continued, "From bits and pieces from people I had talked to, I discovered that the followers of Mithra were originally comprised of a group of thirty or forty middle class men. Women were not allowed as members. The cult was originally founded in Ostia, the wealthy port city to the northwest of Herculaneum, but spread to several neighboring cities over a decade or so. They worshipped an Eastern god named Mithra who promised salvation for the faithful. Mithra was said to have been involved with the original introduction of evil into the world at the dawn of creation. I think his followers chose to follow his evil path to gain money and power. Their secret ceremonies were said to be extremely brutal and involved beatings and self-mutilations. Unlike the Egyptian deities, Mithra is an angry God, and he is believed to feed on misery. It was said by some that a few of their members were involved in the slave trade and took money from the prostitutes. Others claimed their followers threatened and harassed shopkeepers, who had to pay them "taxes". It was rumored the Mithrans had acquired great wealth and material goods, but they became too greedy and failed to pay their tribute to Rome, and the capital finally noticed. I could glean only little bits of information from the townspeople, who were generally reluctant to speak of what they knew. I was finally sent to a small house on the mountainside which was owned by an older man named Blandus. He had been imprisoned for many years for being a member of the cult, but he had only been a minor disciple and had been released. Apparently, he was repentant and had long ago instead followed a different religious path. He asked which gods I followed, and when he discovered I was of the Egyptian faith, he opened up to me and told me some of the early history of the Mithra and some of its leaders."

Everyone listening was now transfixed with the story and implored Zahret to continue, but he coughed severely and had to pause. He drank the last of the bowl of water and sat quietly for another minute regaining his strength. After several more moments, he began again. "Having heard all of this in the day leading up to my meeting with the old man, I asked Blandus many questions about the Mithrans and their exploits. Blandus told me that the Mithrans of Herculaneum had no temple. They met in caves at the base of Vesuvius. Mithra is said to have killed a giant bull, so sacrifices often used that great beast of burden, but only after contests with the bull, where the followers were often bloodied. He was reluctant to talk about any crimes and claimed to know nothing about any atrocities or illegal activities by followers of Mithra, but he did talk about the ceremonies and organization of the cult. The old man explained to me that they had various stages or levels of progression through their ranks represented by raven, lion, serpent, scorpion and dog. There are still pictures of these totems drawn on caves on the mountainside outside of Herculaneum. The Mithrans had to go through brutal initiation rites to move higher in their ranks. The old man denied it, but I have learned from others since that these rituals involved torture of innocents and other crimes which eventually caught the notice of the Romans. They apparently gained control of the entire town of Herculaneum and extorted money from some of the patrician class, becoming quite wealthy in the process. As you probably know, however, the Roman soldiers finally came and the cult members were mostly killed or imprisoned. Over twenty years later, I guess that there are still remnants of their faith left in Herculaneum, and indeed in Pompeii, but no one knows where they hid their amassed fortunes. The Roman soldiers never found any of the wealth of their cult. Many have died in the past two decades searching for it in the dangerous caves below Vesuvius."

Everyone looked at each other in wonder, and Loreius seemed especially skeptical, until he looked again at the man's bleeding shoulder and the spot where the other priest had been killed. He must have considered how precious an object was to push a man to assault three innocent people.

The bearded man drank thirstily from the cup of water and after finishing the bowl, he coughed a few more times. The cool draft appeared to give him renewed strength. "I discovered from Blandus that the medallion and its companion jeweled dagger were ceremonial objects, used in the rituals performed in the caves below Vesuvius and had been with the cult from its early days, even in Ostia. The objects had been made by a Persian who had founded the group and he supposedly added magic symbols to protect them. The Persian moved the group to Herculaneum after being run out of Ostia and was apparently their leader. Blandus would not even mention his name and must have feared him even in death. He said the Persian could read the ancient writings and knew of many tales of the Eastern gods. The Persian was killed as soon as the Romans came to free the city over two decades ago, but not before he must have been able to hide much of the Mithran wealth. The Roman soldiers never found neither the medallion nor the dagger, nor in fact anything but a few small clusters of coins in some of the cult member's houses. Blandus refused to admit to any personal wealth and said he was only a religious follower when he belonged to the group. He said he had never heard of a man called Tarquinus, but when I described Tarquinus and his features to the old man, alarm came into his eyes. He said that my description and the approximate age of the man fit the description of Palindus, who was high among their ranks until breaking ties with the group. Palindus was apparently a thoroughly devious and dangerous man. Blandus said that among Mithrans at the time it was known that Palindus was the individual who sold out the Persian and other leaders to the Romans. He afterward fled overseas as a coward to save himself from Roman wrath. Blandus told me that I was lucky to be alive if I had encountered Palindus on a lonely ship at sea. He was not above strangling me in his sleep. He said that if Palindus had the medallion, he probably was returning to Herculaneum to pass on the medallion and its secrets to his heirs. He had two children at the time of his disappearance and the imprisonment of the cult, but Blandus could only account for one of them. Blandus said the older child was imprisoned by the legion in his teens. This elder son died several years ago, still in jail. The younger son was apparently a drifter and Blandus did not know his whereabouts. Palindus' wife had died in childbirth. Like many others of the cult, the wife of the Persian was also tortured to death by the Roman soldiers, in an attempt to find their hidden wealth."

Zahret was wincing now and was holding his shoulder with his other arm. He was obviously in great pain and there was blood in the corners of his mouth. Loreius urged him to finish his story. He sent the priest Dorian for some linens to help bandage the man's wounds. A few minutes later he returned and shredded several of the towels into thin strips, which he proceeded to wrap around the bearded man's chest with the help of the female healer. Zahret was too wounded and weak to protest and now let the healer help with his injuries. Within only a few minutes the bandages were already soaked in the dying man's blood.

"Please continue, sailor!" said the Prefect.

Zahret stared up into the eyes of the magistrate and nodded slowly. "The old man Blandus seemed to get misty eyed when he talked about all of this, but I understood why. He himself faced similar torture while in captivity. He showed me the scars on his fingertips where his nails had been torn out by his Roman captors and he even lifted his tunic to show me the fibrous scars all over the skin of his back. He said he was tortured intermittently for a few months, but after several years in a prison cell, he was finally released. He said he hadn't heard anything about the medallion in decades. I believe he was hiding something because he cut me off every time I asked about the Persian or physical descriptions of any other followers. He warned me that anyone looking for rich hordes of wealth was likely to be very dangerous, whether they followed Mithra or not. Before I left him, I was told by the old man what the Persian had told him long ago, just after the Romans arrived, but before he was crucified. The Persian had told Blandus that the deepest secrets of the Mithra would be revealed when the medallion was placed with its companion dagger. I asked if he thought the objects were magical, and he said he didn't know, and had long ago quit trying to decipher what that last message from the Persian had meant. He just said the Persian had always maintained that the power of the two objects lay in their coupling."

The Prefect's eyes were now as wide as dinner plates and he was leaning over towards the bearded man, to the point of almost falling. Livia and I just stared at each other. We noticed several men in the corner of the temple were now carrying the dead priest out of the building. Livia looked horrified and came over to me. We hugged tightly and she buried her head into my shoulder. Zahret watched all this and wanted to rest for a while, but Loreius urged him on in between coughing fits. Zahret finally composed himself enough to continue. "With the knowledge of the Mithrans and their relationship to the medallion, I hurried back to Pompeii at rapid pace, for I feared for Vibiana's safety. I realized that in my ignorance, I had been too public with my questions, and had spoken openly about the medallion to many listening ears. I figured there were now potentially many dangerous men who knew the medallion was back in Pompeii. What I didn't know was that the owner of the dagger had already paid Vibiana a visit, and had already heard rumors of the medallion even before I had entered Herculaneum, originating from its presence at the festival of resurrection."

Zahret again tried to raise himself, and this time both Primus and Crispus helped him to his feet. The healer looked at the bandages and checked his eyes and mouth. I'm not sure what she was looking for but Zahret spat up a large amount of frothy blood and collapsed into the arms of the two soldiers. He asked to be taken to a table to lie down, but the Prefect protested.

"Turn him over. Sit him down. We must find out more about this murderer!"

Zahret was breathing very heavily and he looked quite pale. He told the magistrate he would continue his tale but he needed more water. Loreius pointed to Crispus and said only, "You heard him. Go!"

It was several minutes before Zahret could continue. Both Primus and Loreius were now kneeling close to the wounded man as his voice had become little more than a whisper. We all circled him closely to be able to hear.

"I returned to Pompeii only three days ago and was extremely concerned when Vibiana told me of the visit by the large man. I told her I would stay with her for protection, and she was greatly relieved. At length we decided the medallion was too dangerous to keep in her possession, and believed that it would best be hidden in the temple under the protection of the priests of Isis. We took the medallion to Tacitus and tried to explain the legend of the Mithrans to him, but he was only blinded by its beauty and possible magical properties, and cared not for the danger that accompanied it. We left it to the safe-keeping of the Egyptian priests, and asked all over the city about the stranger. No one from Pompeii recognized the man who visited her, and he never offered her his name. She described him to me as having a big frame and dark oily hair with a dark complexion and black eyes."

Livia looked intently at the bearded man and said, "I saw that man two days past. He came to the shop asking if we were working on a chain for a medallion, but I told him no, and that he must have the wrong metalsmith. He left disappointed."

Everyone shook their heads in acknowledgement. I looked at her in alarm. I considered how lucky she had been that the man had not killed her and tried to search our house on his own. Livia saw the concern on my face and said simply. "Don't worry. It was nothing. I was in no danger."

Zahret looked at her and waited for her to continue her story but she only shook her head and let him speak again.

"I did not leave Vibiana's side for a full day afterward, as she needed comforting and her nerves had gotten the best of her. I believe that she had already foretold her own death.

Then early yesterday afternoon, the man returned once more." Loreius looked relieved. "Finally." "We get to hear why he killed her."

Zahret moaned and grabbed his neck and shoulder, but after a few minutes continued, "I believe he meant to rob Vibiana of her medallion, thinking that it had come back to her after having a new chain attached. In fact, she never got around to adding a chain, and the medallion was now safely out of the villa and under the protection of the priests. He was very surprised and angry yesterday to find that I was with her at Vibiana's house when he arrived. He obviously thought I was a client and offered me money to leave him with her for the evening. He was wearing the dagger with the bull headed scabbard on his belt. When I refused to leave, he pulled the knife on me, but I was prepared for danger and had my own blade. I pulled it from my own belt and faced off with him, knife in hand. I told him that I was a ship's captain and was no stranger to combat. He thought better of confrontation and lowered his weapon. I then asked him his name, but he only sneered at me and told me it was none of my affair. I told him that I knew he was a Mithran outlaw and that he wanted the medallion to find their hidden horde of treasure. He looked astonished with my knowledge of his background and purpose there, and then glanced down at his dagger again. I asked him if that was the dagger of legend and the companion of the medallion. He asked me what I knew of the dagger, and I told him I knew that when coupled with the medallion it would share the secret of the riches of the Mithra. He seemed extremely agitated at that point that I was aware of his plan and knew all about the legend. Vibiana told him that we had sold the medallion and were no longer in possession of it, but he didn't believe us. I said that he could fight me, and even if he won, a search of the house would prove we no longer possessed the medallion. He stared around the room and calculated what to do, but after looking at my knife and seeing he was not in the superior position, he retreated out the door. After the Mithran man left empty-handed, it occurred to me that we needed to get the medallion to a safer location. I figured the priests could be in danger if he discovered its location, and I needed to warn them again."

At this point several other men entered the building, including two more soldiers. I did not recognize them, but they were obviously important. They came over to us and looked down upon the bleeding man on the floor and were about to ask something, when the magistrate silenced them. He looked sternly at each in turn and they backed away.

"Please go on, Zahret."

"While we were planning to move the medallion, I thought again about the legend Blandus told me and wondered about how or why the dagger and the medallion would need to be brought together to obtain the secret of the hidden horde. I didn't like the Mithrans or their god, and I had not heard of any sorcerers or other users of magic among their count from my discussions with Blandus. Even the Persian sounded to me more like a thief and scoundrel than a priest or sorcerer, despite what the old man had said. If it was not an ancient relic from the gods, I doubted it had any magical powers. I surmised that if one could use the dagger to pry the large central jewel from the base of the medallion somehow, perhaps the inside of the metal would have the location of the riches carved in runes on the exposed side. It seemed more logical than ascribing mystical powers to something owned by gangsters in Ostia. Vibiana sent word for the blacksmith to come and we would try to break the medallion apart to find its secrets. I went towards the temple of Isis to again retrieve the object from the priests, while Livia entreated you to come to her villa, Blacksmith."

He pointed at me and everyone looked in my direction. "Unfortunately, as you know, it is half a millarium from the Lupanare to the temple of Isis. I underestimated the devious mind of the Mithran. He hadn't left and was just hiding down the block in an alleyway and waiting for me to leave her house. He intended to perform a thorough search of her rooms to find the medallion, or maybe he wanted to scare her into telling him who she had sold it to. He charged back in to Vibiana's villa late in the afternoon, and tore the place apart. The Mithran tried to beat its location out of her while I was gone. I was nearly to the temple of Isis, when I got a bad premonition about her safety and turned around. I believe it was a divine message to me from Bes, the Egyptian god of the home, warning me of Vibiana's impending peril. Had I considered the man's ruthlessness, I should never have left her alone. I didn't trust the black haired man and I felt stupid for leaving Vibiana unguarded, even if the Blacksmith was to arrive quickly. Instead of heading on to the temple, I immediately turned around and ran back at full speed towards her house. I entered her villa and found the dark haired man lying on top of her on the floor of the bedroom, threatening her with the point of his dagger. She kept telling him that the medallion wasn't in the house, and that she didn't have it anymore. But I think at this point he was enjoying her torture and wanted to prolong her suffering. I crept up to him in the bedroom, surprised him from behind, and we fought viciously. Unfortunately, I had left Vibiana with my own knife for her protection, and I had no weapon on my person when I returned. I grabbed his neck from behind and wrenched him off of her before he had an opportunity to cut me. I hit him squarely twice in the head before we separated. Several times he came close to stabbing me with the wretched dagger, but I was able to fend off most of his blows by blocking his stabs with hands and arms. I still had several cuts from his vicious attack. I picked up a small stool near me and brandished it like a spear and blocked many more of his slashes with return blows of my own to his forearms and shoulders. We traded deep lunges toward the other, and I parried thrust after thrust, swinging wildly with the wooden chairlet until two of the legs broke off. While we were so engaged, Vibiana was able to rush out the door past him. He turned and was about to run after her, when I tackled him, but as we went down, he twisted quickly, and landed on top of me in our struggle. I had both hands wrapped around his right blade hand to keep him from slitting my throat, and while my attention was drawn to the hand with the dagger, he took a small statue of Isis to his left and used it to club me with his other hand. I'm afraid it knocked me out completely and I did not wake for several minutes."

"That was why the villa was in such a shambles!" I offered. Everyone looked at me for further explanation, and I said, "I was at Vibiana's house just after their struggle. Everything was broken and laying on the floor. I even saw the broken statue of Isis right where Zahret was hit with it. There was blood on the floor."

Loreius was staring at me now, and frowned.

"Convenient that you corroborate each other's stories so nicely, Blacksmith." His eyes pierced through me with cold indignation and there were several seconds where no one said anything.

Zahret coughed loudly and that seemed to break the tension. He continued, "I had no idea where Vibiana or the man had gone. I was lucky he didn't kill me while I was unconscious, but I think he was more concerned with chasing down Vibiana. He may have saved from killing me only because he did not yet know the location of the medallion. After I awoke and gained my feet, I worried for my Vibiana and I stumbled out into the night air to attempt to find and protect her. I searched the surrounding streets for what seemed like an eternity. When I returned, after less than an hour to the villa, I saw a man coming out of her front door towards the terrace. He questioned a small boy in the front vestibule and then headed off. It was you, Blacksmith, but I had never met you and

thought you a possible accomplice to the dark haired man. My head was foggy with the earlier blow to the head and I had somehow forgotten that we had sent for you. When I saw the blacksmith keep looking around suspiciously up and down the street, I assumed he was a Mithran and still searching for the medallion. He carried a satchel, and I thought it might hold more weapons. I followed him at distance, hoping he might

lead me to the large dark man. He walked cautiously down the vicolo, and kept turning back to look for anyone following, which only made me more suspicious. I had to stay in the shadows a full block or two behind him to avoid being seen. When he reached the forum, I lost track of him for a few minutes and was looking all over the plaza from a vantage point adjacent to the temple of Vespa. It was then that I saw a crowd beginning to gather at the front of the Temple of Venus at one end of the forum square and I heard several shouts and cries. I became fearful that Vibiana had been found by one of these two Mithran men, so I ran out of my hiding place towards the temple. I raced up the stairs only to find my Vibiana lying dead on the vestibule floor, her abdomen slit from stem to stern. I bent down to her and held her in my arms and cried. I kissed her repeatedly and asked the bystanders which one of the Mithran scum had killed her. One of them said it was Titus. I did not recognize that name, and thought it could have referred to the name of either of the Mithrans. I had been following you, Blacksmith, so I assumed you were the assailant. I am sorry again that I jumped to the wrong conclusion."

Everyone looked again at me, and I didn't know how to answer. The story was confusing me. I said, "But I saw you, hiding behind the column in the sanctuary. You were already in the temple when I got there. You killed her! This whole story is a lie."

Livia grabbed my arm, and Loreius and the two soldiers were glancing back and forth between Zahret and me, trying to decipher who was telling the truth. I think at that point in the story, the Prefect was still convinced I was the killer or at least somehow involved. I'm pretty sure Loreius would have liked to have the bearded man implicate me further in the murder somehow, but if so, he was disappointed in the bearded man's words that followed.

Zahret smiled at me directly, and said, "No, blacksmith, the man hiding behind that column was indeed the killer, but it was not I. That was the dark haired Mithran man."

"But I fought you, not him." I protested.

"I did not arrive at the temple until you had left Vibiana's body and had retreated further into the cella. That must have been about the time that you spotted the Mithran by the column and pursued him. When I sat holding my dead Vibiana, I became more and more enraged. The vestal virgin standing there eventually told me you had just run back towards the inner sanctum, so I left Vibiana's corpse and chased you down. I saw you creeping slowly towards the back of the sanctuary and I tackled you from behind. In my rage, I wanted and needed the satisfaction of finding and killing the Mithrans for hurting my beautiful love."

He looked directly at the magistrate and explained, "When I caught up to the blacksmith, I took pleasure in hitting him, for all the imagined hurt he inflicted on my future bride and for ending our dreams prematurely. I was misguided and fueled by passion and hatred. Fortunately for the blacksmith, I was both exhausted from a previous fight and I had underestimated his skill in barehanded combat. He fought valiantly and surprised me with several blows."

Crispus looked over at me and grinned and nodded his head at me, but Livia looked at me with great concern.

Zahret continued, "On other days perhaps I could probably easily beat this blacksmith in a fight. With a bump on the head and having already been bested by the Mithran, the blacksmith and I were both lucky, through the mercy of the gods, for both of us to leave the temple with our lives. I would have fought him to the death but for something that caught me by complete surprise. The blacksmith, who I had thought was a Mithran hooligan, looked at me with rage in his eyes and called me the murderer and said he would avenge Vibiana."

Zahret said he lost focus for a second and stared into my eyes. He saw there not the cold eyes of a killer, but the pained expression of one who had lost one that they loved. Everyone was now staring at me and especially into my eyes. In response, I looked down at my feet so as not to look into Livia's accusing face.

He said, "I realized then that this was an innocent man who had only come to see Vibiana and found her villa trashed and had worried over her. It was only then that I remembered we had sent for a blacksmith to help us with the medallion, and

I understood at that instant that this man was Vibiana's friend who she had sent for. I wondered for a second how and why he had come to this temple, and remembered Vibiana mentioning this man at other times in the past. I guessed that he saw the condition of her rooms and feared for her life as I had. He found the temple by accident in his search for her. He too must have loved her and when he saw her body, must have wanted to avenge her. Perhaps he had even seen the killer in this temple, and he apparently thought that man was me."

We all were silent while we contemplated the meaning of his words.

"All of this came to me in second of realization. I quit fighting the blacksmith and looked quickly around the temple from my vantage point behind the great statue to see if the Mithran was still in the vicinity."

I felt embarrassed even though much of what he said about me was true. Everyone was looking at me, especially Livia, so I said to all who would listen, "I have never slept with Vibiana. She was only my friend, but it is true I loved her like a sister." Livia grabbed my arm and gave me a knowing glance of reassurance. I didn't see jealousy in her look, but only understanding and pity. I smiled back at her and nodded.

Zahret replied, "Then I have wronged you, blacksmith, and was almost the cause of your execution. I am sorry for our fight, and especially for not telling my story sooner, for I truly loved your sister-friend."

He looked at me with deep sorrow.

"If I could have, I would have prevented your executions," he said to me, "but I was preoccupied with several other tasks." He looked around at the listeners and continued, "Just as I was about to explain to the blacksmith that neither of us were the killer and our feud was pointless and misdirected, I spotted the Mithran opening the side door to the temple and running out into the twilight. I did not want him to escape so I chased after, leaving the blacksmith there in the temple."

He went into a very long, harsh coughing spasm and ended up spitting a large amount of bloody sputum from his mouth. He groaned loudly and fell to his side. Crispus was holding his head and looking at the man with the deepest of concern. No one in the room thought the man would live much longer.

Loreius said, "Wait, Zahret, captain of Egypt, wait. Tell us about the medallion and the murderer. Where did he go? Why did he stab the prostitute?"

It took several minutes for the bearded man to gain his composure. He was struggling to breathe and his chest was heaving rapidly. Blood was everywhere. I was becoming sick with so much injury and death and I could taste bile in the back of my throat. Loreius told Primus to get him more water. At length, Zahret sat back up but he struggled severely to continue his tale. He shook his head in anguish.

"I don't know why he killed my Vibiana. She probably ran to the temple because it was close to her house and she thought there would be many people there in the forum for protection. It was well over an hour between the time she left her villa before she was found in the temple of Venus. She must have been hiding somewhere nearby and decided it was safe to come out in the open. Since the man likely knew of her connection to the Egyptian temple from the ornamentation of her villa, I'm sure she didn't want to go there for fear of running into him. It may be that he lost her and just came to the town center hoping to catch her going to the Prefects office in the public administration building across the forum plaza. Maybe that was where she was heading too, she just never arrived. I assume he saw her there in the forum and chased her into the temple just minutes before the blacksmith here entered the plaza. He must have caught up to her just as she was at the top of the steps in the vestibule. I believe at that point, he must have finally figured out where the medallion was hidden or perhaps in her fear, she finally confided to him its location. Deciding he no longer needed her, he dispatched her with his dagger in the most horrific and brutal fashion."

Everyone considered this for a minute, before I asked, "Why was he still in the temple after he killed her, even up to the time we fought?"

Zahret spoke slowly and thoughtfully, "He was probably hiding at first, trying to keep from being seen as the murderer. I think he was confused by your presence, blacksmith, following him, and wondered what part you played in all of this. He stayed and watched you from behind the column to detect your purpose. I'm sure he was even more confused when he watched us fight each other. Once he overheard the blacksmith accuse me of the murder, I think he became alarmed that everything was to be explained and his identity and motive would be revealed. He probably reasoned that he would soon be outnumbered and so he ran into the night."

It was the Prefect who was now asking most of the questions and they came in rapid succession. "Zahret, where did the murderer go? Did you chase after him? Why did he come here for you? What did he do with the medallion?" Loreius' was almost frantic. You could see his mind working feverishly to put everything together. He was desperate to find out about any potential treasure and where it might be, and he watched as the bearded man was slipping closer and closer to death. "Why did he kill the priest?  Where is he now or where is he going?"

Livia suggested we let the man rest and to quit further pestering him with questions, but Zahret shook his head and said he was nearly finished anyway.  He looked at Loreius for a few moments, thinking about his questions and whispered softly, "I do not know what happened to the man for the remainder of the evening.  He quickly lost me on the back streets of Pompeii north of the temple.  After a short time of looking for him, I had to return to my Vibiana and to take care of her burial arrangements.  That is why I could not come to your aid later with my story for the Prefect.  I went back to where Vibiana lay and convinced two of the local men to help me carry her body down the Via Consolare to the tombs of the Herculaneum gate just outside of the wall of the city.  There I spent several hours cleansing her body and preparing it for her immortality.  I had her placed in one of her finest gowns and buried in the necropolis there.  I had to return to her villa to obtain the dress, several amulets and a papyrus containing images and verses of the book of the dead so that she could complete her journey to the west bank of the Nile and the afterlife.  He groaned again and then asked that we do the same for his body when he died.  He told us that there were many coins on his ship docked at port and at Vibiana's villa in a wooden box under the bed."

I told everyone that I had seen that box lying empty in the bedroom when I had been at Vibiana's last night.

Zahret just shook his head and said "Murderer and thief."  He coughed again several times.

"Please continue!" urged the magistrate.

"When the Mithran had killed Vibiana and still had not obtained the medallion, he must have wanted to go directly to the temple of Isis. Even if had I wanted to go there and wait for him, it was more important to ensure that Vibiana would reach the afterlife. It was morning before I arrived in the temple from the necropolis outside of the city wall."

He paused and we all considered this version of events, and everyone was shaking their heads in understanding. The high priest named Dorian then added, "We saw the man sneaking around the temple last night, but there were many priests and revelers about, in anticipation of the Venusian festival today, and he left when he was confronted."

"Unfortunately, after the fight with the blacksmith, I could no longer worry with the motives of the Mithran man and cared not any more for the medallion. I was heart sick with the death of my beloved, and was praying to Isis and Osiris for her safe trip to the afterlife." Zahret went into great detail about his beliefs concerning the underworld, and the preparations necessary to ensure that one's soul reached the desired resting place. He lamented the fact that there was no one in any of the neighboring lands who could perform the embalming procedures necessary to transform Vibiana's mortal remains to those of the Egyptian mummies. "Indeed," he said, "there are few left even in my homeland that have the knowledge of the ancients in the art of mummification. Only the pharaohs of the family of Ptolemy and Cleopatra in the century past have been able to revive some of these ancient arts, and there are but a handful of practicing priests with knowledge of the special herbs and elixirs required. Few of the citizens of Alexandria can afford such luxuries in death in the current times."

It was Dorian who was now most interested in the conversation and he actually sat down beside Zahret and held the man's hand.

"While she could not be mummified in the ancient tradition, at least she had the proper enchantments and vows given at her passing." The bearded man then looked at Dorian and said, "I must thank you, priest, for agreeing to perform the Egyptian rites and rituals for my Vibiana last night, so that her soul may be judged correctly by Osiris and be at peace forever in the afterlife."

Dorian stood up and bowed low, and then said almost under his breath, "If I had not, then I would not have been delayed arriving at the temple this morning, and would have met the madman when he arrived. Like Tacitus, I would too have my throat cut." He shook his head in disgust.

After another long pause and several bouts of wheezing and spitting up blood, Zahret continued, "It was only this morning, having finished the details surrounding Vibiana's burial, that I thought again about the circumstances of her death. I surmised that the Mithran was very likely to visit the temple of Isis to search for the medallion. When I came here at sunrise and spoke to the priest Tacitus, the man had not yet arrived. I warned the priest about the Mithran and his ill intent again, but Tacitus said it was nonsense and that he had already heard the murderer was caught. I left the temple to go find out about his possible capture. I discovered only a short time later that you had arrested and imprisoned the wrong man and were going to execute him this afternoon." With that he pointed an accusing finger at the magistrate, who scowled back.

"I was doing my sworn duty," said Loreius indignantly.

"I hurried back late morning here to the temple and waited in the shadows hoping for the Mithran to return. He took his time. I guess he thought he was in no danger, with the blacksmith in custody. While the ceremony was occurring in the

Forum several blocks away, he finally showed up here to look for the medallion. Before I could reach him, the Mithran had accosted Tacitus and wounded him severely. I confronted him again, with blade in hand. I found my own knife lying on the floor of the villa when I had gone back for a burial gown and protective amulets to bring to Vibiana's tomb. I would not go about without being armed. When he saw me approaching, the Mithran turned his attention and his blade again toward me. We took turns slashing at each other and marked each other's legs and arms with bloody gashes. In my rage, I became impatient. I tried to finish him with an overhead downward strike to his left shoulder, but I underestimated his skill with a blade. A lesser fighter would have tried to block the death blow with a raised left arm, while trying to stab with the dagger in their right hand. That move I expected, and was ready to counter with my own left arm sweep. Instead, as I lunged with the dagger overhead in my right hand, he sidestepped to my right, blocked the downward blow with his right forearm and dropped his dagger from his right into his left hand. Before I realized the cunning nature of this move, he buried the dagger in my right breast with his left hand. I am afraid it will finish me before the day is finished." He shook his head at his own failure and closed his eyes again.

Zahret was laboring now over each word. He paused between each sentence to take a deep breath and his eyes were glazed over as if he was unable to focus. He only continued speaking after further prodding from Loreius.

"Please finish your story, Zahret." asked the Prefect, but the dying man's words were now barely audible and he paused several times to wince in pain.

"As I dropped down to my knee after the mortal blow, I

cried, "I failed you Vibiana, but I will join you soon." I lay here helpless as I watched him corner Tacitus, who was already wounded, and extract the exact location of the medallion from the frightened man. I cried out to Tacitus not to tell him anything, as I knew he would be killed as soon as the medallion was found. The Mithran moved quickly to the back of the sanctuary and when he came out of the cella, he carried the medallion wrapped in a linen cloth. Before leaving, he promptly slit the priest's throat and left us both dying on the floor." Zahret was now really struggling to breathe and the healer had moved in and was seeing to his wounds again. However, the bearded man was beginning to lose consciousness.

"I, I am done," the bearded man managed to say briefly, before his eyes closed. His face lost all expression, then he coughed heavily one last time and he fell dead.

## CHAPTER 8: PREPARATIONS FOR THE JOURNEY

"But we never found out who the other man was, or where he was going." lamented Loreius. "We will never find the medallion again."

"Herculaneum," I said. "The legend says the hordes of the Mithrans were buried in secret caves outside of Herculaneum."

The magistrate looked keenly at me and his eyebrows furrowed. "You seem to be an expert on this issue, blacksmith." "In fact, you seem to know a lot more than you have been telling me. How do I know you are not involved?"

"Did you not listen to the bearded man's story?" "I am only a bystander. The bearded man and I were strangers before yesterday and fought each other fiercely only last night."

The magistrate thought about this and said, "In which case, you may have been in league with the Mithran all along. He fought the bearded man as well."

I protested my innocence again, before he added, "We must follow the dangerous Mithran man to Herculaneum and catch him before he finds this great treasure" and then he said quietly to himself "or retrieve these riches from him after he locates the treasure." He looked around the temple at no one in particular and stated, "We will bring him to justice, and then Pompeii will share in the riches of this forsaken cult."

I was thinking what a good idea that was until the magistrate added, "and you, Titus the Blacksmith, will go with my soldiers, since you have such intimate knowledge of this case." "If you do not, then I must assume you are in league with the Mithrans and I will have you executed after all, despite your apparent miracle in the temple of Venus earlier today."

I was about to argue with him, when Livia grabbed my arm and interdicted. "Your lordship is most wise. My husband is great working with metal and may be able to decipher the secret of the medallion, as the Alexandrian had wished. I was born in Herculaneum and know the area and the caves well. Prefect, though I am but a simple blacksmith's wife, I will accompany my husband and your soldiers, if I have your leave."

The magistrate looked long at my wife, and finally smiled. "You are much more than a blacksmith's wife, I gather, Mistress Livia. I should not be surprised that you continue to make demands of your own of me, even when faced with your own death. You think yourself clever, blacksmith's wife, but I don't trust your motives."

He then considered a little longer and said, "However, your knowledge of your hometown may yet prove useful, so I grant your request. Be prepared to travel by first morning's light tomorrow." With that, he told Primus and Septimus, who was now waiting patiently behind the magistrate, to put together a burial detail and to take the corpse of the bearded man from Alexandria out to the necropolis of the Herculaneum gate to be entombed beside his lover.

Dorian began to collect implements for performing two additional Egyptian burials. He looked again at the dead

Alexandrian with pity, and at the spot where his fellow priest had been slain on the other side of the sanctuary, and mumbled a short prayer to himself. Everyone left the temple at once, each with their respective tasks.

Once we were a few blocks clear of the temple, Livia grabbed me and gave me the longest, firmest hug I had ever received. We stayed in that embrace for several minutes before moving on. She was crying uncontrollably and just kept saying, "Thank the gods. Thank the gods." I could feel her trembling under my arms. She looked up into my face for several seconds.

"I thought we were both dead today. I thought we were going to orphan our baby. I, I,"

I put my finger to her lips and shook my head. "I know" was all that came out of my mouth. I was visibly shaken by the events of the day and emotionally, completely drained. We had barely survived execution, and had been witness to two brutal murders in addition to the death of Vibiana last night. I was in a fog, and Livia was on the verge of emotional collapse. The walk back to our villa and shop was slow, and we barely spoke. Both of us were deep in thought. We traversed the cobblestone streets of the Via del Fortuna (avenue of Fortune), passing a few horses and carts as we went. We turned down the Via Stabiana towards the house and passed the central Pompeii Thermia bathhouse on the corner. This was much larger than the Stabiane bathhouse several blocks closer to my neighborhood, but it reminded me that I desperately needed a bath.

I told Livia as much, and she agreed. "After your night in the amphitheatre catacombs, you smell worse than the street

sewage!"

"Thanks," I replied, and said that I would go to the

bathhouse as soon as I could.

When we finally arrived at the gate to our dwelling, we stopped again.

I looked at her and said, "As bad as today was, and as much as I would like to sit and do nothing but cuddle with you tonight after I clean up, you know we are going to have to prepare for the trip tomorrow."

I had spent the last few blocks of our walk worrying about it. Of course, I was greatly relieved to no longer be considered enemy of the state and fodder for the ghoulish entertainment of the Pompeii festival goers, but I was dreading the journey to which we had been volunteered. It was a full half day walk to Herculaneum without a horse or wagon. While I had been there several times, I had seldom ever ventured farther than a league away from Pompeii. I was not an adventurer like my brother. I owned no sword to protect me, and I knew nothing of the Mithrans beyond what I had just heard. This whole idea of sending me sounded like a crazy vendetta by the magistrate.

"Why would Loreius want me to go to Herculaneum? It makes no sense!"

"He was mad at you for making him look bad." said Livia when I explained my misgivings. "If he had his way, we would both still be on the docket for execution this afternoon. It is only by the grace of the gods that we escaped our misfortune."

I reflected on that and had to agree. "I guess it really was a miracle of the gods. If the priest Dorian had been murdered along with the others, he never would have reached the forum and notified Loreius and we probably would have been stoned to death tonight or tomorrow anyway.... And the earthquake helped."

Livia agreed, but added, "Aule and Alycia were great back at the temple, and they really helped persuade the crowd of the message of justice from the goddess. I think Aule would have done everything he could have to save us from the gladiators and amphitheatre. We must go to him and thank both he and his wife."

"First I must eat. I am weak with nothing in my stomach."

She smiled in pity at me and put her hand to the side of my face. "I am sorry, Titus," said Livia. "I forgot. Let us go into the house and I'll find you something."

I was about to move into the eating area and pick up some fruit to quiet my stomach, when Livia grabbed me and hugged me again. She started crying again. "Today was terrible. We almost died. Those poor people in the temple. I never want to have another day like that."

I didn't want to think about today. I never wanted to think about it again. Just the sight of all of that blood was enough to make me queasy and if I had anything in my stomach I probably would have vomited in the temple. After several minutes of silence and more hugs and tears, we separated. While Livia considered what she was going to put out for some food for us, I pondered what tomorrow's adventure would bring. At least it kept my mind off of the ugly and tragic events of last night and today.

"How are we going to find the dark man when we don't even know his name?" I said, more to myself than to my wife.

Livia shook her head as if to say she didn't know, but she was deep in thought about something else and didn't reply out loud.

"It will be good to see my family again," she exclaimed,

and I finally understood why she had volunteered to come with me and why she was so deep in thought. She missed her parents and was looking forward to an excuse for a visit. She noticed that I had dwelt on her reason for volunteering, and added, "It wasn't just to see my parents, it was to help protect you, too, Titus. If you were alone with the soldiers on this adventure, I would worry about you constantly. At least this way, my family and I can keep you safe." She was about to hug me again when her face contorted into frown and her eyes rolled.

"Oh my god," she said suddenly, "I forgot all about Dania. I must go to Aule's and feed her and bring her clean linens."

She hurried out of the front door, ran through the front gate off to the east, and I lost her to the dark. I looked after her from our courtyard for several seconds, thinking to myself. I had almost lost my wife and been responsible for both of our deaths. My emotions waivered from grief to joy and back again. A loud growl from my stomach sent me back into the present. I walked back into the villa and began collecting food on the table.

I devoured everything I could find in the serving area. There were two small round flat loaves of bread and some olive oil, and several olives and figs, which I swallowed as quickly as I could pick them up. I was famished. It was late for Prandium, and still early for the Coena meal, but I had nothing in my stomach for a day and a night, and I couldn't wait for Livia to return. I poured some wine from a pitcher into my wooden cup and drank it almost in one gulp after finishing the other items. I would sure enjoy some meat or fish right now, I thought to myself. Since I had rarely been on extended journeys from

Pompeii, and at most only for a day or two for plumbing jobs, I had no idea how to prepare or pack for a trip like the one we were about to take. I considered the possibilities and then concentrated on just what we would need. I went over some necessary items in my head: water to drink, some food for the journey, and a weapon. I wondered how Livia and I were going to be able to keep up with the soldiers on a forced march, when they were used to such exercise. The folly of including Liv and I on this expedition seemed ludicrous. I considered for a minute asking Loreius again if we could back out based on our lack of usefulness, but I thought better of it. I did not need to give him any extra excuse to send us back to the amphitheatre. It was fortuitous that we could stay with Livia's relatives while we searched Herculaneum for the Mithran man. Unlike citizens of the elite classes, I had never been involved in a hospitium, where travelers stayed in the homes of those in other lands, in return for hosting those same individuals in their own homes at a later date. I wasn't even sure how that arrangement worked. It seemed to be something only the patrician or equestrian classes could take part in.

I remembered many details of the city from my earlier visits to Herculaneum. It was not a terribly long walk, only a few hours on the road. The cobblestone thoroughfare is well kept and well-traveled, but not nearly to the degree of the Via Appia. The Appian Way is utilized by soldiers, traders and merchants to go by land from north to south throughout our lands. It is paved and wide for much of its course, allowing chariots or carts to pass by each other without stopping. It sits just to the southeast of the Sarno gate. The Herculaneum road is not as wide and doesn't get as much military traffic as the Via Appia. It is largely used by merchants traveling only between the two towns. It occurred to me then to consider the potential perils that we might face on our travels. Outlaws and rogues would not dare attack a group of soldiers. In a half day, about the most danger we probably would face would be foot blisters. I still wished I owned a sword. I thought to myself that I should definitely start work on making one as soon as I am back from this adventure. I couldn't think of anything else I might need, but guessed that Livia would probably think of several other things. I was tired and I was still not thinking straight. I decided to wait for Liv and then go directly to the bath house.

Livia returned about an hour after I had finished eating. She looked tired but relieved. I asked her what had transpired.

"I fed our daughter and put her to bed."

"Why is she not with you? Is Dania sick?"

"No, she is fine, if a little cranky. I'm worried that the trip would be too hard on her. I want to be with her, to bring her, but we could face all kind of dangers with this mad man running loose in Herculaneum. I know we will be protected by the soldiers, but I don't think this journey is fit for an infant."

"Aule and his wife are going to keep her with them until we return. Aule was elated to see me and hear that our names had been cleared of all crimes. He firmly believes the goddess intervened on our behalf. Perhaps she did at that."

She started to well up with tears. "Do you think I am making the right decision? My mother would love to see Dania again, and we could leave her with my parents while the soldiers look for the man. Maybe we should just take her with us anyway. I can go back and tell Aule I changed my mind."

I considered both options for a moment, but a vision of the Mithran with a knife and two dead innocent victims flashed through my head.

"No. This man is too dangerous and has no morals. He would have no problem in abducting or even killing a baby if it would help him escape. I don't want my daughter anywhere near that man. I will miss her too, but she is very young to have to go through such an ordeal, and we would have to carry her for the entire journey. Leaving her with Aule is for the best."

Livia hugged me and shook her head in agreement. "I hope we won't be gone long. I hate being away from my baby."

I kissed her on the cheek and said simply, "I know. You are a great mother."

She smiled and lifted a small reed basket with some smoked fish inside. "I'm sure you are hungry. Aule offered you this."

I replied that Aule was a true friend. She smiled and reminded me that there were many people who supported us at the temple today and all tried to push for our release. She said simply, "I took note of several individuals that I will have to thank personally when we return from Herculaneum."

We sat in silence for several more minutes holding each other while lying on the cushion next to the table. I was exhausted and didn't really want to think about how I was going to handle the trip to Herculaneum, but we still needed to prepare. I asked if she had any ideas about what we should take on our journey.

"It is only a half day walk on the road. If we leave at sunrise, we could be at my parents' house by the midday meal. I'm sure they will make us a feast. It has been Dania's birth since we have last seen them. I'm sure they will be disappointed that we could not bring her."

I replied that I still didn't know what to pack for our adventure.

"We are not bringing carts nor horses to carry belongings. We need to bring as little as we can get away with. I hope to query my parents for the identity of the man, and perhaps find out where he lives. When we can give that information to Primus and Crispus, then our duty to the magistrate should be fulfilled, and it will be up to the soldiers to capture and arrest this man. We are not armed, nor are we capable of bringing such a ruffian into custody."

Her logic was sound, and I agreed that I didn't want to have to carry a large knapsack of goods to a city eight millarium away. I replied, "There are some beautiful villas in Herculaneum. It will be nice to see them once more. I'm glad we are leaving early in the morning. The walk there will not be so hot and sticky."

Livia just nodded and was laying out the fish on the table. I was still hungry, so I tore apart the dry flesh, lathered it with the garum fish flavored sauce Aule provided, and ate greedily. I left the bones on the table. I still had some wine left and washed the rest of the meat down.

I said, "I am filthy and need to go to the spas. Will you join me?"

"I'll be there directly. I need to see about clothes for my journey. I want to look nice for my parents."

At the Stabiane bathhouse, or thermae as we call them, the men and women have separate entrances and even separate pools. I walked down the few blocks to the bath house and entered through the colonnaded foyer, going further through the complex to the changing room. I laid my tunic and thongs on the bench where several others lay adjacent. I stared down at the mosaic on the floor. It showed two twin nymphs, each pouring water out of large amphora into a central pool. I always enjoyed my time in the baths here. The architecture was beautiful and the artwork added to the experience. I stared at the painting on the wall for a moment before heading towards the spa. I passed by several large marble statues and walked past the doorway to the large sweating rooms. One held dry heat and I noticed several men inside talking, while the other room next door was the wet sweating room that we call the sudatorium. The thick steam emanating from that room obscured whoever was inside. To get to the hot pool room, I had to walk through the exercise room. It was one of the largest chambers in the entire thermae complex, but had no pool. Mosaics of athletes in various competitions covered the floors and the walls. In one corner there was a very muscular man who was lifting large round bricks of various sizes. His arms strained against the weight and he dropped one of these with a thud onto the floor. He was sweating profusely and the oil on his skin made his entire body shine. In the center of the room, there were two young men wrestling on mats padded with straw sewn inside of linen sheets. Even across the room I could hear their grunts. I was a pretty good grappler in my youth. I could generally beat Crispus or Primus, but my brother used his weight and strength advantage and I usually ended up being pinned to the ground by Gallianus. I smiled at the two wrestlers as I thought of those earlier times with my older brother. I watched the two as they circled each other and one hooked his arm under the other's and suddenly flipped his opponent to the ground. That looked like it hurt. They continued to roll and grab at each other as they garnered for position. I hurried past them and into the next room.

A separate attendant slave came over to me and asked if I would care to have my skin oiled. Most often I get oiled prior to exercise, but I didn't have time to run or otherwise exercise tonight. However, I love the sensation of the oil before a bath, and it is considered poor etiquette and poor hygiene to bathe without cleaning the body with oil first. The attendant escorted me into the preparation room. In many bathhouses, you have to apply your own oil, but at Stabiane thermae it is performed by the slaves. He slowly and carefully covered me in the olive oil, and massaged it in with his large hands. After several minutes to allow the oil to moisturize the skin, the attendant took a thin metal strigil and scraped the oil from my back, legs and arms. He used a thin leather wipe to remove most of the remainder of the excess and handed me a linen for my face. It felt luxurious and especially so after the tight muscles and bruises I had from my fight last night. The oil ensures the skin remains healthy and cleans some of the dirt from the body so the pools do not become soiled. I left the small preparation room and ventured toward the hot room (calidarium). I was feeling very tired from lack of sleep the previous night, and I hadn't even reached the bathing pool yet.

I said hello to the attendant slave who was holding fresh linens at the entrance to the calidarium and entered into the large ornate room with a hot water pool at its center. The raised floor of this room was suspended on narrow pillars composed of circular bricks. The floor was covered in square tiles and decorative mosaics with aquatic themes. I splashed my face with warm water from the open basin along one wall before I entered nude into the warm soaking bath. Slaves in the level below were stoking the flames and the water was lusciously warm, with steam rising off of its surface and drifting out through the lone round window on one wall. I relaxed for the first time in two days, and let the liquid envelop my skin. I dunked my head under water and rinsed my hair. There were a couple of men from the area that were also present in the bath and they acknowledged me. We exchanged pleasantries, and while both seemed expectant that I would tell them the entire story of the previous two days, I chose to bathe in my own corner of the pool and they left me to my own thoughts. I spent several minutes staring up at the domed ceiling and the flame-proof terracotta bricks which lined the pool. After what seemed like an hour, but probably was only half of that, I left the pool pruney and grabbed a linen from the same slave standing by the entryway portal. He asked if I was going to proceed to either the cold pool in the frigidarium or the notatio, which was the large open air swimming pool in the inner courtyard. Both women and men could bathe in the courtyard pool but at different times. Apparently at this hour, the notatio was still under the men's domain and he told me it was available if I desired and could proceed on to the courtyard. He told me there were acrobats performing tonight in the courtyard around the notatio and that there were some food vendors as well in honor of the festival. I politely declined and told him that soaking was enough for tonight. After drying, I handed the linen back to him and walked back through the complex into the changing room and sat down on a nearby bench where I could put my clothes back on. I needed to get home to Livia, so I hurriedly dressed and left the building. I could hear lots of people laughing and talking from the echoes of the courtyard. As I entered the night air I got goose flesh from the difference in temperature from the warm bath waters. On the walk home my thoughts again went to the journey ahead.

    I was still apprehensive of going to Herculaneum. I didn't mind the travel and would enjoy getting into the countryside and seeing Livia's relatives, but I dreaded the prospect of meeting the dark haired Mithran man face-to-face. He had already killed at least three people, and possibly many more, carrying out the criminal deeds of their evil cult. I wondered if he already had discovered the secret of the medallion and was even now carting away horded treasure acquired over decades from Roman citizenry. I dressed quickly and soon was back in the evening air heading for my villa. There was no sense opening the shop tonight and trying to get some work done. The furnace was probably down to cold ash and would take some effort to light again, and I had completed all of the metal forming I could do on the current project.

"Goat's beard" I said to myself, I hoped I didn't run in to Gordianus again. I looked around several times and was happy he was nowhere to be seen. If he showed up, I would have to come up with another excuse why his saddlery was delayed yet again. I was considering this as I turned the corner and strode toward my house. I heard someone yelling for me down the street. It was Crispus. He was coming towards me and carrying my tool satchel.

"Hi Titus. I picked this up in the Prefect's office and thought you might need it tomorrow. We might find the Mithran man with the medallion and we should try to find its secrets before we come back to Pompeii."

"Thanks for bringing this to me, Crispus." "It is a good idea to bring my tools in case we find the medallion." What I actually was thinking was that it would be a great idea to have a weapon on me when we run into the Mithran, but I kept this thought to myself.

Crispus said that Portius was going to come with us. He was an older soldier of the guard who I knew, but he was not what I would consider a close friend.

"Is Septimus coming too?" I asked.

"No, he said he needs to stay here and maintain the guard of the wall and that he can't be off wasting time on a manhunt," said Crispus, "but I really think he didn't believe or trust the Egyptian's story and suspects the killer is still on the loose in Pompeii."

I shook my head and said, "He may be right. In fact, I hope he is right. I think Septimus could take him in a fight."

Crispus pulled his gladius from its sheath, held it up in the light, and said, "Yeah, well I hope to take the dark haired man in a fight before he gets the chance. One on one. His little bitty dagger is no match for my sword."

I was going to argue that the Mithran man was a crazed killer and was purported to be a very large, strong man and a worthy opponent, but I decided against arguing with my friend. I was just glad that Crispus and Primus were there to protect Livia and me. We said our goodbyes, and I went back to the house. I never heard Livia come home. I was in the bed sound asleep minutes after going through the front door. The next thing I knew, Livia was shaking me to get up and meet our party at the Herculaneum gate.

## CHAPTER 9: THE ROAD TO HERCULANEUM

We arrived to find the three soldiers, already packed and ready to leave. As we suspected, there were no horses, carts or chariots, but all three were carrying backpacks that looked stuffed with goods. I wondered what they had brought, and was somewhat worried I had forgotten something important. I had only my tool satchel, with a small skin of water and pieces of smoked fish from last night that were wrapped in thin linen. I did not know what Liv had with her but she also carried a small bag. Everyone said good morning to each other and after acknowledging we were ready, we walked under the arch of the Herculaneum gate and towards our destination. A guard from the parapet on the tower to our right yelled something and waved at us, and Crispus and Portius both waved back. Primus seemed to be deep in thought and hardly noticed. In fact, it was an hour before he even talked. We ambled on the paved road past the necropolis on our right. There were two extremely large villas, actually palaces, across from the catacombs on the left side of the road that belonged to wealthy citizens. The courtyards of these two mansions were larger than my entire shop and villa and were decorated with many exotic plants and flowers.

At the entrance to one of the tomb tunnels on the opposite side of the road, I saw Dorian the priest preparing to enter. I yelled after him a greeting and he turned to wave at me. I thought to myself that the man must never sleep. He said he was performing rites of Osiris for the dead Egyptian man and preparing his body for his travel to the afterlife. He seemed to be going to a lot of trouble for this man and his dead female lover, and then I remembered the wealth of the Egyptian and wondered if part of the interest might involve taking some of the dead man's estate for the "good of the temple". I suspected that the magistrate had already confiscated the Egyptian's ship and most of its contents "for the good of the state." Maybe I just was being cynical, but greed, or at least money, seemed to drive much of the political and religious institutions in this town.

We continued on the cobblestone path, past the tombs of the north side and towards the great mountain in front of us. We passed another palatial villa on our right just past the necropolis complex. I didn't know who that belonged to, but they must be very important. I looked again to the mountain in front of us. The entire top of Vesuvius was enshrouded in clouds this morning and the air seemed to be heavy with dew and mist. The farmers and slaves who worked the fields on either side of the road had not yet come to their pastures to start the day's toil. We saw a few shepherds herding goats and sheep. Most likely they had slept in the pastures with their flocks all night. It was strangely quiet and few birds were singing. In fact, we heard nothing but the caws of the magpies and huge flocks of crows as they moved in unison towards the south. I found that a little strange to see so many crows all moving with conviction in the same direction. It is said that crows are portents of bad tidings. I thought of several things that could go wrong on this journey, starting with the Mithran and his accomplices catching us unaware and surprising us in the night. I put those thoughts out of my mind as we walked along.

We travelled for about thirty minutes longer before we met a group coming toward us in the distance. As we neared, we noticed two horses pulling a four wheeled cart, carrying a rather dignified man and two children in their early teens. In the back of the cart were an old woman and several objects. Behind the cart was a younger man pulling a much smaller two wheel cart filled with furniture and there were a variety of men and women walking behind them, all carrying satchels, bags or other objects. Presumably, most of these were the man's slaves as they were dressed in much more modest attire. As we were about to pass the man, Portius moved to the center of the road with his arms outstretched and stood in front of the cart and barred his path.

"Halt, please. I need to ask you a few questions." The man in the cart eyed us suspiciously but slowed his team in front of the soldiers.

"Why do you stop us, soldier? We have done nothing wrong."

"I'm sorry to bother you, good sir." said Portius in a polite tone of respect. "There is a murderer on the loose and we believe him to be heading towards Herculaneum."

"Murderer, you say? He will not find it pleasant in Herculaneum. There are many who are fleeing that town. "We have seen no others on this road moving in your direction."

Crispus looked at the man quizzically. "Why are people fleeing? What is happening?" Portius looked alarmed.

The man looked at each of us in turn, and then said, "The omens are bad. The spirits and sprites have come back to the mountain and their campfires are lit at night. We have seen these fires shining all over the mountain after twilight. I am taking my family and slaves and fleeing far away to the south. I hope the road is clear to Pompeii. My servants and I would like to be there before early morning. We are traveling further south and hope to be in the far southern provinces before nightfall."

I was looking at the man and thinking he must have gone crazy somehow. It seemed silly that so many people would be leaving Herculaneum just because of a small earthquake. I didn't see any train of refuges behind him but his servants, so I wondered what had scared him so badly into leaving his hometown. When I considered how many servants he had, I decided he could not be a lunatic and changed my mind. I figured someone of that much importance must know of what he was speaking. Something was definitely wrong there.

Portius asked if the Mithrans were behind the trouble in Herculaneum.

The man looked at Portius as if the soldier instead had lost his mind and then said, "Young man, the Mithrans have not been a problem in Herculaneum for decades. These bad omens are due to the god of the mountain. I still remember when the ground shook many years ago and our villa almost collapsed at my feet. It took months to rebuild. There was another quake yesterday. I will not wait for another catastrophe. No, we have upset the gods and in their anger they have recalled the spirits of the mountain from the underworld. Vulcan has unleashed his hammer on the earth."

I looked at him intently to try and understand of what he spoke. I could see the mountain behind him, but it looked about like it always did, with a few more clouds today than normal. I remembered the big quake years ago, although it did much more damage in Herculaneum than in Pompeii. I was in my mid teens and was terrified during that event. About every few years since we have had an episode where the ground has shaken again for a few seconds. Other than some terra cotta tiles falling and objects falling off of shelves, this has not been too upsetting and most people just go out into the streets to watch. The earthquake yesterday was very mild in contrast and didn't do any damage to Pompeii.

The old woman in the back of the cart sat up and said, "The signs are everywhere. The wells are steaming, and they say there is a foul stench on the mountain. The birds are fleeing in large flocks to the north and south, and yesterday a shepherd on the mountain found half of his flock dead in the field. One can hear the god of the mountain moaning in the night air. Hades is unleashed and ruin is upon us."

I have heard prophets talk like this on the streets of Pompeii. Maybe this old woman was also a prophet and had convinced her family and servants to leave their house and flee to the south. I have to admit it was somewhat alarming.

Portius seemed disinterested in their story and finally asked, "I need to ask you again. Have you seen a large dark haired man traveling on this road this morning towards Herculaneum?"

The man driving the cart only shook his head and said, "I told you. You are the only ones we have passed heading towards the mountain, but we have passed a few other travelers fleeing Herculaneum for the south. Those who remember the legends of old know the strength and danger of the god of the mountain and are heeding the signs. You would do well not to tarry in Herculaneum, but flee back towards Stabiae."

Primus and Crispus had had enough of the man and with Portius. They walked around his cart to the line of servants traveling behind. They tried to ask more questions but the servants just lowered their eyes and shook their heads negatively. Livia and I bid the man in the cart good travels and followed the soldiers on the road toward our destination. It took two more hours of walking before we neared the gate. We were only a millarium from the city when we saw a man on a white horse having difficulty getting his animal to behave. I knew exactly of our distance from Herculaneum as the white round milestone was visible on the side of the road. These mark each millarium between the two cities, and actually are present along all of the great highways of the empire. The man barely kept from being bucked backwards off of his horse. He was atop a basic saddle with little anchoring straps and a thin girth. He had both hands clinched on short reigns. The horse was visibly disturbed and whinnying heavily, while shaking its head side to side and up and down. The horse reared twice as we watched. After a minute of prancing about in tight circles, the man finally settled the horse and moved toward us.

He said, "I would stay clear of my mount, soldiers. He seems to have come down with brain fever. I can't seem to control him. I was only going a short distance this morning but may have to turn back to the stable as he is so agitated. This is very unlike him."

I remembered what the old woman in the cart had said about the animals and the omens and I was increasingly getting concerned about our proximity to the god of the mountain. I kept looking towards Vesuvius, but all I saw was beautiful scenery and thick clouds. We were close enough now that the mountain was off to our right, but we could still not make out the peak of the dome. The man got off his horse and after pulling the bridle over the horses head, led the animal back towards the city gate. Our group walked some distance behind him.

We entered Herculaneum from the southeast and stopped just past the city wall and the large palaestra to our left. The mountain loomed large on our right. We stopped long enough for the soldiers to discuss their next move, and Portius pointed toward the left and toward the large buildings lining the beach. We walked toward the bay for a few blocks then turned back along a wide boulevard paralleling the beach, past several beautiful rich villas on our left and our right. Herculaneum is actually a much older city than Pompeii, but it is smaller, situated as it is between the mountain and the ocean. The thick outer city walls are similar to Pompeii, but they don't surround the city, and the villas and palaces of the elite citizens are also lined by tall walls of brick and painted lime plaster. The effect is to shade the vias and vicoli from much of the hot sun. A cool wind off of the water blows between the villas as you pass. Most homes have two stories with balconies facing that same ocean breeze to help cool them in the summer. We have a patrician class in Pompeii, and the villa of the magistrate is quite large and impressive, but these houses are on a much grander scale than those in my hometown. Many probably belong to patrician families who have left Rome for the quiet and peaceful solitude of the beach here or they keep these houses as vacation retreats. They have brought their wealth with them. There are tall trees and fantastic garden terraces everywhere. I looked in amazement at the painted plaster of the nearest villa on the left. The pink shone brightly in the sun and nicely countered the somewhat darker terra cotta tiles on the roof. There was a balcony on the second floor lined by bricks. Flowers of several different colors adorned the railing. On the other side of the street, an even larger villa had 3 floors and was covered in the whitest of plaster which looked almost like marble. A fresco adorned the wall, with a rendering of Neptune and his trident astride two dolphins. The wall painting was easily 12 cubits high and nearly as wide. Most of the courtyards contained olive trees for shade and a variety of growing vegetables.

The city of Herculaneum sits on a beautiful sandy beach and the scenery is spectacular, with its grand views of the mountain on one side and deep blue green water of the sea on the other. There are many fishermen here, but the marina does not have the traffic of those in Pompeii or Ostia, and it is not a major trading port. We could see the marina in the distance jutting into the bay. There were several boats docked there. After a few blocks, Portius decided to turn back toward the mountain and the northern part of the city. We followed a two lane boulevard northeastward towards the city center, with the bathhouse, markets and forum in front of us. We passed a few shops and markets in the center of town but few people were out shopping today. We crossed the plaza of the forum and viewed the beautiful temple there on our left. A statue of Hercules and a fountain containing variously shaped fishes were placed as showpieces in the center of the forum in front of us. The marble of Hercules was especially impressive, with bulging muscles and hands tearing the jaws apart from some serpent.

We passed these slowly and admired the workmanship. The lavish temple to our far left was lined by marble columns and held a triangular roof, which sat prominently atop a line of marble figures. I tried not to think about the previous day's experiences in a temple, but instead just marveled at the imposing walls and the small figurines that were carved into the base of the roof. The marble had a slightly pink cast which made it blend perfectly with many of the other nicer villas in this town. As we past, I looked at the statue of Caesar Augustus on the front step of the temple. It was unusual to have such a statue on the grounds of a sacred temple, but this was different. As I looked closer at the figures around the temple, they were mostly related to battle scenes. I realized that this was a temple to Augustus himself, where the former emperor was venerated as a god on earth. I had heard of such a place in Herculaneum, but didn't realize until now that it adorned the most prominent location in the city forum. It was even more grand than the shrine to Augustus west of the forum in Pompeii. My eyes moved past the temple to the large dark shadow behind and above it. Mount Vesuvius towered over the city to the northeast and dwarfed everything below, providing a backdrop for all of the buildings in its vast shadow. I could still not make out the top of the peak, due to the cloud cover surrounding its summit, even though we were so close. I thought again of the old woman's words, and I secretly hoped the mountain god remained quiescent while we were here.

I was now really aware of the lack of people on the plaza, especially considering it was mid morning. I was about to say something about it to Livia, but she signaled to me that she had also noticed the lack of bodies. We just shrugged at each other. We continued northward for a few blocks towards the base of the mountain and my legs reminded me that the trip was mostly uphill. The lavish villas with their flower gardens, terraces and statuary were replaced quickly by the more familiar surroundings of simple brick and mortar buildings typical of the plebeian classes. The houses in this area were generally of one story and were built very close together. Most had very small yards in front and few had any courtyards or terraces. Still, there were many planted flowers and a few olive trees lined the cobblestone center of the street. Some of the roads to the left and right were little more than alleys and most were dirt and mud. A few children played in the alleyways, but the city did not seem busy. Portius took the opportunity to ask the few individuals walking around the forum if they had seen a man fitting the description of the Mithran, but he received no leads. We stopped again to decide upon our strategy.

Livia told the soldiers that we could go to her parents' house for a mid-day meal, since it was so close. Everyone seemed to be in agreement, since we didn't know exactly where to look. Unlike in the city center, in this neighborhood we began to attract attention from the local populace. People were staring out of windows and coming out into the street to watch us pass. It wasn't just because we were strangers, but likely because a group of soldiers in battle dress probably piqued their interest. We moved past a small wine bar in the northern part of the city and took one more right turn past a row of small, but nice looking, brick houses. I recognized this neighborhood above the forum, and very shortly we reached the modest home of Livia's parents. She ran the short distance from the road to the front door and into her mother's arms. After a big hug and some small talk, Livia introduced the three soldiers.

"How are you, Titus?" said Livia's mother.

"It's good to see you, Cassia." I managed to blurt out, but before I could say anything else, she proceeded to tell me I was working too much and I looked tired. I only smiled and gave her a hug and a kiss on her cheek. She invited us in and told us that Livia's father and brother were out on the boats with the fish nets and would not return until after sunset. We reclined on the triclinia couches aside the table while Livia and her mother proceeded to make us a great meal of fish, eggs and fruit. There was no wine, but we drank goat's milk out of a large ceramic flask. I was happy to get off of my feet. Three and one half hours of walking had made my soles hurt. We ate heartily at prandium and it was a full hour before anyone was ready to consider doing much. Crispus had discovered one of the neighborhood stray dogs in the yard in front of the house, and was spending all of his time petting, running or chasing it. The dog was black and white with a big bushy tail and seemed to be enjoying all of the attention. Every time Crispus tried to stop and come back in the house, the dog would bark loudly and get in his way, blocking the front door. Another couple of minutes of running and chasing would then ensue. Livia was catching up on all of the family news and gossip, while trying to explain to her mother all that had happened to us in the past few days.

Her mother was visibly shaken with the story and kept putting her hand to her mouth and saying, "No! No!" She kept staring over at me and shaking her head.

I hoped she didn't blame me for putting her daughter in danger. While this conversation was going on, Primus and Portius were over on the other side of the room quietly discussing strategy for finding the Mithran. When they had finished speaking to each other, Portius walked over to the ladies and asked Livia's mother if she recognized anyone who fit the description of the killer—large, dark oily hair and dangerous.

"Well, I don't know about the dangerous part, but most of the men of Herculaneum have dark hair. It is a small city, so it shouldn't be that hard to locate him if he lives here. Are you sure that it is this town that harbors the murderer?" she asked.

"We are not sure of anything, except that he is the killer and he is a Mithran," I said. My comments confused her, as Livia had obviously not gone in to that part of the story with her, and she looked at each of us in turn.

"The Mithra? What have they got to do with this? They broke up long ago and there are no active followers left in the community. The Roman soldiers took care of that."

Livia said, "So we have heard. But we also heard there is a man here who knows much of the Mithran lore and might know who this man is. Do you know of an old man named Blandus?"

Livia's mother frowned and looked at her daughter with dismay. She replied, "Of course I know Blandus. Everyone knows Blandus. He is nice, harmless old man who never hurt anyone. He could not be your killer. He couldn't even lift up a sword, poor old man." She looked at the two soldiers and implored them to leave the man alone. "Most people around here have to give him food every so often. He is in poor health and can't go out with the fishing boats. I don't know what he does for income. His shack is up at the top of the city on the hill, near some of the mountain paths." "I do hope you don't bother him. He is frightful around soldiers in uniform. The Roman soldiers hurt him and his family badly."

Portius explained that we did not intend to hurt him,

only to get information from him and especially to help find the identity and possible whereabouts of the murderer. "Have you heard about the magical medallion of the Mithrans?" asked Portius.

"Magical medallion? No. I don't know anything about that." and then she added, "The Mithrans who survived the purge of Nero are all poor and most are old and alone. I do not think you will get much useful information with them. I doubt that any of them have enough money to buy a medallion. The few that are left don't have enough coins to buy bread."

Primus and Portius thanked her for the meal and her information and told us we needed to try to find the house of Blandus. Livia asked if she could stay and talk with her mother while the soldiers interrogated Blandus. Primus agreed, but he emphasized that we needed to get explicit directions to the old man's house. Cassia told them they would probably get lost in that part of the city due to the blind alleyways, and then said she needed to go to the market anyway for some food for the evening meal. She also needed to stop at the bakery to buy loaves. She coaxed Livia into escorting the soldiers to the old man's house while she went to pick up food. She told us that although the house of Blandus was nearby, the only way to get there was through a circuitous route to the west, looping back around north and east along dirt paths. She assured us we would get lost without a guide. I think her mother sensed that Livia and I were still in trouble with the Pompeii magistrate, and wanted us to cooperate as much as possible with the soldiers. Livia begrudgingly agreed to leave her mother to her shopping and after getting explicit directions from Cassia; we exited her house and headed up the street toward the northwest end of Herculaneum.

As we entered the front terrace area of the parents' house, Primus yelled obscenities at Crispus and chastised him to get back to work. Crispus put his helmet back on and fell in rank with his fellow soldiers in our march up the street. The black and white dog followed about fifteen cubits behind, his white tail wagging happily side to side and his tongue hanging from the right side of his mouth. He barked aloud every few minutes or so, and Crispus did his best to keep from playing with the dog on the trek up the hill.

## CHAPTER 10: BLANDUS AND HIS PAST

We walked for four blocks parallel to the mountain until we could see the semicircular open air theatre to our left and somewhat below us as we looked toward the beach. It is a very nice venue, and although smaller than the grand theatre of Pompeii, it is equal in size to the theatre Del Piccolo there and much more ornate than either. It has beautiful statues everywhere including two of the city's benefactor, Marcus Nonius Balbus. One of these bronzes has him riding a great stallion. I wondered at the craftsmanship in working with the metal to form such a wonderful structure. While I am pretty gifted at working with metal, the art of sculpture is one I haven't yet mastered.

At this point we turned right toward the mountain and walked steeply up the hill for several blocks on a nice tree-lined boulevard. The smooth cobblestone vicolo soon turned to a dirt path. The houses in this neighborhood were in poor condition, with missing plaster and exposed red bricks. Some had linens covering windows or holes in the terra cotta roofs, and most were missing doors. We had to backtrack for a couple of blocks back in the direction of Pompeii, towards the house of Marius and Cassia. We were walking on a small dirt road which eventually turned steeply uphill again toward the mountain. We eventually came to a small one story house at the end of the dirt pathway and ambled as a group up to the open doorway.

Portius yelled, "Blandus. Blandus of Herculaneum. We would like to speak to you."

We heard some movement inside and someone yelled back, "Yes, please wait. It takes me a while to get to the door. I don't receive many visitors."

A stooped, white haired gentleman in a soiled, tattered tunic came to the portal but stopped in horror when he saw the soldiers waiting outside the door. He was visibly upset, and said "Oh no, please, I haven't done anything. I'm just an old man. Please leave me be. I don't know anything. Don't hurt me." He was shaking uncontrollably and was almost in tears.

Livia comforted him and said, "It's OK, Blandus, we are only here to ask you a few questions about the Mithrans and their medallion. We need to know what you told Zahret."

He stopped shaking long enough to look up her. He kept staring at the soldiers and pacing back and forth. Finally he looked back at Livia and said, "I don't know him. He came here asking questions. I didn't know anything. Please go away and leave an old man to himself."

He tried to turn and back away but Portius grabbed him and shook him. He said, "Listen old man, we've come all the way from Pompeii on the trail of a murderer, and you had better tell us what you know."

At that the old man looked at each of the soldiers in alarm and started shaking again. He said he had never even been to Pompeii and didn't know anything about any killings. "I have rarely ever had any visitors in as long as I can remember," he said, and then he started whimpering and begging the soldiers not to torture him. He was really pitiful, and started mumbling to himself. Both Crispus and Livia tried to comfort him, but it didn't seem to help. He retreated into his house with several of us following him. He was shaking and now crying loudly. It was Crispus who finally calmed the old man down enough to reason with him. Crispus said, "Blandus, we didn't mean to disturb you. Perhaps you could sit down with Livia and Titus here, and answer a few of their questions. We soldiers will wait outside."

He put his hand on the shoulder of the other soldier and indicated with a jerk of his head for them to move out into the yard. The three armed soldiers exited out the man's entryway and into the street. Crispus waved at Livia and me, and said they would be asking around the neighborhood for the dark haired man. The black and white dog was jumping up and down all around Crispus as he talked. I admired Crispus for his ability to understand and empathize with people. He had figured out before any of us that Blandus was petrified of soldiers and uniforms, and that the old man was obviously reliving his days in captivity. I think he would have gone into fits of seizures if the soldiers had remained. A few minutes after Portius and company had departed, the old man finally settled down enough to at least stop shaking. He wiped his face, then sat on a bench in the small room and eyed us carefully.

Livia was first to speak, "Blandus, a few days ago, an Egyptian man named Zahret came to see you."

The old man only nodded.

"Yes, well, he asked you about a medallion that he had acquired in Alexandria from a man named Tarquinus."

Blandus looked at her and only nodded again. After a

few moments his demeanor seemed to change. He asked if Livia was the bearded man's lover, the woman who he had given the medallion to. Blandus added, "Zahret said you were beautiful."

Livia thanked him, then explained that no, she was only an acquaintance of Zahret and not the object of his affection. He seemed confused by her answer, and generally distracted by the whole conversation. I watched him intently as he fiddled with his soiled tunic. It was hard to maintain his attention and several times Livia asked the same question.

"I'm afraid both Zahret and his mistress Vibiana were killed by the same man, a man who apparently lives in Herculaneum, and a man we believe is a Mithran" Said Livia.

The face of Blandus changed from disinterest to one of alarm, and he looked up. The change in his demeanor was not only sudden but severe. His tone was defensive. "I don't know anyone who would want to kill the man, he said. I'm not involved. He came here on his own accord. He asked me several things and I told him. That's all. Don't send me with the soldiers. Please! I don't know anything!" He began to cry again, and put his head in his hands.

Livia put her hand on his and said, "No, its okay. The soldiers are not here for you. We are trying to find the man who killed them. We thought you might know who he is, or at least you could tell us what you told Zahret that might have led to his murder."

Livia was obviously trying to help this old man get through this rough experience, but Blandus kept looking at me wondering if I was going to hit or otherwise hurt him.

Finally, I said, "The killer used the jeweled Mithran dagger to kill them, and stole the medallion."

Blandus quit sobbing and looked up at me with red eyes. After rubbing his face on the sleeve of his tunic, he gained his composure. "Then he was not of the Mithra." he said matter-of-factly.

We both looked perplexed, until he added, "I know of the knife of which you speak. The ceremonial dagger was an object of great importance to our religion." "One of the faithful would never have used it to slay another human being. It was to be only removed from the scabbard during our rituals to the god, and only for taking the blood of the bull."

We both looked at him skeptically. I said that the killer had used it for not one, but three separate murders and had apparently been wearing it on his tunic belt when he was first observed in Pompeii.

He shook his head several times and looked down at his hands. Even from where I sat I noticed the scars on the skin and that most of his fingers lacked any nails. He seemed to take a few moments to assimilate what I had told him and it was a while before he looked up at me. "How old was this man?" he asked.

I answered that I had never seen him personally, and Livia had only met him briefly. We described him as in his mid or late thirties with black hair and eyes and that he was in good enough shape to win in hand to hand combat against an Egyptian ship captain.

The old man looked at us and said, "There are none left of the Mithra who fit that description. We were slaughtered mercilessly in the reign of Nero the tyrant. Those few who are left are old and bent like me. This man is not of the Mithra." He wiped his snotty nose on his sleeve again as he finished the sentence.

"He must be." I protested. "He knows about the legend of the medallion and he had the dagger."

The old man then asked about particular features of the man's appearance. We explained what we knew, and he dwelt on one aspect specifically. "You said this killer was very large, a big man with dark eyes?" he asked.

"Yes that is what we heard."

He looked down at his hands and said simply, "Scaevolus. I am sure you are looking for Scaevolus. Only he would have such cruelty. He is a criminal and has no morals."

Livia and I looked at each other, and then asked, "Do you know where to find this Scaevolus?"

"He lives in the rundown villa of his father, but I doubt he spends much time there. Instead he is more likely to be in the brothels or taverns, or sneaking into the grand palaces to steal material goods. He is often at odds with the law, but they are afraid of him ...and with good reason."

"You said he lives in his father's villa. Is his father still alive?" asked Livia.

"No", said the old man and he wiped his brow with his wrinkled hand. "He died a few years ago. I did know his father, but I detested him. He pretended to be a follower, but was only drawn to our religion for its mystique. He used his position in the group for his own gain."

"So he was a Mithran leader, like the Persian or Tarquinus?" I interrupted.

Recognition seemed to spark in the old man's face when he heard me mention the Persian. He stared at me blankly for a few seconds, and then said, "Sartarus was no leader and knew nothing of the old ways. He never got farther than the level of lion."

Livia then asked, "So this Sartarus, you think he is, or was, the father of the murderer?"

Blandus looked at her blindly as if he was deep in thought, and answered casually, "If the killer is Scaevolus, then yes, he is the son of Sartarus. And Palindus, or Tarquinus as you and the Egyptian called him, was no true leader of the faithful either."

The old man noticed the confusion on both of our faces and went on with his story.

"At first, Sartarus listened eagerly to the teachings and took part in the ceremonies. Over time, he became a disciple of Palindus and fell under his sway. They thought they could use the network of middle class men who made up our cult to form their own private army to support nefarious criminal activities with which Palindus was involved. This had nothing to do with religion and more to do with greed. Palindus and Sartarus were criminals. They were both kicked out of our order and left to their own evil devices. I think they continued to extort money and steal from the locals after leaving the Mithra. They were furious with the Persian and eventually vented their combined wrath towards him. They were responsible for all nature of crimes that were blamed on others in our order. Sartarus was not as devious as Palindus, and I think Palindus came to consider his partner a rival. When Palindus betrayed and decimated our order, Sartarus was also turned over to the Romans. The treachery of Palindus was complete."

"You sound as if the Persian and the Mithrans were guiltless, as if they were not even involved in any criminal conspiracy." I said.

The old man smiled at me, showing only a few teeth remaining in his mouth, and said, "Like your Egyptian friend, you listen but you do not hear, and you look but do not see."

Livia and I just stared blankly at the tanned, worn face with deep wrinkles and the wet red eyes. The old man went on to explain,"You know nothing of the Persian or our religion. You know only what has been written by those who would like the truth smothered."

Livia countered, "Tell us, Please. I grew up and lived here in Herculaneum and heard only the old rumors. I would like to know the real story."

"Over half a century ago, the Persian, as everyone called him, came to Ostia from the far east. He actually did not come from Persia, but from even farther in the distant lands beyond Babylon where there are elephants and tigers and ancient peoples. He brought with him relics of his religion and great texts. You see, he could read Sanscrit and Greek and was quite a learned scholar of the Eastern gods." He paused and smiled to himself. "He came to the great harbor of Ostia by ship over the seas from those distant lands with his father. They did not stay there in Ostia, but traveled on to Rome to join others of the Mithran faith. This was almost three quarters of a century ago. They started practicing their religion with others in Rome at that time, which included the worship of Mithra, who was one of the most influential of the Eastern gods."

I said, "Yes, I have heard that Mithra first brought evil into the world", before Livia punched me in the arm and frowned at me.

Blandus only shook his head in pity at me. "The god Mithra brought knowledge and learning into the world, which some other jealous gods saw as evil. Many of the gods did not want mortals to have any sacred knowledge, but instead to keep us in the darkness."

"Oh," I said in wonder.

He continued, "The Persian, whose actual name was Radijah, studied the ancient texts and after he had attained adulthood, moved from Rome back to Ostia to attain some more religious freedom. Tiberius had initiated strict moral practices and started purges of religious beliefs that he felt countered the morals of the Olympian gods. Both he and Caligula, who followed him, had many followers of lesser religions put to death and they each persecuted Mithrans as well during their tenures as emperor. This was somewhat hypocritical considering the depraved orgies that they were supposedly involved in. In Ostia, the Persian acted as high priest to some of the few original Mithran faithful, as he was very learned in the ancient texts. But because of the climate of intolerance under the emperors of that time, the local inhabitants were very suspicious of foreigners and the secretive practices of the religion bred contempt and false rumors. To escape further religious persecution, the Persian and his new wife Vimala left Ostia after only a few years and settled in Herculaneum. They had no money to build a temple, and in fact, were discouraged by the ancient texts from doing so. He and a few of his followers met in caves at the base of the mountain and practiced the sacred ceremonies. Radijah had reached the level of dog, which is the highest degree of enlightenment among our faith. As word spread of this "secret society" and its mysterious rituals, more men joined, some out of pure curiosity, some out of a quest for ancient knowledge. I was of this faith from an early age. I used to listen in wonder while the Persian told the old tales." Blandus smiled again to himself while he reflected on his past.

While he was deep in thought, I looked around his small cramped villa. It was more like a room, and there was dirt and litter scattered everywhere. A cloth rug covered the center of the room. Other than the sofa in which we sat, and the bench in which he cowered in the corner adjacent to us, there was no other furniture in the room and no central table for dining. I looked back at Blandus when he finally spoke again.

"Later, Palindus came to muscle his way in to the group, and he began to take on leadership roles as he ingratiated himself with other fratres and patres of Mithra. Palindus attempted to gain higher rank among the group by intimidation and actually boasted of his own levels of enlightenment, but without any scholarly effort or attempt to achieve those accomplishments. He was supposedly at the level of scorpion, but in fact was little more than a raven. The Persian tried to set him on the correct path, but in vain. For a time, he influenced others to follow him, including Sartarus. His criminal activity was at odds with our teachings, so he was finally expelled when those grievous acts came to light. That decision to ban him from the order turned out to be disastrous for everyone."

"How did Sartarus die?" I asked.

Blandus answered immediately, "He was imprisoned for several years by the Roman soldiers, and was sickly for most of his life. He died of the plagues of old age. He was obsessed with finding the secrets of the Mithran order and spent much time after his release in the caves searching for ancient treasures behind this house in the mountain. You see, he never got very far studying in the religion. With his fascination and early devotion to Palindus, their development and knowledge of Mithra became stunted. I think in his elder years, he thought he could find riches in those caves based on misinterpretation and innuendo he and Palindus had gathered from our ceremonies."

"And you do not believe there are riches to be found?" asked Livia.

Blandus answered, "If there are secrets there, they need to be left alone. The search for Mithran riches has led to nothing but bloodshed and misery."

I couldn't argue with that. "You sound like you really loved and respected the Persian and his knowledge and devotion to the ancient religion." said Livia.

He looked at her for a very long time without saying anything. Finally, he spoke. "I was wrong about you, mistress. You see and understand much. What is your name?"

"I am Livia, and this is my husband Titus."

"Well Livia, I will tell you something that I have not revealed in a score of years. Not to anyone. But I will only tell you on one condition."

"Name it."

"You must never tell the soldiers who accompany you. Never. Or I will be tortured again or killed." stated Blandus with a serious face.

"I agree to your condition, Blandus." She said.

He looked at her again and then paused while staring at me, until I finally said, "me too."

"Radijah was my father. Vimala was my natural mother. That is why I was imprisoned so long ago when still only an impressionable young man."

It took a while for his words to sink in. "Oh great goddess" said Livia, "No wonder you don't want us to tell the soldiers."

He nodded then said, "When Palindus was expelled from the Mithra, he continued his rampage on the local populace and all the time boasted that it was in the name of our cult. In his deviousness, he meant for our downfall and ruin. He sent word to Rome of our great riches and hidden wealth, and that we were not paying our taxes. At that time Nero was emperor and in the very first year or two of his reign. He was only in his late teens, but everyone knew of his tendency and fondness for excess. He had also inherited some of the past debts of Claudius and Caligula, his forbearers. Given the large palaces that lined the shores of Herculaneum, it did not take much imagination for the young emperor to conclude that the cult was fantastically wealthy. He bought into the vicious lies of Palindus and perpetrated great horrors on members of our religion in the pursuit of wealth. Of course, none of the palaces belonged to the Mithra. It didn't matter. He sent his troops to find the riches for himself, and to take them by force to replenish the Roman coffers.

My father and mother were the first to die, and did so without even understanding their crimes. All of the great texts were burned or lost, and the ancient artifacts were dispersed. Palindus gave up the names of everyone he knew to be of the faith, including eventually his former criminal partner and friend, Sartarus. I don't know how or when Palindus and Sartarus got the medallion and dagger, but I assume they stole them from our villa after my parent's arrest. I think they each originally shared the stolen artifacts and had one or the other item in each of their possession, possibly as a pact of trust between them. But Palindus, in his greed, betrayed Sartarus to the authorities in order to steal the dagger from his partner and have both sacred objects for himself. Disregarding any magical power, the two relics were worth a fortune due to their jewels and gold and bronze character alone. Before Sartarus was jailed, he must have hid the dagger somewhere and Palindus had to flee across the oceans before he could find it. The local elite had by that time convinced the Romans that the captive Mithra were telling the truth and all of the perceived evils of our order were actually the actions of only the two expelled men. Despite years of torture and imprisonment, Sartarus never told anyone where he had hid the dagger. I doubt the Roman centurions ever even knew about the existence of the medallion or dagger to ask about them. Once Sartarus was released to freedom, he obviously retrieved the dagger at some point. Palindus and the medallion were lost to us all. After our release from prison, Sartarus came to me many times in the ensuing years asking for information that would help him to find the secret horde of treasure from the east that he imagined was hid in the mountains. On more than one occasion he asked about the medallion or if I had heard any news whether Palindus had returned to Herculaneum. He must have heard from somewhere about the coupling of the dagger and the medallion as the key to the secrets of the Mithra. He was under the impression that the Persian had many more ancient objects from the Fareast hidden somewhere. For my part, I blamed him for the death of my parents and never helped him in his quest or with his questions. I never knew of any other objects. When he died, I assume he must have bequeathed his dagger to his son Scaevolus."

We pondered all that he had said, and after a minute I finally spoke and broke the silence, "Tell us more about the son,

Blandus. We need to find out as much as possible about this killer."

Blandus reflected a moment before speaking, and then began, "Scaevolus wasn't always a scoundrel. He was relatively young when his father was initiated into the order, and it was only a few years later that Sartarus was imprisoned. Due to his youth and lack of knowledge, Scaevolus was not considered a threat and was never incarcerated. I did not know his mother but it is possible she died of natural causes while Sartarus was in prison. The wife of Palindus had died in childbirth and had also left a young son a little older than Scaevolus. The older son of Palindus died on the executioners block in the arena. I believe Scaevolus and the younger of Palindus' boys were friends in their youth, and due to their family notoriety, they were both largely shunned among their peers in Herculaneum. With little or no income in their families, they could have starved to death or been sold into slavery at a young age. Instead, they turned to criminal activity in their teens and Scaevolus has been in and out of trouble for years. Had there been a constant Roman security presence in Herculaneum this past decade, he likely would have been caught and probably already executed. We only have a few armed soldiers in our village to keep the peace and protect us. Even so, Scaevolus was doing occasional illicit favors for a prominent citizen in town living in the palace district, and I think he must have been protected for the past several years from arrest. From what you tell me, it seems of late he has run amok and that protection will likely not be enough to keep him from execution in the gladiator's arena this time."

I asked if he knew the name of the boyhood friend of Scaevolus and if they were still potential accomplices, but he said he didn't know and tried to stay as far away from them as he could.

Livia said, "Blandus, do you think Scaevolus killed all of those people only for the medallion? It seems such a waste of life."

The old man shook his head, and said, "I think he was originally motivated by greed, and wanted to find the secret treasure that had bewitched his father's soul, but his scars and anger run much deeper than just lust for money. I think he blames the world for his lot in life, and takes pleasure in the misery of others. I think he enjoys killing, and will continue this murderous spree even if he finds the secret of the medallion."

"We must find him soon then." I said to both and they nodded their heads.

Blandus then added, "You will need the help of your soldiers outside. He is big, brutal and dangerous."

I hoped I didn't have to be involved in his capture. Let the soldiers do their duty instead.

"Where does Scaevolus live? Where is his house in Herculaneum?" asked Livia.

Blandus frowned and said, "That is the most painful of ironies. You see Sartarus moved into my parent's house when he was freed from his prison cell about twelve years ago. My parents were both dead, and he took the opportunity to search their abandoned villa for any secrets to the whereabouts of Mithran treasure. I was still imprisoned for another two years after that, so at the time I couldn't protest."

I exclaimed, "But that's not fair! He was older and more involved than you could ever have been. How was it he was released first?" Blandus smiled at me and replied, "Yes, he was older, but he had been expelled from our group, and had really never attained higher than a rank of lion. I was already at the scorpion level. In any case, even as a man in only my mid-twenties, I was the son of the person implicated in the conspiracy, so I was held for a very long time. As long as Nero was emperor, my chances for freedom were very small. After all, I knew the truth of the events of the persecution and the emperor's role in it. It didn't matter to the Roman magistrates that we were guiltless."

Livia and I were the ones frowning now.

"Scaevolus was not on friendly terms with his father and only occasionally shared his house, but when Sartarus died, Scaevolus took the opportunity to move into his father's quarters. The structure had suffered two decades of neglect and the house is almost a ruin now, but it gave Sartarus a place to hide out."

He stood up and stretched. With his thin build, prominent bones and rags for clothes, he looked absolutely wretched. At least he was no longer shaking or wailing as he was when we entered.

"The remains of my parent's house are not far from here. It is only four blocks to the west and a few blocks down towards the port marina. It is near the outdoor theatre." He said as he pointed out the directions.

Livia stopped him and asked, "Blandus, I believe your story and I feel sorry for all that you have suffered. But I am bothered that I have never heard of this version of events before. When I was a very little girl living in Herculaneum, I recollect the round-up of your cult, but I remember everyone was scared of your group. Why is it that all of Herculaneum thought you guilty?"

Blandus reflected on this and said finally, "I think it is due to a number of things. Firstly, people fear what they don't understand. Our religion was different, and our ceremonies were not public, so people imagined wild goings on, when in fact we performed rituals like any of the other religions. Herculaneans made up stories about our beliefs, even though in truth, our religion involved peace, knowledge and understanding. The lies of Palindus fed into this. He spread vicious rumors to discredit my father and our followers so that he could seek revenge for his dismissal. In fact, he was probably responsible for several crimes of which we were blamed. He brutalized the prostitutes in this town and extorted money from others and claimed our secret organization would hurt or kill them if they didn't pay. In fact, his organization included only Palindus himself and Sartarus. Not knowing the truth, citizens assumed they were acting on the orders of the Persian and the other Mithra. People with strong, but different, religious beliefs have often been targets of the Romans. Nero was actually worse than either Tiberius or Caligula for persecuting those of other religions. He hunted the Mithra, but also the Jews and the Christians. Greed, in order to steal their wealth, was only one of his motives. Fear and bigotry were also involved. You know what happened to the Judeans in Jerusalem only a half century ago. By the time of the burning of Rome, there were no Mithra left in either the capital or outlying provinces. That was probably fortuitous, because as it was, he blamed the fire of Rome on the Christians instead of our faith. In addition to destroying the Mithra, the Romans under Nero's edicts also quashed other lesser cults in other cities in this province and tried to confiscate their property and possessions. They replaced those religions with Imperial cult worship. In fact, the temple of Augustales in the city center of Herculaneum is still the largest source of priests dedicated to the emperor's cult across the whole of the empire."

He thought for a while and with seemingly greater conviction added, "Lastly, the smearing of our religion was political expediency. The newly elected Nero was rapidly draining the public treasury of wealth for his own wasteful habits, and he saw in the Mithrans a quick way to acquire substantial new income. He could not risk overtaxing the patrician and equestrian classes in Rome and Herculaneum, for which he depended on for support. The Mithra were middle and lower class men, with no political power, and hence we were a convenient target. Unfortunately for the young emperor, he never found any riches for all of his efforts in eradicating our group. He kept hoping for several years of course that riches would come to light, which is why he never wanted Sartarus or myself free of our prison cells. The elite rich along the beach district probably knew in their hearts we weren't guilty of anything, but they also did not want to openly confront Nero and his soldiers. It was easier for everyone to blame us for all of Herculaneum's troubles at the time. Everyone in the city simply accepted the official version of events and that made our religion out to be thieves and vandals."

"When Galba seized power of Rome from Nero, and then Otho succeeded him shortly thereafter, I thought I might yet survive my captivity. It was not until Vespasian the Great came to power that I was finally removed from my cell."

I said, "But Rome has never been fond of imprisonment or keeping any prisoner alive for more than a few days or weeks. What kept you out of the gladiator's arena or away from the crucifixion stake?"

Blandus thought for a while and then said, "Only two of our order survived for more than a short time without being killed, Sartarus and myself. I think the centurions kept the two of us alive and captive because they thought we were possibly the only two who might know where there were riches to be found. I am sure that somewhere there must have been someone who thought they could find some buried treasure, for otherwise the Roman soldiers would have surely killed us. They took no pleasure in keeping us alive."

Livia then asked about the little girl who disappeared when she was small. She reminded us that her death was blamed on the Mithrans.

"It would not have been due to the Mithrans. We did not perform human sacrifice, and women were not even allowed to visit our ceremonies. Who can say for sure who took that little girl?" said Blandus "but if it was not some evil ploy of Palindus to lay blame at our feet, I would wager that Lucius Battalius had some hand in it. He owned, or rather still owns, the most elaborate villa in Herculaneum. In his younger days, he was a frequent visitor to the island retreat of Tiberius and Caligula, and shared in their depravities. He always had a proclivity for young slave girls. The younger, the better. Even in his old age, he is of uncertain morals, and yet he is praised as a pillar of our community and is an elder. It is he who sponsored and protected Scaevolus for many years."

"But did no one ever confront this man about the disappearance?"

"None would ever publicly accuse him of anything, as he has many friends in high places and may even be related to the emperor. He has also been the Duovir of this town off and on for years."

Livia shook her head in wonder, and whispered, "I have held these false perceptions of your group for most of my life. I feel ashamed that I did not ever seek deeper for the truth."

Blandus looked at her again intently and put his hand to

her cheek. He said, "Livia, though you do not remember me, I do now remember you. I can see your mother Cassia's eyes in you, and you speak as she does. Your family has always supported me, even in the dark days. I am glad that I can count you among my friends who know the truth." He escorted us to the door of his little villa and squinted as he looked into the sunshine outside. He looked old and beaten. He paused at the portal and tried to sneak a glance to one side or the other, obviously looking to see whether the soldiers were still there to harm him. He wished us well and told Livia to give his best to her family.

Livia and I were amazed by the story Blandus had told us and we greatly pitied him. He had given us valuable information that would complete our quest. We now knew the name of the killer and had an idea of where he lived. We needed only inform the soldiers of the guard of our findings, and Livia and I could go home.....or so we thought.

## CHAPTER 11: RUMBLE IN THE CITY

As we strode slightly down the hill for a few blocks and then made the turn southwestward toward the house of Sartarus and potential hideout of the murderer, the serenity of the morning was about to change dramatically. We saw the 3 soldiers coming toward us, when we heard a low rumbling sound coming from all directions. I felt as if I could no longer stand. I became queasy and then the ground started to shake.

Livia ran to me, and said, "It is another earthquake! I know these signs. You must stay in the street. This is a much bigger one than yesterday."

Portius and Primus were huddled together looking at the sky, and the black and white dog which had been following Crispus suddenly jumped into his arms and started whimpering. All around us, there were crashing noises and people hollering and running out into the street, some holding their small children. Wagons were moving of their own accord. There were tiles coming down everywhere and I could no longer stand up. Livia and I sank to the ground in the middle of the road and clutched at the earth with a free hand to keep from falling further. This earthquake seemed to be as bad as the event I remembered as an adolescent. That quake had caused severe damage to buildings in Pompeii and many had to be rebuilt from the ground up. Many people were hurt at that time. I held my eyes shut for several seconds trying to get those images out of my head. As quickly as it had begun, it was over. People were still yelling and screaming, but the surrounding buildings appeared to be standing and relatively undamaged. The dog was licking Crispus in the face, and the soldier carefully let the affectionate canine out of his embrace on to the pavement.

Primus looked at me with a very serious face and said, "I do not like this, Titus. The signs are bad, just like the man on the road said. I think the god of the mountain is angry. We must find this killer today and quickly return to Pompeii where it is safe."

We took a few minutes to gather ourselves, and we continued down the street towards our destination. Actually, we had earlier passed very near to the house of Scaevolus on our way from Cassia's villa to see Blandus. When we were only a block or so away, we spotted a large man with long coal black hair and bushy eyebrows coming from a small dilapidated building near the corner. He was wearing a shabby tunic and was heading directly for us. He looked up just in time to see the five of us staring back intently at him. Livia whispered that that was the man who had visited her in the blacksmith shop. He knew from our posture and the presence of the soldiers that we were trailing him, and he took off running at full speed back towards his house. Crispus, Portius and Primus at first hadn't recognized him as our target, at least until Livia told them and he turned and ran. He therefore had a substantial head start. They yelled after him and drew their swords, moving swiftly in unison in his wake. Livia and I walked cautiously behind, letting the soldiers do their sworn duty. We arrived at the small villa that Scaevolus had run to. It fit the description of the house Blandus had described. It looked barely livable and was missing part of the roof. The villa of Blandus was a patrician's palace in comparison to this structure, which was leaning slightly and had little plaster covering the bricks and mortar of the walls. Missing bricks were everywhere and there were chunks of rock lying on the ground. We looked inside but saw no evidence of either Scaevolus or the three soldiers and the house looked to be deserted. There was a back door which was wide open and must have been the route of escape. Everywhere people were in the streets still recovering from the quake, so it was hard to see where our companions had gone. Livia and I decided that we would head back to her mother's house and ensure that her family and their villa were unscathed from the shaking ground. I hoped the soldiers had caught the killer. I didn't want to happen on him by mistake. As we walked, we passed several people standing in their yards examining their villas, and a few people who looked as though they had been hit by flying debris. When we got back to the parents' house, we found Livia's mother picking things off of the floor. Cassia had just returned from the market and the contents of the evening's coena meal were scattered everywhere. There were chips in the plaster, cracks in the wall and the small black and white mosaic on one wall had a few missing tessera pieces that had fallen to the floor. We helped her clean up the mess and she hugged us both after wiping away a tear.

"I don't know what is happening. There are strange happenings everywhere and now this. It is as if the gods are trying to warn us off. We have had earthquakes two days in row. That is a bad sign. We need to go to the temple and pray."

We stayed for a short while then decided we probably

should try to find the twins and Portius. We strode up the block and turned the corner and I saw a shadow dart behind one of the houses to the west. It was Scaevolus. I silenced Livia with my fingers and pointed towards the direction in which the man had gone. I whispered to her that we should not try to capture him due to the danger, but if he didn't see us, we could follow him and find out where he went. Slowly we moved to the spot where he had been. I hesitated for a second before sneaking my head around the corner. He was about a block ahead moving in and out of the shadow of houses, past more people loitering in the streets. We continued

our pursuit and watched him eventually head into the theatre. It was difficult to follow without being seen so we had to stay almost a block behind. We waited for several minutes at the top of the steps of the amphitheatre. Just as we thought we'd lost him, we saw him skulking at the back of the stage below. He looked all around and then sped in a full run towards the north side entrance which ran behind the stage. We had to move with some speed down the steps of the theatre and by the time we got to the stage and peered through the door behind, he was nowhere to be seen. We decided to head northward for a few blocks, since that was the direction he was last seen moving. After a few minutes we spotted him again sneaking in and out of alleyways. He was moving back northeastward on these dirt roads and alleys towards the house of Blandus and the mountain. We were careful to stay at least a block behind him, and keep to the breezeways or behind porticos of the villas so that he remained unaware of our presence. Eventually he did reach Blandus' house, but he did not enter. Instead he took the dirt mountain trail beside and behind the old man's house and moved up towards the crest of the mountain. It was too difficult to follow closely without being seen, so I sent Livia back to the town center to see if she could find the soldiers. I told her I would stay well behind Scaevolus but would try to see where he ventured. Livia kissed me and told me to be careful and reminded me that the man was a murderer, as if I needed the warning. She ran back down the hill, off towards her house, and I crept to the corner of the old man's house and peered to the east where the trail led up the mountain.

I considered waiting for Portius and the twins, but Scaevolus was getting farther and farther away on the trail. He was carrying something, which I guessed to be the medallion and dagger. There are some hunters who are marvelous trackers and can glean the direction and distance of an animal looking only at its tracks, but that knowledge and skill is unknown to me. Instead, I simply hoped for darkness and moved slowly and deliberately up the trail, hoping that I maintained a safe distance behind my target. I had followed the dark haired man for about thirty minutes when I finally spotted him above me on a switchback. Luckily he didn't see me and I quickly moved into the brush and waited for him to put greater distance between us. As I sat lying in the bushes by the dirt trail, I noticed that there was a faint stench of rotten eggs drifting in the air, and much of the vegetation along the trail was dead. My thoughts drifted back to my brother's stories of this mountain. I wondered if the man on the road today was correct, and the evil spirits had been let loose by the god of the mountain. I was scared, but intent on my mission. It was getting late in the day, but due to the late summer months, the sun had not yet set in the horizon. I continued the pursuit for several more minutes. About every five hundred cubits or so, there was a large boulder present on the left side of the trail. Many of these had a figure of an animal painted on their flat surfaces. I recognized immediately that these included figures of the Mithran stages of enlightenment, and we passed in turn elaborate paintings or sometimes crude figures of several different animals. I couldn't remember what I had heard about all of the levels of the Mithra, but I remembered lion, serpent and raven, and all of these icons were clearly painted on boulders scattered along the trail.

When I had reached the boulder with a scorpion painted upon its surface, I heard a voice to my rear. I ducked down behind the large rock and saw the three soldiers and Livia jogging up behind me. I motioned to them to be quiet, and we all stopped by the boulder to discuss what had transpired. Livia was out of breath, but the other three were also visibly tired. They had obviously been running uphill with their packs for the better part of an hour or more. Livia explained that she had found them searching the neighborhood just south of Scaevolus' house and had brought them back to the house of Blandus where she had left me to follow the murderer. They saw my footprints going up the trail and had decided to follow as fast as they could. The dog that had followed Crispus all day had also come along and was now licking everyone in the face, each in turn. I was not sure if having the dog was a good or a bad thing, but it appeared that we had no choice in any case, as the dog had become part of the company. They explained that the town had suffered only minor damage from the quake.

Portius said that they had pursued Scaevolus for several blocks, but that he had extensive knowledge of the alleys and terraces in the town, and had eluded them.

Livia added that it had taken her about fifteen minutes to find Primus and Portius, and only another five minutes to find Crispus because she had heard the dog barking. As if he understood his name, the dog went immediately over to Livia and licked her face.

I told them that Scaevolus was staying to the trail and was only about ten minutes ahead of us. I also mentioned the painted figures of the animals on the boulders and told them about my theory about their relationship to the Mithrans. I had not seen any cave entrances as of yet. We decided to go as a group and continue following Scaevolus to wherever his destination was. Perhaps he would lead us to the treasure. The soldiers all unsheathed their swords and I pulled the hammer out of the tool satchel I was carrying. Livia stayed at the rear, unarmed. We passed some other symbols painted on boulders by the trail. One of them I didn't recognize. I wondered if there were more levels of enlightenment in the Mithran religion than Blandus was aware of. After another half hour of strenuous hiking up a steep trail, we passed a sheer rock cliff face, where we saw the last of the Mithran figure paintings. This figure was composed of a beautifully painted abstract rendition of a dog. It was painted in multiple colors on a huge slab of rock embedded in the face of the cliff lining the trail. We examined the rock closely and looked beside and below it for any evidence of disturbance that might indicate it was the site of buried treasure. It looked as if the ground around the cliff had never been disturbed, and in fact the bedrock of the ground was so hard it would not have been possible to bury anything there anyway. We moved up the mountain for another fifteen minutes and noted the trail was beginning to traverse slightly to the north instead of just to the east. There we found a small cave about sixty pedes above the trail. We considered going up to check it out, but the dog was intent on moving farther up the trailhead, and Crispus convinced us that this probably meant we should continue forward. After another several minutes of following the trail (which was becoming smaller and smaller), we noticed a large outcrop of stones and a large cave just beyond. Portius whispered to us to be quiet and we paused to see if there was any sign of Scaevolus. We waited for about a minute before finally moving forward. Crispus was trying to hold on to the dog, which was extremely anxious and wanting to run forward into the cave. The dog did not bark, which we were thankful for. The dog was obviously agitated, and was whimpering slightly and looking back and forth from the cave and back towards town.

The rotten egg smell coming from the mouth of the cave was overpowering, and it even made the eyes burn. I was not enthused about following anyone into the tunnel. After a minute or two, we moved forward slowly, with Portius in front, followed sequentially by Primus, myself, Crispus and the dog (who Crispus was holding by the scruff of the neck), and Livia staying put in the rear, many cubits behind. We were just about to enter the cave and look around when Scaevolus stood up and suddenly appeared behind the rock outcropping above and to our left. Crispus and I saw him first, but the two soldiers in front of us were unaware until we yelled out in warning. As we did so, he raised a large melon-sized rock over his head, which he held in both hands. He was only about five cubits to the left of

Portius and twice that far above him. He suddenly launched the projectile in his hands and hit Portius directly in the head. Had the soldier not been wearing a helmet, he would have been killed instantly. Instead, he was knocked completely off of his feet and rolled for some distance down the side of the mountain to our right. Chaos ensued. Crispus ran to help Portius. Primus advanced a few feet to his left, towards the position of Scaevolus, but he could not directly climb the sheer face of the outcropping to engage the man in battle.

Scaevolus had picked a perfect defensive position and held the high ground. The only way to get there appeared to be a circuitous route around the cave entrance to the right, climbing up and over the upper rim of the cave mouth. Instead, Primus was left exposed on the face of the rock outcropping, just under the dark haired man. Scaevolus picked up another small boulder to throw and launched it at Primus. Primus moved to his right just quickly enough to keep the large stone from hitting his head, but it looked to have landed on his shoulder. The dog was directly adjacent to Primus and just missed getting crushed. It was barking incessantly at the man behind the outcropping and jumping on its hind limbs trying to get to the attacker. Livia had moved out of range of the projectiles, but was frantically hand waving and prodding me to do something. I threw her my satchel, and with my hammer in hand, I ran past the opening of the tunnel to the right and squeezed in between two large rocks. I climbed over a third, then a fourth boulder and followed a thin footpath up and above the cave entrance. It required a bit of stretching and climbing around some additional big rocks but I made steady progress towards the murderer. By the time I had moved far enough to reach the position where Scaevolus was shielded behind boulders to the upper left, he had already inflicted significant injury to Primus. I didn't know how many boulders or rocks he had thrown, but one of them had obviously knocked the helmet off of the twin, and Primus was holding his left arm limp as if it had also been struck. He was standing back several pedes away from where Scaevolus had taken refuge. I did not see the dog, but Livia was crouched in fear further back on the trail. She had my satchel open and was holding a pair of hoof shears out in front of her as a weapon. I approached Scaevolus from his left, but I had to go slow as the slope of the mountain was extremely steep over the cave entrance, and the footing was precarious. The dark haired man turned toward me with a crazed look in his eye and pulled the dagger from his tunic. I raised my hammer as I approached. I expected him to try to stab me, but instead he simply held the knife out towards me and kept looking below him at the injured Primus and then at Livia. I guessed he was trying to decide if he was trapped or in the better position. I decided to act and swung wildly with my hammer. He simply backed away slightly and I missed hitting anything except the rock in front of him. I advanced again with a backhanded swing of the hammer and this time it barely missed. He countered with a slashing motion of the knife, and as I backed away from his lunge, I lost my footing and fell backwards. I dropped the hammer and rolled from my back to my stomach as I slid over the edge of the cave entrance. I grabbed at whatever stones or ledge I could to keep from falling and breaking my legs.

I was hanging precariously with my legs dangling over the mouth of the cave for a brief moment. I would not consider the thought of dropping the ten plus cubits or more below to the hard ground, so I pulled myself up by my own weight. As I crawled back to my feet, I fully expected Scaevolus to launch another fatal stabbing blow, but he did not. I was now unarmed, and in no position to fight off his dagger attack. Instead he had moved off away from me to the southwest on the little footpath, out behind the outcropping and towards Livia. In a surprising move that I failed to understand, he slid down the soft earth on the slope of the mountain on his rear end, towards her. She screamed and ran at full speed down the trail. I cried out to Primus to warn him of events, and tried to pursue, but both Livia and Scaevolus were already a long way in front by the time I had slid down the rock face to the trail to follow them.

## CHAPTER 12: THE CAVE OF VESUVIUS

I was met on the trail by Primus who had both his gladius and my hammer in one hand. He no longer was wearing his backpack and he still had no helmet. The hammer must have fallen on to the ground at the opening to the cave floor and he had retrieved it for me. He looked terrible. He was bleeding from his head and looked dazed.

He said only, "Go!" and instead of giving me my mallet, he handed me his sword.

I could not hesitate long enough to stop and examine his injuries, for fear of what would happen to Livia. I didn't even know the whereabouts of the other soldiers in our group. I had to chase down this madman and save my wife. I grabbed the gladius, nodded, and ran off down the trail. I couldn't understand why Scaevolus would be chasing Livia in the first place. I heard barking behind me, and then that crazy black and white dog came running up beside me. I didn't know whether the dog would be any help in a fight or not, but I was glad to see him anyway. I was maneuvering down the hill as fast I as could without losing my balance. I did not want to fall down the steep sloping mountainside to my left. There was little vegetation on either side of the trail in this location, so I was not worried about an ambush, but I still couldn't see either person in front of me. Livia must have been running like Mercury. I wondered again why the man was chasing her. After only a few minutes we arrived at the small cave, and the dog stopped and barked. I looked up above me to the cave and just saw the back side of Scaevolus entering the cave entrance.

"Goat's mother!" I said out loud.

I couldn't believe Livia had climbed up and hid in the cave. It was a dead end trap, with only one way in or out. There was no way the dog was going to be able to climb the steep slope, with a thick layer of gravel in between the boulder field. The dog barked at me again twice as I climbed up the mountain deliberately but quickly. I was worried and I made a silent prayer to Jupiter for Livia's safety as I climbed. It took only a couple of minutes to make it up the forty cubits of rock and arrive at the ledge where the entrance to the small tunnel began. The dog watched my progress and then headed back towards Primus. I had never had a dog as a pet, but I was impressed with this one. He seemed to think like a person. I only was familiar with the stray dogs of our town who begged for food in the restaurants, or the herding dogs of the shepherds, and they seemed to know only how to protect and keep sheep and goats in groups. I was thrilled that Primus had given me his sword, and I brandished it in front of me as I entered the cave. It was dark and smelled terribly, but the small entrance belied a much larger cavern inside. I needed a torch to see. I realized that anyone in the cave could probably see my outline against the light of the outside if I stood too long at the mouth of the tunnel, so I quickly moved farther inside. I instinctively reached to my left and right to find the walls, and my sword banged against rock on my right. I took a few careful pedes in that direction and then traveled slowly along the right wall deeper inside. I was using my hand to keep a consistent distance from the wall and to feel for any side passages, but I was virtually blind. The air was stifling and I wanted to cough, but dared not for giving away my position. I decided to stop and listen. I heard distant footsteps ahead and slightly to the left. I looked around and saw nothing but shadow, and thought to myself that Livia could hide in here for a long time without being seen. This was not such a dumb idea after all. I whispered for her in the front chamber of the cave, but did not hear anything, and decided to follow the sound of the footsteps. Slowly I walked along and beside the right wall. I had transferred the sword to my left hand and was using fingers of my right hand to maintain contact with the wall. The cavern in here was pretty large and I did not have to stoop over to walk. At length I hit a wall in front of me with my foot. I used my right hand and felt all around and in front of me. The cave seemed to be taking a hard turn to the left. I looked in that direction and could see a faint light farther to the left. I couldn't imagine what that light was.

I whispered again for Livia several times but there was no answer. I looked behind me and could also see the faint light of the cave opening. I had to make a decision. Should I wait here in the dark, go further in the cave in the hopes of finding Livia or Scaevolus, or should I return to Primus and the soldiers and we could try to confront the killer together. At this point, I was regretting ever coming on this journey and especially the stupidity of bringing my wife along. I cursed myself over and over and sat for several minutes trying to decide upon the best course of action.

After several minutes of indecision, I was beginning to imagine that the cave was filled with all nature of wild animals, dangerous insects and spirits of the underworld. I had no idea what to do when or if I could find Scaevolus in the deeper part of the cave, and I had no idea where Livia was hiding. Then suddenly the cave became much brighter. There was a strong light coming from the same area where before there was only a faint glow. I had to make a decision quickly now, just in case the dark haired man came back up this way. He would surely see me crouching in the corner. I worried then that if he could see me, he could also see where Livia might be hiding, so I proceeded to walk slowly towards the light with my sword held in front of me. I was shaking with fear, but I had to move forward or face losing my wife to a killer. As I crept forward the level of the tunnel was moving downward slightly and it was getting a little harder to breathe. However it was definitely getting lighter. The rotten egg smell was overpowering.

The tunnel took another sharp right turn and I halted at the corner and as quick as I could I snuck a peek around. There was a small oil lamp lit in the middle of a large cavernous room and several torches were lit and were sitting in staff holders attached to the walls. There were several designs and paintings of gods and monsters on the walls that were backlit by the flame of the three torches. It created an eerie effect. Two smaller tunnels were at opposite ends of this subterranean gallery. There was absolutely no sign of Livia anywhere, which made me a little more at ease. There were digging tools and utensils lying against one wall and Scaevolus held the medallion and the dagger in each of his raised hands. He didn't seem to know what to say or how to use them. He kept looking at each of the ceremonial ornaments in turn waiting for something to happen. He was banging them together and walking over the entire floor of the cavern holding them aloft as if they would suddenly start glowing or make some sound. Nothing happened no matter what he did. I was paying too much attention to these weird actions of Scaevolus, and not enough attention to staying hidden. When he glanced in my direction, I was too slow in pulling my head back around the corner, and I was pretty sure he saw me. I began to back step towards the entrance of the cave. Suddenly I saw him turn the corner. He had a small oil lamp with him and when he held it aloft, he saw me staring back at him with the sword in my hand. I pointed it toward him and he pointed his dagger at me in turn. He must have left the medallion back in the cavern.

He squinted his eyes at me, and said, "You again. You were with the soldiers at the other cave. Why do you follow me? You're no soldier."

I was so nervous, my hand was shaking and the sword was wavering back and forth. I replied, "I am here on behalf of the magistrate. We are going to take you back to Pompeii and account for the deaths of Vibiana and Zahret."

He looked at me and laughed. "You are here on behalf of the Prefect of Pompeii. Isn't he the one who was going to execute you? I recognize you now. You were the one who fought the Egyptian. You were the one who was holding the whore in the temple. You are the one they thought killed her. How did you manage to get off?"

I didn't answer but glanced back at the cave opening. It was still many cubits away.

"I guess that stupid Egyptian pimp ratted me out. I should have finished him in the whore's villa. I thought I left him dead, but he kept following me around like you're doing.

You'll end up like he did." He smiled menacingly.

While he was talking to me, he was trying to circle to my right and cut off my escape. I kept backing up and working to my left so he could not get behind me. He grinned again and asked where the soldiers were. I told him they were coming, that they were right behind me and even now climbing the slope of the mountain to the cave entrance.

He looked over my shoulder to the dim light a few hundred cubits to my rear, and said, "I think you're lying, mister. I don't think they're coming at all. I hurt two of them pretty bad back there, maybe killed them. They won't follow. No, instead, I think you are here to steal my treasure for yourself."

I was really getting nervous now and looking around left and right to see if I could turn and escape. I said, "I don't know about any Mithran treasure." But as soon as I said it I realized that I had slipped when I mentioned the Mithrans.

"I knew it. You're a thief like all of the rest. I'll kill you quick."

He lunged with the dagger, but my sword hand moved in a reflexive arching motion that parried his blade and made a nice slice in his hand. He yelped once and backed up.

He grimaced at me and said, "So you think yourself a swordsman. We'll see".

He moved the blade to his other hand after setting the oil lamp on the ground beside him. He started circling again, and taking small steps toward me left and right in feint after feint. I was gaining my courage with every second, and I started throwing blows of my own. I followed a downward strike with an upward reverse cut to his right, then immediately did a crossing cut from right to left that he barely managed to back away from. He began talking to me, probably to distract me.

"Where did you find out about the Mithran treasure? Was it from the Egyptian?"

He could read from my face that that was true. "Ah, of course, he said, but where did he find out about it, and where did he get the medallion. It must have come from Palindus."

He was thinking as he was fighting, but he could do the two together and it did not detract at all from his skill in combat. As he said "Palindus", he lunged forward and slashed straight across my body in a deadly right to left attack with the dagger, this time with the blade back in his right hand. My left shoulder and the left side of my chest were both cut. I made a mental note to myself, not to trust either side, as this man was deadly with a blade in either hand.

"That's it, isn't it? You're working for Palindus! I should have guessed. Well, he's an old man by now, and I can take care of him."

Before I thought about whether I should engage him in further conversation, I said, "Palindus is already dead, and I don't work for him."

He slashed again from my left to my right just as I finished the sentence, but I countered with a reverse cut of my sword starting from my right hip and moving up across his chest in an upward stroke. The force of this cut parried his dagger thrust and made a fairly significant cut in his hip, stomach and chest. He was bleeding, but still in the fight, and now he was angry. He kept thrusting at me and asking questions as he went. I only kept backing up and slashing with my sword to prevent him from getting too close.

"Who are you doing this for," he kept asking. "Who knows about the medallion? Are you working for the elders? They want to steal my treasure?"

I had a question of my own. I said, "Why were you chasing my wife? "Where is she at?"

He seemed to hesitate for a minute, and then in a very soft threatening voice said, "Your wife? You mean that little tart that ran down the hill towards town? I wasn't chasing her, I was only trying to get to this cave and complete the ritual with the medallion."

Awareness suddenly came over his face. "Oh, that's it, is it? You thought I was going to bring your little wench up here to the cave and spoil her?" He threw me an evil grin and said, "I wasn't planning to, but now that you mention it, I think once I finish you, I'll go down and have my way with her. Then I'll open her up just like a fish, the same way I did to the whore. You are going to wish they would have executed you in the arena when you see what I do to her."

He was trying to bait me into losing my temper and making a stupid move in my anger. It worked brilliantly. I began lunge after deep lunge, and thrust after thrust. He kept backing up with half or full steps to avoid being perforated by my gladius, but he was also moving slowly and steadily to my left side and was now parallel with me in the cave. Instead of backing up any further, he jumped to his right and was now standing between me and the exit to the cave. Worse yet, we had moved some distance away from the oil lamp, and he was getting increasingly harder to see. This made blocking the thrusts of his dagger very difficult and put me in a much more dangerous spot. It was my turn to stall. I was tiring, and I needed to slow the pace of the fight in hopes that the soldiers could find me and catch up.

He asked again what I knew of the medallion and the dagger.

I said I only knew that they were supposed to hold the

secret of the Mithrans and that they needed to interact somehow for the magic to work.

"How," he said, "How do they interact with each other? Tell me and I might not kill you."

I began to think that if I sat here and talked to him a while, I might not have to keep fighting for the next two hours. That was a prospect that would likely end in my death. I embellished upon the facts that I knew in hopes that I could trick Scaevolus into wasting more time. "Palindus told the Egyptian everything. He sold him the medallion, and before he died, he gave the Egyptian the secrets. Unfortunately, you killed Zahret before learning all that he knew."

Scaevolus looked down at the dagger and turned it over in his hand. He said, "I don't need to know what the Egyptian pimp heard from that back-stabbing cowardly old goat, I have the dagger AND the medallion."

"But you don't know how to use them together."

Scaevolus threw a quick thrust in my direction but I easily sidestepped it and backed further into the cave.

"Tell me all you know, stranger, and I will allow you to live."

I knew, of course, that he was lying, but I needed to buy time. I said, "The Egyptian said the medallion is a map, if you can read the symbols, and the dagger is the key to that map."

I spoke confidently to Scaevolus, in hopes he might keep me alive longer to find out all I knew. "Didn't your father tell you the story of the hidden treasure of the Mithrans and how the dagger and medallion could lead you to them?" I asked.

"My father? I barely knew him. He spent half of my life

in a Roman prison and another several years crawling around these caves trying to get rich while I half-starved doing the dirty work of the patricians down on the beach. The only way I knew anything about the legend of the horde was from Aerulius."

He was still moving slowly side to side with dagger outstretched, and waiting to see how I would respond. I moved my sword from my right hand to my left, as my arm was getting tired holding it. With the wound on my shoulder, that was probably a mistake as the arm felt much weaker. I matched his leg movements.

"Aerulius, who is that?" I questioned. "Another Mithran?"

"Let's just say he was somebody who knew some of the old tales, but he's not around anymore to share in the spoils." said Scaevolus.

I wondered who his former accomplice could be, until I remembered what Blandus had told me about Palindus having another young son who befriended Scaevolus in their youth. "He's Palindus' son, isn't he?  He was the one who told you what your father was looking for in the caves." I asked.

"Figuring it all out, are you?  Well you don't know everything, and neither did Aurelius. I'm gonna take it all and live big. I have the dagger and the medallion both now. I just need you to tell me how to use them. I might even give you some of the treasure and let you go."

I didn't believe that for a minute, nor was I going to drop my guard. I asked again if Aurelius was his accomplice and if he had killed him too. He said only, "The time for stories and explanations is over", and then threatened that if I didn't tell him what I knew he would "gut me like the whore".

I told him that all I knew was that the dagger and medallion had to be brought together for the secret to be revealed.

"I tried that." "Nothing happened."

I said that Zahret had thought to use the dagger to break apart the medallion to find the map. He quickly looked down at the dagger then back at me. Again he looked at the dagger and seemed to examine the blade more closely. The dagger had no writing that I could see, but the handle had lots of carving and there was a large ruby and emerald on the pommel. Scaevolus was looking back at the large cavernous area behind me now, where he must have left the medallion. He was wondering if the medallion had a map. I was cursing myself under my breath for giving him any extra ideas, especially those that might lead him to any conclusion to finish me off quicker. I decided to engage him in further conversation.

"You got the dagger from your father after he died?" I asked.

He grinned and said when he heard Sartarus was gone, he went to the house to take possession and he found the knife hidden amongst some of his father's things. This was only a few weeks after Sartarus death, while he was scouring the house for valuables.

"And Aurelius had already told you about the dagger and medallion?" I asked again.

Scaevolus was in no hurry to kill me now that he had blocked off my escape, and he seemed to relish in our conversation, as if it was enhancing the pleasure of his impending kill. He talked leisurely for several minutes as he continued to move the dagger back and forth between his hands.

"Aurelius had overheard his father talking about them

when he was a small boy, right before Palindus took off. Palindus thought their magic was enhanced when put together. He was reminded of their worth again after my father got out of prison and approached him. Sartarus wanted to see if Aurelius knew where Palindus might have hidden the medallion, or any clues to the whereabouts of the treasure horde. Sartarus said the Persian had brought back all kinds of ancient treasure with him from the East. We knew my father was looking all over for treasure, and Aurelius and I planned to take it from him as soon as he found it. But he never did.   When Aurelius found out I had possession of the Mithran knife, he tried to take it from me by force. He'd given up on the treasure and just wanted to hock it for coins, but he underestimated me. Nobody takes anything from me.  He paid for his mistake with his blood.  His body is lost in the caves and that's where you're about to end up if you don't help me."

Scaevolus grinned nastily, and I was reminded that I had to keep my wits up, as this man had killed many times before. "Why did you kill Vibiana?" I asked. "She was in the temple and didn't even have the medallion anymore."

I threw a half hearted thrust in his direction which he laughed off as he backed away easily.

"I killed her because I wanted to.  It felt good.  She acted all haughty and dignified, but she was just a whore and deserved to die.  The look on her face when I stabbed her was priceless.  She was so surprised.  It was the same look that stupid priest gave me in the Egyptian temple.  He really believed I would let him go when he told me where to find the medallion."

He laughed a diabolical, guttural laugh that made my skin crawl.  This man was evil and insane.  I was in real danger, the longer I stayed in this cave.

"And now I'm gonna kill you." he said and he laughed again.

This time as he laughed, however, he lunged right at me thinking to catch me unaware. I was not nearly as fast with the sword in my left hand and my parry was weak from my bloodied shoulder. As I tried to block his blow, he pulled the dagger back and around my arm to the outside and with a quick slash put another large gash in my left shoulder. I cried out in pain and moved the sword back to my right hand. I was sweating and coughing now and deep in the cave I found it difficult to breathe. The heat was getting worse, or the exercise from fighting was making it feel that way. I was not going to last in a fight much longer with this bigger man. As I backed up further, I felt the wall of the cave against my back foot and realized that I was trapped unless I could work to my right back toward the cavern or get around this man somehow.

"You're done thief." he said, "You don't know any more than I where the treasure is, or how to use the knife to find it. You have no more worth to me except as another notch on my belt."

He was about to thrust at me, when I swung the gladius right to left across his body, then wildly back and forth across his chest two more times to gain some room between me and the wall. He countered, but I quickly sidestepped to the right and thrust my sword in a hacking motion towards his left arm. He blocked the blow with the metal of his dagger. When the crosspieces of my sword met the hilt of his dagger, the forward movement of the gladius was stopped briefly. He was able to grab the blade of the sword near the handle and crosspiece with his left hand, and was trying to wrench the sword free of my grip. I surprised him by pushing the sword strongly towards him and to my left and then letting go of it. He followed the movement of the sword so as to take it from me, but in that instant when his body was partially turned, I ran past him and straight for the cave entrance before he knew my intention. I needed to get as far away from the cave as possible as fast as possible. When I hit the light at the opening, I moved swiftly down between the rocks, jumping several feet at a time. Within a minute I was back on the trail, but unarmed. He hadn't followed me out of the cave yet. I looked to the right and the left and could not see anyone on the trail. I hesitated only long enough to decide on direction. I took a deep breath of fresh air, coughed twice again and started running for Herculaneum. I hoped Livia was alright for the present, but as long as Scaevolus was free, I figured we were both still in danger. After several minutes, the ground again shook and I was afraid I would be buried by falling debris from above me on the mountain. I huddled down as low as possible as several rocks and boulders rolled past me. Fortunately this was a very mild quake and lasted only a few seconds. When I was sure it was over, I thought it best to get off of the mountain as quickly as possible and I ran at full speed down the trail.

## CHAPTER 13: THE END OF THE SON OF SARTARUS

As I made my way down the hill, the sun had set and the stars were just beginning to appear. Although it was relatively late in the evening, the region was enjoying the long days of mid to late summer and the twilight still allowed me to see the trail as I hurried downward. I passed several of the boulders containing painted figures to my right and at the point I was at the pictogram of the scorpion I noted two figures up ahead, moving slowly downhill. I heard a bark and then noticed the dog with them. As I neared I could make out the distinct outline of Crispus and Primus. They were leaning on each other and carrying several things in their hands. I approached and yelled a word of greeting.

Crispus turned to me and said, "Oh, Titus, it's you."

As I reached them I could see that Primus was visibly hurt and though he was wearing his helmet, it looked very misshapen. His left arm hung completely limp and he had his right arm draped over his brother's shoulder for support.

"Hi Titus." he said weakly.

"Where is Portius?" I asked.

"Dead. We buried him." was all Crispus could manage,

but his twin brother added, "Up in the cave, where we were ambushed. He fell a long way down the hill and his body was broken when Crispus found him."

Crispus explained that he ran to help him, but Portius couldn't move from the fall down the mountain slope, even when he had taken the pack off of the back of the mortally wounded man. "He began having trouble breathing and lasted only a few minutes longer before his soul took the long journey. I had to wait for Primus as I couldn't get his corpse up the hill to the trail by myself."

Primus then added, "We thought of bringing him back to Herculaneum, but I wasn't that much help in lifting him, with my arm the way it is."

He looked down depressingly at the limp limb dangling from his left shoulder. The dog was wagging his tail and trying to move in and out of my legs.

Crispus said, "We were right there at the mouth of the cave anyway, so we brought him in, thinking to leave him and return later with a burial detail. We couldn't go any farther into the cave because of the foul vapors, but we didn't need to go more than a few cubits from the mouth because there were already several large holes dug into the floor of the cave. We simply enlarged one with the tools from your bag and covered him with dirt. We left his leather lorica and greaves on his body, but brought back the bronze helmet and sword to present to the Prefect. It seemed the proper thing to do."

I only nodded as Primus handed me my satchel. It now included the gladius, attached balteus (trooper's belt) and the helmet of Portius, as well as my blacksmith's tools. I took them from Primus and thought how much of a burden they must have been to carry with one arm.

Crispus then asked me about Livia. "Did the madman

catch her? What did you do to him?"

I replied that no, he hadn't caught up to her and explained that he was only trying to escape us and to try and quickly find the treasure in the smaller cave near the trail and really wasn't trying to chase her. I told them I had no idea where Livia was at present.

"The treasure is in the small cave?" asked Primus.

I answered that as far as I knew, Scaevolus had not yet found any treasure, and didn't appear to know how to use the dagger and the medallion. He was as clueless as we were.

"You are bleeding" noticed Crispus.

"Yes, I found Scaevolus in the cave. I was careless and he spotted me spying on him. He attacked me and I was barely able to keep him from killing me. He got a pretty good slash in on my arm." I reached up and held the wound with my right hand. I added, "It'll be all right. I just need it bandaged. I got a lick or two in on him, as well. His stomach, chest and shoulder are also bleeding."

That seemed to cheer up both men and Crispus smiled and slapped me on the back as we walked downhill. "Where is the man now?" asked Crispus "Did you wound him enough to immobilize him?"

"No, I answered, he is still dangerous and capable of causing any of us injuries. He stayed in the small cave, in order to try and find the Mithran horde. I think he doesn't know any more about the medallion than we do. I'm wondering how he knew enough to go to Pompeii and try and get it from Vibiana."

Primus asked if I was in the cave when the latest quake had happened.

"No", I said, "Fortunately, I was out here on the trail. It seemed to be much less violent than the one we experienced in town today."

They both agreed, but then Primus smiled broadly and said, "You said Scaevolus was probably still in the cave when the earthquake happened. I hope it buried the goat bastard."

We continued talking about what else had transpired in the cave and how the fight had gone as we walked further down the trail. We all speculated wildly about what Scaevolus might find if he could decipher how to use the medallion. After several minutes I spotted Livia waiting impatiently, pacing back and forth near the trail's end. She saw the three of us coming up in the distance and ran to me. We hugged tightly and she gave me several kisses amongst her tears.

"I was so worried about you, Titus. So worried. I thought the man had killed you. He was so evil....." She stopped when she saw the blood on my right shoulder and asked what had happened.

I told her it was alright and I was fine, but that Primus was going to need a healer. I explained that I had fought the man with a sword that Primus had lent me and that we had traded blows. I said that the only important thing was that I was still alive and relatively unharmed. I then remembered that I had lost the sword at the end of the fight.

"I'm sorry, Primus." I said as I explained why I no longer had his gladius in my possession, "The only way I could escape was to drop the sword and run. It saved my life."

Primus was looking off in the distance, deep in thought, and said only, "It doesn't matter, my arm doesn't work anyway. I'll be lucky to ever fight again or even to be able to remain a soldier. My arm is numb and won't work. I can't protect the city with one arm."

Crispus tried to comfort his brother by telling him we were going to a healer and that his arm would be fine, but

Primus could not be raised out of his melancholy. He lamented to himself, "I am a cripple and a broken man. I will end my days as a one-armed beggar."

To change the subject and quit dwelling on Primus' poor state, I asked Livia how she came to be there.

She replied, "I went to Blandus' house and stayed for a while with the old man. I decided to send him to get more help from the town elders. I figured they could bring more soldiers. I was there for a long time at his house, but I couldn't wait any longer. I had to see if you were alright so I came up here a short way up the trail to wait. I don't know what I would have done if Scaevolus had shown up."

She looked around, and then frantically asked, "Where is Portius?" She cried when we told her of his death, and I gave her another hug. "So much killing" was all she could answer.

The dog stood on his hind legs leaning on her chest and licked her tears. As we neared the base of the trail, near the house of Blandus, Livia had looked back from where we had come and cried out, "Look. Look there. It is Scaevolus."

He was moving down the trail about a hundred cubits behind us. Before Scaevolus had even time to realize or process what was happening, Primus broke free from his brother and started running at full speed towards Scaevolus.

Crispus took off after his twin, yelling, "Primus, wait. Wait for me. We'll fight him together."

The dog ran at full speed and closed the distance in seconds. It was barking loudly. Crispus at least had his sword in hand, but Primus had appeared to drop everything and was running unarmed toward the murderer. When Scaevolus realized he had two soldiers in full leather and metal gear heading for him, he turned quickly and started moving uphill, back towards the caves along the trail. We had the advantage of surprise this time. Primus had closed the distance incredibly fast and was only a few pedes away from Scaevolus when the larger man decided to turn and fight. He had the sword of Primus in one hand (that he had taken from me) and pulled the dagger from under his tunic belt. In two-armed combat against an unarmed opponent with one limb immobilized, it should have been an easy fight for the bigger man. However, he had misjudged the speed of the wounded Primus and did not count on the dog. Before he could mount a sufficient defense, the dog had clamped its jaws around the wrist holding the sword. Scaevolus screamed in pain. Primus dove at the big man and wrapped his one strong right arm around the hip and waist of Scaevolus and with the force of his legs, was driving him towards a ledge on the right side of the trail. Scaevolus was flailing his arms wildly trying to get the dog to release his right arm and to hack at the soldier with the dagger in his left hand. He still had the weapons in each hand but he was losing his balance and couldn't get the right angle to inflict much of a wound on Primus. He turned his head just in time to see that they were about to fall off of a cliff. Within seconds the two men and the dog tumbled off of the edge. Crispus screamed loudly at his brother's disappearance from the ledge, and I left Livia to run and see what had happened. I arrived at the edge of the cliff moments later, and looked over to see Crispus carefully climbing down over the rocks to one side. The ledge was an overhang which was only about eight cubits above a level area. From there the mountain had a gentler slope down to a tree line below. As I peered down through the growing dark, I could see the two men in heaps a few pedes away from each other just below me. Neither was moving, but Primus was groaning loudly. The dog was lying near Primus licking its front paw. I followed Crispus and crawled down carefully over the rocks to the level space below.

Both men appeared to be stunned, but Primus had apparently landed on top of Scaevolus and so had taken less of the brunt of the fall. Crispus went to his brother and lifted him up onto his lap to try and help him. Primus had the dagger embedded in his left thigh, which Crispus immediately withdrew. There was a spurt of blood coming from the wound, so Crispus held his hand tightly to the wound.

"Where are you hurt, brother?"

Primus smiled and said, "Everywhere, but at least I got the best of that goat's testicle."

I went over to check on Scaevolus. He was not moving and appeared to be dead, but I kicked him heartily in the chest to be sure. There was still no movement. I then turned to help Primus a few pedes away. Crispus was still holding the wound on his twin's thigh, but was trying to get Primus to move his other limbs.

Primus was intermittently groaning and mumbling to himself. He said, "I still can't move my arm, and I can barely feel my legs." He looked at Crispus and me in turn and then apologized to both of us for transgressions against us when we were young. He said he should have been a better brother. Then he apologized again to me for mistreating me when I was imprisoned yesterday. He said that I held the favor of the goddess, and that because he had offended me, he had offended Venus herself and she had sought vengeance on him. He said he deserved this punishment, his broken body. Then he smiled and explained that in fighting Scaevolus twice and protecting Livia, Crispus and I from further harm, he had hopefully redeemed himself to Venus and the other gods. He then implored his brother that when he died, which he thought was imminent; he was to be buried in his uniform in the Necropolis at the Vesuvius gate in Pompeii. This was where all of the gladiators were entombed and was just north of the necropolis where Vibiana and Zahret had been laid to rest. Crispus was crying, but shook his head and promised that he would fulfill the twin's wishes.

I was preoccupied with trying to determine how we were going to get the wounded Primus up the rocks to the trail. While I had never been fond of Primus, he had certainly shown himself to be a brave and worthy companion in the last few hours. Crispus was right when he said that Primus had become a believer. The miracle of the tears in the temple of Venus, however contrived, or maybe the series of earthquakes, had transformed him from a bully to a true friend and champion of my cause. As I was thinking this, the dog sat up and barked loudly and I noticed a sudden change on the face of Crispus. His eyes got wide and he managed to shout "Look out." As I turned around, two things happened in quick succession—I saw Scaevolus reaching for my neck with his outstretched hands. I was preparing to back up and raise my hands to keep from getting strangled, when I heard another loud, piercing scream. In the air behind Scaevolus, a giant eagle with a shining outstretched talon had grabbed Scaevolus from above and behind. He fell and his right arm was severed completely from his body. He turned and gazed in horror at the figure who had buried a sword up to the hilt into and through his shoulder. It was then that I discovered that the eagle was in fact my wife, Livia. She had seen Scaevolus get up and come behind me to strangle me, and without thinking she had dove off of the ledge with Portius' gladius in her hand. She had landed blade first on his right neck and shoulder and the force of the blow had completely cleaved the man's arm at the joint. Scaevolus was writhing in agony on the ground as blood came pouring out of his shoulder like a spigot. He finally went limp and his eyes closed. Livia had twisted her ankle with the fall and was limping severely as she came over to me. Crispus stood up with the dagger in his hand and he thrust it into the chest of Scaevolus at the level of his heart.

"Not this time," he said as he pulled the blade out of the man's chest. "You will not live to hurt anyone else."

The son of Sartarus would not get up again. Crispus kicked him several times, all the while cursing him. Amazingly, Primus was still alive and was grinning at both us.

"We got him, we got him," was all he could say.

We passed around the water from one of the packs. It tasted great and helped wash the sulfur taste from my mouth, a burning, bitter essence that had lingered in my throat from the time in the cave. We had to wait almost an hour before Primus had enough strength to be moved up the rocks off of the ledge to the trail. I actually lifted the dog up the rocks to the ledge above. I owed the dog that. On our way back down to town, Crispus was carrying Primus on his shoulders, and the dog limped along besides us. I tried to help lift Primus, but my shoulder wound was exceedingly tender, and I was of little usefulness. Crispus wouldn't let me carry his brother anyway, and seemed so happy that Primus was still alive that he didn't even seem to notice the extra weight. We found the medallion wrapped in linen just under the tunic belt of Scaevolus and put the dagger in the linen beside it in one of the backpacks. We

gathered as much of the things in the backpacks back on the trail as we could and Livia and I carried them downhill. It was close to midnight when we finally arrived at Livia's mothers. Livia's father and brother were there and helped stitch up wounds on my left shoulder and arm and on the thigh of Primus. Fishermen were the best with needle and thread in the land, as they had to constantly fix their nets. Even the healer was amazed at the quality of their surgery skills. She came as soon as Cassia had summoned, applied liniments and herbs to our wounds and wrapped everything such that the bleeding had stopped. She stayed and looked after Primus for the remainder of the evening. The healer sent Livia down the street to another home with a baby for relief. It had been almost a full day since she had nursed Dania and her chest was engorged making her very uncomfortable. When she returned she felt better physically, but she was missing her own baby terribly. Surrogate nursing had only made her pine for seeing Dania, and she was very anxious to return to Pompeii.

We had a very late dinner and I had several glasses of wine. The wine was a welcome pain reliever, better than the healer's herbs, and I hoped it would help me sleep tonight. When I finally had finished eating and drinking, I looked around the house and noticed it was still a shambles from the two earthquakes earlier in the day. There were some broken pots and several cracks in the walls. At least the roof was intact, and the triclinia that Primus and I were laying on felt great.

Livia was also gazing at the broken pots and looked troubled. "Do you think the earthquakes caused damage in Pompeii? I hope our house and Aule's are both OK."

"I'm sure the houses are fine. So is Dania." I knew she was only thinking about the baby, and didn't really care whether the villa was damaged or not. I decided we would return to Pompeii at first light.

Just before everyone was thinking of retiring to bed, we

heard a knock at the door. Livia's father answered and let in a young man in a well groomed tunic. He was a male slave, in his late teens, and a servant of one of the city elders. He told us that we were to meet at the villa of the city elder, Lucius Battalius, in the morning, and to bring the medallion and dagger. We were to be met there by the Praefectus Urbi of Pompeii.

We wondered aloud what that was all about. Livia suggested that the Prefect must have learned about the events of the evening from the town elders. She reminded us that once she had run down to the base of the trail away from the murderer, she had found Blandus and she had sent him to get help and more men from the town elders. She didn't know where Blandus was now. I added that the elders may have heard some of the story from her father and brother, who had already broadcast various versions of the story throughout the neighborhood.

"But how did the Prefect in Pompeii know so quickly that we had killed Scaevolus and more importantly, how did he know we have the medallion and the dagger?" Crispus asked everyone.

Livia's mother said that Lucius had paid informants everywhere and as one of two Duovir (deputy magistrates) ruling over the Herculaneum Decurion council, he knew all that went on in the city. "Mind your manners when you are in the presence of Lucius Batallius. He is no mere aedile managing the city's buildings." said Cassia. She reminded us that the Duovir elders in Herculaneum reported directly to the Prefect in Pompeii. Although they were elected annually from among the elders, the small size of Herculaneum meant that Lucius had served in this capacity repeatedly over a twenty year span.

"Loreius governs not only Pompeii, but Herculaneum, Sarno and Stabiae. The Duovir must have sent word to Loreius right away." said Cassia.

Crispus was shaking his head and said, "But it is still impossible that the Prefect knows of these events. We just fought Scaevolus only a few hours ago, and it takes that long to get the message to Pompeii from here."

Livia answered, "Regardless of his means, I can't believe the Prefect couldn't wait one extra day to at least allow us to heal before he sent for us. He probably is going to make us go hunt for the treasure..."

"The treasure!" I interrupted. "I forgot about that. I wonder if there ever was any buried treasure at all. Perhaps it is just legend."

Primus seemed to stir a little bit and without sitting up said, "I've had enough of that mountain. I don't want to return. I don't like caves, I don't like quakes and my whole body hurts. The god of the mountain can keep his treasure."

Everyone in the room seemed to ponder that for a while. I was too sore to go to sleep, despite the hour, and there wasn't much room in the house for all of us to lay down anyway on the klinia. Livia was busy with something in the center of the room.

Livia had the dagger and medallion sitting on the table in front of her, and she was staring at them intently. She mentioned that she had been thinking about them since she had come back from nursing the neighbor's infant, and had tried to decipher their secret meaning. She had finally succumbed to her curiosity and decided to take them from the backpack and place them on the table for a better look.

"I don't recognize any of the symbols on either object."

Each of us in turn looked at them closely on the table,

but I really didn't want to touch them, and it was only Crispus who would pick them up. Livia pointed to some small tongues of metal that were holding the central onyx stone in place on the medallion. A few of these small clasps appeared to have been bent away, as if to remove or release the central stone from the piece.

When she saw me examining the clasps, Livia said, "I didn't do that. Those little metal grips were already bent like that."

Crispus suggested that Scaevolus may have tried to remove the stone to sell it.

"No, I think he was trying to remove the stone, but not to peddle it. He wanted to see if there was a map hidden underneath."

Livia asked me where or how he would have come up with that idea.

I put my head down, and said "I kind of suggested he do that when we were talking in the cave." I explained that I was trying to distract him.

I felt pretty stupid, until she said, "Actually that's a pretty good idea. Not the distracting part, the thought about having a hidden map in the medallion. I think the Egyptian thought about that. You two may have been right about that. Scaevolus apparently didn't have time to finish removing the stone."

Crispus said, "Primus, you said something earlier that might be correct. He may have run out of the cave when the second quake started before he could pry the stone and look at the map."

Primus turned his head and grinned. "He probably was trembling in his tunic that the walls were going to crumble in around him. I bet he just grabbed the medallion and sped out of the cave."

Livia then said, "Titus, find a suitable tool from your kit and see if you can pry this stone off."

I said something about my fear and unwillingness to touch a magic medallion, but Crispus took a tool from my bag and started manipulating the metal clasps.

It took a few minutes but he was able to lift the onyx off of the base. There was nothing but gold underneath, and so we put the stone back in place, fearing the prefect would arrest us for vandalism. We had just about given up on the medallion and dagger and interpreting its symbols and meaning, when Crispus reminded us that the scabbard for the dagger was still in my tool satchel.

"I noticed it was in there when we were grabbing things by the cliffs."

I had forgotten all about the scabbard, and figured it had just been left in there when I got my tools from the Prefect's office. I thought the scabbard should be placed back with its blade to house and protect the dagger. The magistrate would demand it back anyway. He pulled the scabbard out and we all looked at it in detail for a while. It was beautiful and contained a bronze emblem of a bull on the leather shaft, with an emerald and a ruby eye. There were swirly signs and other symbols I did not understand.

"Oh great goddess", said Livia. "I think I recognize that symbol".

She was staring at the bull. She immediately grabbed the medallion and put the two side by side. She pulled the blade from the sheath and examined the sharp tip of the metal shaft, which contained a small star engraved in the bronze. She put the dagger back in its sheath and noted the star corresponded to a place around the bull's lower jaw. She smiled broadly and handed both objects back to Crispus.

"Everyone, I think I know where the secret lies."

## CHAPTER 14: TREASURE ON THE MOUNTAIN

Crispus, Livia and I got up just before sunrise the next morning and headed back through town and past the small house of Blandus. Primus was still too banged up to move more than a few feet from his perch on the triclinium. We arrived at the small house and Blandus greeted us warmly. Livia thanked him for helping her yesterday, even if the extra soldiers he had requested from the town elders had not arrived in time to save Portius. She asked him who he had been able to contact, and it was not the same elder that had summoned us. In fact, he had nothing but contempt for Lucius.

"I actually went to the other Duovir, a man named Pollius, who I trust deeply. I have never liked Lucius, but I am sure that it was Pollius' duty to inform Lucius Batallius and the Prefect in Pompeii in due course. I told Pollius that you and soldiers from Pompeii were under orders of the Prefect to capture Scaevolus who was wanted for murder. I informed him that he had ambushed and attacked your group, and that you were requesting help."

Livia assured him he had done exactly as we asked and thanked him again. I wanted to ask him more about this Lucius, but we needed to get going. I couldn't really understand his reservations about the city elder, but it was one of many quirks associated with Blandus. I shrugged it off. Livia then told him we had a surprise for him and needed him to accompany us up the mountain. Blandus was uncomfortable around soldiers in uniform, and he was not enthusiastic about going anywhere with Crispus. However, with some further coaxing from Livia, his curiosity took over, and the old man decided to accept our invitation to escort us up the mountain trail. I actually didn't know he was coming with the three of us. Livia had not told me much about her plan or theory of where the medallion was hidden, so it was going to be a surprise for me too. I wasn't worried about Scaevolus anymore, but like Primus, I had had enough of the mountain and its danger, and was happy to have some more company on this trek. Somehow, it seemed safer with Blandus along.

We followed the trail for well over an hour towards the two caves. We were banged up and Blandus could only walk slowly. As we had the day before, we passed by the big boulders on the side of the road with figures of raven, lion, serpent, and finally, scorpion. Livia told us that if her memory was correct, the next figure would be a bull. We then came to the boulder with the figure in question. Sure enough, there was an abstract painting with a head, two horns and a red and green eye.

Livia asked Blandus, "Do you know who painted these?"

Blandus said that they were here when he was only a child. "They may have been painted by the Persian, or one of other early followers." As he said this, he looked directly at Crispus and then back at us. I realized that Blandus did not know the identity of Blandus' father, and the old man was trying to make sure we didn't slip up and reveal his secret.

Livia understood immediately and said, "Well, it doesn't matter who painted them, only that they have been here since the Mithran purge in the reign of Nero."

Blandus continued, "This is on the way to caves where the Mithra held ceremonies. I always supposed the figures acted as a sort of signpost or a kind of a map.

She stopped and pointed and said, "Didn't you say, Blandus, that the levels of Mithra were raven, lion, serpent, scorpion and dog?"

He nodded.

"Then, why is the bull here? It is not one of the levels of enlightenment. It seems out of place."

Blandus explained that the God Mithra had conquered a giant bull and that he sometimes took the form of a bull when visiting the earth. It was therefore natural to see the bull in Mithran iconography. He didn't think it that strange.

Livia countered, "OK, but why not paint it farther up trail and put the figure of the dog here, as in the proper order?" she asked.

Blandus shrugged, and said he didn't know because he wasn't the artist. I really didn't understand where Livia was going with all of this and had trouble following her logic.

Livia continued, "And did you notice how beautiful and intricate the paintings of the other animals are. They were done by a true craftsman, a really talented painter. This picture of the bull lacks the skill of the other works. It is hastily drawn."

Everyone examined it closely and agreed she was right. This was not the same artist. She asked, "And what is this one?

All of the other figures are five hundred cubits apart, but this one is only thirty cubits from the bull."

We approached the figure and looked at it closely. It didn't look like any animal at all. It was a series of circles within circles. The center contained a kind of strange shaped abstract figure with traces of orange paint still present on its weathered surface. It was even less artistic than the bull. The two boulders with the bull and the circular diagram were indeed much closer together than the other figures, but no one could have lifted them and put them here, so I didn't really capture their relevance. I looked behind them and both had small spaces separating them from the cliff face behind them.

Livia looked at each of us in turn, and said, "Do you recognize this figure?"

Blandus, said "I don't know. It could just be graffiti and not related. Many people have come up here. Someone might have just drawn this."

Livia smiled broadly and answered, "Maybe." but then she pulled out the medallion and placed it directly beside the figure on the rock.

"Goat's teats!" I said, "It's a picture of the medallion!"

We all crowded around the figure and put the medallion in various perspectives. There was no question, that this was a picture of the medallion. Crispus was patting Livia on the back and congratulating her on her ingenuity.

Livia said, "I saw this yesterday and it stuck in my mind. It wasn't until last night looking at the medallion up close that I remembered what it could represent."

I said, "Yes, but this doesn't necessarily mean we have found the treasure."

Livia agreed, but then took out the dagger and the scabbard and placed them side by side. We all then backed up and I gasped.

I said with surprise, "The bull on the dagger matches the picture of the bull on that rock over there. The bull painting we just looked at."

Livia nodded, then asked Blandus, "What is it you said you're… uh …uh, the Persian, told the Mithra?" Livia looked away to cover her near mistake with Blandus and cursed to herself that she had almost exposed the identity of Blandus' father to Crispus.

"The secrets will be revealed when the two objects are together." said Blandus. He didn't seem to notice or care that she had almost revealed his secret. He was too entranced with the revelation of the figure on the rock.

"Look at the scabbard of the dagger. It has a bull's head and the eyes are ruby and emerald jewels just like the red and green eyes in this painting. If you put them together, what do you get I wonder?" She unsheathed the blade and noticed the point of the dagger was pointing down like an arrow. "I think the star on the point of the dagger is the location of the secret. If I put the bull's head of the scabbard here on the bull of the boulder, it means that the star is somewhere down here."

She pointed to the base of the rock. There was nothing on the front of the boulder and the ground there seemed very hard. I looked again at the space behind the boulder at its base.

I exclaimed with surprise, "There is a faint picture of a star on the back of this boulder!" I touched the earth and added, "The ground back here is very soft and we can dig in around it."

Crispus moved forward and said, "We must have found the treasure!"

I looked again at the space and shook my head.

"There's not enough room there to hide a large horde of treasure."

"Exactly," said Livia. "So maybe the secret of the Mithrans does not lay in treasure but in something that can be hidden in a small space."

We four all dug around in the one cubit gap between the boulder and the cliff side with one of my tools. Sure enough, after about only a half pes deep we hit something hard that made a clanking sound with my spade. We carefully moved the dirt from around the object. We kept digging for several minutes and finally unearthed a small clay amphora pot approximately one or two cubits in length. It took some time to pull the jar out intact. We all looked at each other with anticipation, but Blandus was in tears.

I asked him if he knew what it was, but he only said, "It is my father's work!"

I looked over at Crispus, but he didn't take notice of the old man's words. Livia carefully took the lid off of the pottery jar and gazed inside at its contents. There she slowly pulled out two papyrus scrolls. Blandus actually gasped when he gazed upon them. We dusted them off and partially unrolled one of them just enough to find beautiful designs, multicolored paintings and inked words in a language that I didn't understand. Blandus was giddy.

He said to Livia, "These are the lost scrolls of the Mithra that Radijah brought from the old lands. They are ancient and contain many of the stories of the great god. I thought the religion was dead. There is no one to teach us the old ways, but now if they can be translated, we may yet relive our past and seek enlightenment."

Crispus was about to take the scrolls from her hands. He probably would have directly turned them over with the dagger and medallion to the Prefect, but Livia stopped him.

She said, "Crispus, these are not treasure, and their worth is lost on the magistrate. They are priceless icons that belong to those of their own faith."

Livia then looked to me and back to Crispus. "Blandus should have these to keep and protect. They are his birthright. We cannot tell the Prefect or anyone else of their existence. Enough people have died or been hurt based on a hunt for something that never was."

Crispus looked long at her, then back at Herculaneum where his brother laid mending with grievous wounds. He finally shook his head and said "I will not tell. It is our secret. Blandus, keep them and use them well."

We walked in silence all along the mountain trail and back to his small shack by the mountain. As we left him, he waved to us, still grinning and went inside to examine the parchments at length. We walked the extra millarium to Livia's parent's house. Her father Marius, and brother Leto had decided to stay at home instead of going fishing that day. They needed to start repairs on their villa after the quakes. We ate some figs and melon and finally decided to begin the walk over to the grand villa of Lucius Batallius and our appointment with the Prefect.

## CHAPTER 15: THE PALACE OF LUCIUS BATALLUS

As we made our way downhill toward the ocean and the villa of the Duovir, we noticed that there was significantly more damage to the shops and homes of Herculaneum than we had noticed yesterday when we were following Scaevolus. Apparently the combination of earthquakes had weakened many of the structures. We saw several collapsed roofs in Livia's parents' neighborhood and passed a small building with two walls that had also collapsed in toward the interior. It appeared to be a bakery based on the exposed brick oven. I hoped that no one was inside when the building fell. We worked our way across the forum, and saw three giant Doric columns lining the eastern peristyle, which had fallen with a portion of the attached roof of the atrium. The quake here in Herculaneum must have been much worse than it felt while I was up on the trail. Perhaps I was just so preoccupied with my fight with Scaevolus that I didn't appreciate its magnitude. It was still relatively early morning and few people were outside yet. We saw a few tending to their homes, mending doors or windows or patching ceilings and roofs.

We walked down the beautiful grand boulevard of

Herculaneum past the central bath house, past palaces and fine villas of the city elite with their beautiful marble cladding. We turned back south near the sea for a block or two until we reached a tall wall on one street corner and could see the mansion behind it. There was an arched gate with a large wooden door at its center, and bronze handles which I stopped to admire. Those looked like the work of my grandfather. I appreciated the twisted columned rows and knew how much work went into them....and these were just the door handles. I marveled at the masonry of the house itself once we moved opened the doors to the terrace inside. This was truly a magnificent home, and its owner was obviously extremely wealthy and powerful. We walked to the side of the house past manicured gardens. There were several slaves in the terrace doing various gardening or cleaning jobs. They were scantily dressed and all seemed to be quite young. They only looked at us briefly before continuing their duties. The entrance to the mansion was on the southern side of the property facing the sea. The villa had a second floor covered balcony overlooking the vicolo below. We were met at the door by the same young male servant that had given us the message last night. He bowed to us and asked to follow him where his master was waiting.

We entered a large reception room on the first floor with a fine colored mosaic at its center. There was a beautiful fresco of Argus and Io on one wall showing Io in the form of a large white heifer and of Argus with his thousand ever watchful eyes. Mercury was in the background with his sword held high, ready to slay Argus on the orders of Jupiter. There were statues of nude women all along one wall, and a marble of a woman lying invitingly on a bed in the center of the room. We were escorted into the adjacent atrium and saw the magistrate sitting with an older man on two large cushioned chairs. They were both wearing long togas and the magistrate had a Pallium styled robe draped over the top of his toga.

The older man said, "Here they are Loreius. Just as I told you."

We were led into the area of the room just in front of their two chairs by the young servant. Loreius stood up, but the other man remained seated.

"Titus, we meet again. Miss Livia." He lowered his head slightly as he greeted her.

I was staring at the walls of this room which were adorned in pornographic paintings that covered three walls. On the remaining wall behind the two men were multiple shelves containing many beautiful metal figures and small marble statuary. Various other objects were on opposite walls.

Loreius looked at Crispus and said, "I understand your brother is still mending his wounds. I am sorry for his ails, but I applaud both your efforts in finding the murderer so quickly and dispatching him. Crispus bowed low but Lorieus sensed the exaggerated effort and frowned back at him. He looked back at Livia and me and said, "I arrived here this morning. I understand you have recovered both the dagger and the medallion?

"Yes, Prefect."

"And may I see them?"

"Of course, Prefect." Said Crispus again and handed the objects over to the magistrate.

"They are exquisite, and the medallion appears to be made of gold." said Loreius, as if no one in the room had noticed. "Well worth the money you are paying me, Lucius." He then simply handed the dagger and medallion over to the older man and said, "Have the money delivered to my chariot. I am leaving for Pompeii as soon as I have finished prandium. I need to see how much damage these earthquakes have wrought. Pompeii has much to repair."

He then glared directly at me. With that final gesture, he walked out of the room and left us.

Lucius got up, and said, "I owe you three a great deal of gratitude."

We were staring at him with contempt, and Crispus asked, "For bringing the dagger and medallion to the Prefect so he could just hand them over to you?"

Lucius looked bemused and replied, "No, for taking care of Scaevolus for me." He looked at the bundle of metal in his hands and said, "I guess Blandus has told you much of the history of these objects. I actually owned the dagger for a time."

Lucius noticed our surprise and said, "Yes, I bought it a few years ago from Scaevolus, but he stole it from me only two weeks ago when I sent him to buy the medallion. The stupid oaf really thought the objects were magical."

"You had him kill all of those people?" said Livia incredulously.

"No, dear woman. I only sent him to purchase the objects. I gave him enough bronze sestertii and silver denarii coins to pay for two medallions, but I should have known better than to trust the miscreant. He took my money and before he left, he also took the dagger from the shelf right behind me."

I said, "How could you ever trust such a despicable man with even one coin of your money?"

"I have many eyes in this city and in Pompeii. I was not worried about losing my investment, and thought he still might be able to obtain the medallion by one means or another."

Livia then said accusingly, "So you knew he might kill Vibiana and Zahret."

"No, but I suspected he would steal it from them and then I would steal both objects back from him." He continued, "I have had him followed throughout his journey to Pompeii and back here. I knew he would go back to the caves and try to use some stupid spell he learned from his father or Aurelius, in an attempt to find the infamous Mithran horde."

I said, "So you never believed there was ever any treasure?"

"Of course not, young man. I helped the Roman soldiers do the original interrogations of the Mithra twenty five years ago."

We looked at him with confused faces.

"I am sixty seven years old. Although your friend Blandus appears to be even older than I am, he was only in his early twenties when he was imprisoned. I am afraid the years of captivity and toil has aged him well beyond his years." He paused for a minute and looked at each of us in turn. "I was already one of the town council even then, thanks to my status and family history."

Livia couldn't help herself and glared at him.

"Ah," he said, "Blandus must have told you of my time with Caligula on the isle of Capri. Blandus hasn't ever forgiven me for my role in his interrogations and slanders me constantly with that fact. It is true that I spent some time on the isle palace in the latter years of Tiberius' reign before Caligula came to power. I was summoned to their vacation villa when I was only in my late teens. Tiberius was a relative. I could hardly be held accountable for my actions."

"Are you related to the current emperor?" I asked.

"No, not directly to Titus or his father Vespasian, but maybe distantly to their family by cousins through some of the various forced weddings in the imperial family over the past decades. I think Vespasian's family is from Falicranae, north of Rome. I have no relatives there. I did know the Mulio, and I always liked him, despite his rather stern reputation. I was sorry to see him pass. Did you know he actually fell asleep once while listening to Nero play the lyre? That cost him some years in exile."

As he laughed to himself at his joke, I shook my head no. I also thought it disrespectful to speak of Vespasian as the Mulio. It was a disparaging nickname referring to his time in exile as a mule rancher. If he had used that term while Vespasian still ruled, he would have been facing crucifixion. I never understood the ins and outs of Roman politics anyway.

Lucius continued, "You, Mistress Livia, were probably named for my great aunt, Livia Drusilla. A lovely woman by all accounts, and a forceful and fitting counterpart to her husband, the great Augustus."

I marveled again at this man's family connections to some of the greatest rulers in Roman history, and his ability to name-drop in almost any situation and demonstrate his elite status and implied overall superiority to anyone listening.

Livia asked how he could stand witnessing the depravities of Caligula and his orgies.

"If I hadn't dear girl, I assure you I wouldn't be here today. Caligula's detractors didn't live long, especially those he was related to. Tiberius in his elder years was also capable of great cruelty. "

Lucius walked around the room picking up a few of the objects on a shelf. He lingered over a bronze bust of Tiberius. "I was named after Lucius Calpurnius Piso, an extremely important man who lived in a neighboring villa. He was a consul of Rome and a patron of the arts. As a friend of the great poet and epicurean Philodemus, he had a wonderful collection of poems from the philosopher as well as those from Ovid and others in the family palace a few blocks down the boulevard. It remains the finest library in Campania. Unfortunately, his grandson failed to support Vespasian during the year of four emperors and he met a rather gruesome end in the first year of Vespasian's reign. I therefore now tell people I was named after the patron of Herculaneum, Lucius Maximus. You see, one must be careful with whom one allies, and it never pays to meddle in Roman family politics."

Livia finally got the nerve to ask the question that she had thought about since we arrived. "And did you enjoy torturing Blandus…"

"Miss Livia, the Prefect was right, you are impertinent." said Lucius in an indignant tone. "I am afraid you have been grossly misinformed. I never tortured Blandus. I only helped the Romans interrogate their prisoners. It was my way of protecting our citizens. All of them would have been killed immediately had it been up to Nero and his centurions. I knew and liked the father Radijah, and I knew the entire Mithra leadership was being blamed for the crimes of two or three of the wayward cult members. I'm afraid Palindus was even more devious than anyone suspected in his machinations against them. I only found out the truth of his misdeeds and the extent of his crimes during the interrogations. Once I was able to convince the magistrate of the various lies and criminal intent of Palindus, so as to have him arrested, he had already fled to Egypt beyond my grasp. I never wanted anyone from the town tortured, crucified or stoned to death, but the legion soldiers required it. I think they even enjoyed the torture. As you know, Rome has always been entertained with execution. Most of the Mithra were killed in the arena only days after their capture.

Livia was still mulling something over in her mind, and finally asked, "How about that young girl who went missing twenty five years ago? Blandus said you might have been involved in that too. Did she get sent to the isle of Capri?"

He frowned at her and answered, "As to the little girl in question, if it is the one I remember, Palindus abducted her and had her sold into slavery in Rome even before the centurions arrived, as he did with several other women. I had nothing to do with her abduction or bondage."

Livia was still frowning at him and was looking around for his other young slaves. Lucius saw her looking at his slaves and only laughed. He said, "Yes, I like my slaves young and pretty, even the boys, but the girl in question was only in her eighth year at the time. I'm afraid that is too young for my tastes."

He paused and got up and walked to one of the shelves where he had several bronze objects. One of them consisted of lovers wrapped in an embrace. One was of a many armed god, and another was of one of the Egyptian pharaohs. He ran his finger along one of the objects and said, "I am a collector of exotic art and beautiful objects from many parts of the world. I especially like figures of lovemaking, but also those representing mystical gods of other lands. I want you to know this because I don't want you to think I was after any Mithran horde of treasure. I knew the Mithra had no money, and tried to make it clear in the interrogations with the soldiers of Nero that their only crime was religion. I wanted the soldiers to understand they were persecuting these citizens for no reason. For Nero, it didn't matter, and if I had protested too loudly he simply would have imprisoned me and taken my villa and all of the acquired wealth of my family. At that time, my first wife was still alive, as was my son. I could not risk losing everything. As you well know, the Romans favor execution over imprisonment, and it was all I could do to save two of the Mithra from crucifixion.

As time went on, it became harder and harder to keep Blandus and Sartarus alive. Nero could have had them killed at any time, but his curiosity over the unfound treasure horde played in their favor. He left two alive who he thought still knew the secrets. I can never make it up to Blandus, and while his contempt for me is justified, his reasons are faulty. I have tried to help various members of the cult over the years. Not all of them were imprisoned or sent to their deaths. This included Scaevolus and Aurelius, who were family survivors who both lost their mothers. I took them into my house and fed them and allowed them to live among my servants, but as free men, not slaves. Unfortunately, they lacked the discipline of a father figure and became wayward early on. Eventually I could no longer control them, but I still offered them various jobs, especially the nefarious ones I could not risk doing myself. I bought the Mithran dagger from Scaevolus soon after he had found it amongst his father's belongings. I knew of them even while the Mithra were active. Radijah was a devoutly religious man and never would relinquish either object. Sartarus was delusional and believed until his death there was a great buried horde of eastern artifacts.

He knew there was no money, but thought Radijah came from the east with an elephant load of gold, silver and bronze religious objects. He wouldn't sell the dagger, and I lost interest until Scaevolus offered it to me. When I heard about the medallion showing up in Pompeii, I simply wanted it for my collection. I asked Scaevolus to retrieve it for me and gave him the cash to do so. I should have suspected when he was glancing around this room that he intended to take the dagger following on the foolish quest of his father. Had I had enough forethought to hide the dagger, he would not have entered my villa that night and stolen it."

This story became more and more convoluted and I had a hard time deciding who was to blame for what. Crispus looked as confused as I was, but Livia seemed to be following Lucius' version of events.

"I actually sent Aurelius to steal it back from Scaevolus. It is only in the last few days that I fear that was not a good decision on my part, and I'm afraid Aurelius met with some foul end."

"Scaevolus had admitted to killing Aurelius and leaving him in the caves. He didn't seem very upset about it. Actually, kind of proud of himself for killing his friend out of principle."

"I feared as much. I shall be accountable for several deaths that will scar my soul, when I meet the gods one day. I hope they realize I personally meant no one any harm."

He sighed loudly and sat back down. He clapped his hands and a servant appeared. "Bring us some mulsum promptly." He asked.

Mulsum is the honey mead beverage that we drink at festivals and for special cenae. It has a nice semisweet taste. It does not get one quite as inebriated as wine, as it is diluted with water, but it is a refreshing drink in the midday.

Lucius continued, "In any case, Scaevolus betrayed my trust and went to Pompeii immediately with the intention of retrieving the medallion for himself. In a ridiculous attempt to create magic, he would somehow combine it with the dagger and find untold riches. Poppycock. Aurelius told me of the supposed legend of the coupling."

Livia and I were looking at each other but we simultaneously looked back at Lucius when we felt him staring. "I have the two objects in my possession now, but they are nothing more than beautiful things from the Far East. I do not believe they have any magical powers, and I don't believe they are connected to any buried treasure."

"But so many people were killed over these two things." said Livia.

"I am truly sorry for that, but as I said, the man had apparently lost whatever mind he had remaining." "He stole my money as well as some from the Egyptian and our friend Vibiana. The man that I had following you went to his house last night and found a lot of money under Scaevolus' bed wrapped in a linen towel. More money than I had given him. There was enough there for him to live comfortably for years. Unfortunately, in his rage and crazed greed, he left his fortune in his house to go search for the treasure in the cave. Any sane man would have left the province with the riches he had, knowing he was being pursued by the Prefect's guards."

"You had us followed too?" asked Livia.

"There were eyes on you from the time you entered Herculaneum, dear girl." He smiled. "And yes, I knew you went up to the mountain just this morning and know that you

returned with Blandus."

We all shot worried glances at each other. He continued, "Don't worry; I won't take the parchment he was carrying, although I have a pretty good idea what it contains."

We looked at him in amazement and he laughed suddenly. "I owe him at least that," said Lucius. "By the way, which one of you figured out where to find the scroll?"

Livia blushed and bent her head down as Crispus and I looked at her.

"I thought as much. Good. Now, finish your drinks for you have a long walk ahead of you and there may be more quakes today. It seems the ground has shaken much in the past few days. They say the god of the mountain is restless." He laughed again and bid us farewell.

## CHAPTER 16: THE MOUNTAIN COMES ALIVE

It was still late morning when we stopped back at Livia's parents to gather our things, say our goodbyes, and help Primus up to his feet. Livia was greatly missing our daughter and needed to feed her to relieve both of their anxieties (and the growing discomfort in her breasts). Thankfully, the Prefect had placed the extra gear that we had taken from Portius into his own carriage. We weren't going to have to carry much back to Pompeii. That left me free to help Crispus hold up Primus while he managed to limp home. Primus was able to wrap his left arm over my unhurt right shoulder, with his other arm draped over Crispus. Between the two of us, we could almost support his weight. It was still going to be a long slow day of walking. We passed out of the streets of Herculaneum the same way we arrived. The sky seemed dark and overcast for a summer day and I wondered if it was going to rain again. Noon had not yet arrived when we finally left through the city gate of Herculaneum, on our way home on the cobblestone road to Pompeii. I noticed there were a large number of people walking on the road, most of whom were carrying bags of goods, or pulling carts filled with many of their possessions.

"What's with all of the travelers?" asked Crispus. He must have noticed too.

We passed a family of four that were in front of us and Livia asked where they were heading and why.

"We are fleeing the city. Our home was damaged badly in the two quakes yesterday and we have only a portion of our roof. We are going to stay with our relatives in Pompeii." said the woman in the group.

Another older man who was walking nearby and overheard us, added, "My home has only a few cracks, but I remember the last great earthquake seventeen years ago. We have had three quakes in two days and I fear there is going to be another massive one again today or tomorrow. I'm getting out before I get buried in my own house. Do you know that yesterday, the sea by the beach retreated several blocks off shore and left hundreds of fish and other life floundering there in the sand?"

We all looked at him with alarm and drew closer to hear what he said.

He continued, "I saw it with my own eyes. Fish there, lying on the beach. The surf was a full quarter millarium off of the coast. A little while later the surf came back in but with four foot waves that crashed against the docks and tore at the moorings. It was as if Neptune had sucked in his breath and then exhaled the sea back at us. I was terrified. Several of the boats there in the docks were washed up onto the terrace."

Livia looked at me with alarm, but I responded, "If your father's boat was damaged yesterday when that happened, he would have told us. We just saw him this morning."

That seemed to comfort her, but I could tell she was still very anxious about the day's events. I felt sorry for all of these people who had their homes damaged, and hoped they had a place to go. I then started worrying about the family blacksmith shop and our house, and wondered if they too had suffered a lot of damage. Livia must have been thinking along the same lines, as she looked at me and grabbed my arm.

"Do you think Dania is all right? I am worried that Aule's house may have been caught up in the earthquake and then he or Dania may have suffered some injury. We must hurry home."

I tried to assure her that everything was going to be fine, but secretly I was as worried as she was. Even Crispus, who usually kept a very upbeat temperament, looked pretty worried. We heard a commotion behind us and everyone at once had to scurry out of the way and off of the road to keep from being run down by a man in a cart. He was moving his team much faster than was safe on a road packed with people.

Crispus yelled at him to slow down, but his only reply was, "I am getting as far away from that mountain as I can."

After that, we walked more briskly than we had, and even Primus, for his part, was trying to keep up and not lean on his brother quite as much. After about an hour we started to hear murmuring going up and down the road, with groups of people talking among themselves. It was midday, and while the sun should have shown brightly in the late summer sky, it seemed a little overcast and the light was dimmer than I normally remembered it for this time of year. The temperature seemed fine. It would be another month or two before the air would begin to take on a slight chill during the days. The wind was blowing strongly from our right. The group ahead of us, who had been talking, now were turned back towards Herculaneum and were pointing at the mountain. Livia was the first to turn around and follow their gaze.

We had been traveling for about an hour or so when the wind seemed to shift suddenly.

"That's strange," "there is smoke rising from the mountaintop." The dog, which had followed us from Livia's parents' house, let out a low howl, and immediately we all heard a low rumbling sound to our left that could have been thunder if there had been any other sign of lightning. None of us had ever seen anything like that in our lives. There appeared to be a small plume of smoke coming from the mountain. It was a mixture of blacks, whites and greys, and could easily be separated from the surrounding cloud tops.

People up and down the road were turned around staring at the mountain and pointing. Someone said they thought that the top of the mountain was glowing. Another said there were fires on the mountain. I couldn't see that through the smoke, but whatever was going on, this was unusual and frightening. We heard all kinds of wild speculation from passersby about what was happening on the mountain, and which of the gods were angry and which gods were causing the mountain fires. By this time, Livia had seen and heard about all she could take and was becoming hysterical with worry for our baby. She implored us to hurry and move as fast as we could make for Pompeii and Aule's house. This was difficult because Livia had a swollen ankle from her leap off of the cliff last night and was still limping pretty badly. Primus was being held up by the shoulder of Crispus and there was no way he could go any faster than he was at present. Livia looked at me imploringly and then back at Primus.

She said, "We need to move faster, but we can't leave Primus behind."

"Don't worry about us. We'll be fine. Primus here is walking much better." assured Crispus.

We were about to take off when Crispus yelled, "OW", and brushed his arm, as if he had been stung by a bug. It began to get somewhat darker, despite it being only around noon. We noticed that there were small flakes and grains of pumice and ash that were falling as rain droplets here and there.

"That doesn't look like rain. It looks like fire. It is raining fire. This is like the horror stories of old, when the titans fought the Olympian gods." said Primus. "The world is coming to an end. The gods are retaking our world. Jupiter protect us." He bowed his head in prayer.

The flakes of pumice and ash coming from the sky increased steadily over a few minutes, and all of us felt the burning sensation on our heads and shoulders when one of these flakes hit us.

"We must cover our heads!" said Livia.

She borrowed a sword from Crispus and used it to cut her gown off at the level of her mid thigh. She then cut or ripped the remaining fabric into three pieces. She gave one to Primus and I, and kept one for herself, which she placed on her lead like a scarf. She instructed the two of us to do the same. Crispus was already wearing his helmet (so he wouldn't have to carry it and his brother). The flakes of ash were getting a little bit larger and could have been snow had this not been several months too early and several leagues too far south. My eyes were beginning to water, and there was a foul odor of burning in the air. We left our bags at the side of the road. I figured I could always come back and retrieve them.

Crispus told us again that Livia and I needed to hurry back to Pompeii and retrieve our daughter. He insisted that we let them follow behind at a slower pace, and that we would meet up in Pompeii. Primus did his best to look confident and agree with his brother. He was unfortunately still in a lot of pain and was not walking too well, but Crispus maintained they would be fine. They wished us well as Livia and I took off at a much faster pace, with nothing to carry but ourselves. We weaved in and out of refugees on the road. There were individuals and families all up and down the via, with carts, both handheld and pulled by horses or donkeys. Most of these people seemed pretty distraught, and some looked really scared. Children were crying, and their parents were staring at the strange scarves around our heads and the scandalous, torn outfit that Livia was wearing, as we whizzed past at a fast walk. We weren't able to run, but we could still move much faster than those ahead who were dragging their children and belongings.

After almost another hour of speed walking or jogging at a stiff pace, we had to stop and catch our breath. We were within eyesight of the necropolis and could see some of the funerary monuments just ahead on both sides of the road. I could just make out the walls of the city ahead running perpendicular to the road. We slowed to a walk, but had not said much of anything to each other since we had first noticed the plume of smoke on the mountain. Livia was still deep in thought and probably concerned for both our daughter and her family back in Herculaneum. I looked back quickly towards Mt. Vesuvius and noticed that the small trail of smoke had turned into a rather large inverted cone of dark, black boiling clouds. I just turned back southward to face Livia and had taken a few steps towards the nearby catacombs. Suddenly, we heard an incredibly loud explosion behind us that sent us both to the ground. This blast was surely the most violent wrenching of the earth in the history of Campania. We brushed ourselves off and looked back at Mt Vesuvius, still on our knees in the middle of the road. We sat in amazement looking at the mountain to our north. The large black cloud was now climbing to the heavens like a giant tree. The dark smoke was mixed with large bursts or flashes of lightning, and there was fire and flame easily visible at the top of the mountain. I have never seen anything so frightening nor so awe-inspiring. People behind us on the road were screaming, and I could even hear screams coming from Pompeii a distance away to our front.

"Primus was right. This is the end of days. The world is finished." was all that Livia could manage. She was crying, but my will became resolute at that instant.

"We must get our daughter and flee. Aule may have already left the city. Quickly. Run!"

We got up to our feet and ran past the tombs and through the city gate. It was several minutes until we reached the forum and began to scurry across the plaza. There were scores of people moving inside all three of the temples lining the forum. Directly in front of us facing the bay, there was a line moving slowly into the temple of Apollo. Across the plaza on the northeast side, several robed virgins in white were trying to herd people into the vestibule of the Temple of Vesta. Many of these were women. The statue of Hercules in the center of the plaza had fallen on its side and was broken into a few pieces. There was a crack in the forum grounds, running north to south that was many cubits in length. The earth had been torn apart by the force of whatever blow had been dealt there. I didn't know why the Gods were angry, but it appeared they had decided to take all of their vengeance out on our two cities. Alycia, the slave girl who worked at the forum wine bar, came running up to Livia and I as we crossed the plaza.

"Titus. Mistress Livia. I am glad to see you both. I heard you were in Herculaneum and thought you dead. Isn't it terrible? I heard the whole world is exploding. I don't know what to do."

"Alycia, where are you going? It is dangerous outside. You need to seek shelter."

"I am going to the temple of Venus. I hope she has Pompeii still in her graces. I witnessed the miracle of the tears." She wiped her own tears from her face. "The master of my house left us to our own devices. When he heard the explosion and saw the mountain, he told us to close the bar. He was running to the Stabiae gate, and said we should protect his house and business. Two of the male servants are still there, but it is very hot inside the building. I didn't know what to do, so I came here to let the priests try to plead to the gods for our release."

I looked at the mass of people huddled inside the temple and saw Silvanus trying to help some of the older ones. He was praying loudly and repeatedly looking toward the sky. He looked scared.

"Alycia, you should follow your master and run quickly to the south. You must get as far from the mountain as possible. I fear Pompeii is no longer safe. Don't stop until you reach Stabiae."

"But I have never been outside of the city gates. It is forbidden for slaves. I don't know where I am going. It is too difficult. I will stay inside the temple. I will be safe there."

At that moment, a new horror started. Instead of just ash mixed with rain, there started a rain of small rocks. These were light pumice, and most were the size of small pebbles. Occasionally however, a much larger piece would fall and crash to the ground. If one of those hit someone, they would suffer severe injury. All of these small falling pumice stones were hot, so even the smaller ones hurt or burned if they hit you, and there was no way to avoid them, standing in the middle of the street.

Livia grabbed my arm and said we had to go. I bid Alycia good luck and good bye, and we turned to head for the corner of the forum and the main boulevard, with our hands covering our heads. A huge crashing sound came from the grainery to my right. A large rock the size of a rabbit had penetrated the ceiling near the entrance and hit the column supporting the portico. The elaborate entrance to the building had buckled and collapsed onto the ground in front. More screaming from the crowd ensued. Several people from the temples on both sides ran over to see to the damage. There was smoke coming from the wreckage, but no fire. I paused briefly to see if anyone needed help, but it appeared that no one was in the grainery at the time. The giant building was usually guarded by a soldier or two, but I didn't see any soldiers of the wall anywhere right now. Livia again pulled at my arm and we started jogging quickly towards the arch that marked the forum eastern entrance.

By the time we reached the extreme northeastern corner of the plaza, the onslaught from the heavens had intensified. There was a steady rain of gravel, pumice, sand and ash that was falling from the sky. It was getting progressively harder to breathe, and I had welts and blisters on my exposed skin where I had been hit by burning ash from above. We heard a strange wailing sound from above. A large boulder, the size of a sheep, came hurtling down just to my left and crashed through a roof in the administration building. It completely destroyed the roof and one wall of the structure in which it hit, and the force of the impact knocked me completely off of my feet. I landed on the shoulder which had been slashed by Scaevolus only yesterday, and I cried out in pain. Livia had run ahead but turned back to see what had happened to me. I was still sitting down and managed a look at the smoldering ruins to my left. The stone that had crushed the building was visible through the front entrance and glowed red as if it was on fire. As if on cue, the building's timbers suddenly went up in flames. There were small plumes of smoke from other parts of the city, where other flaming stones or boulders must have also hit their mark. This was truly Hades come to life. I expected to see the Kraken or another beast of the underworld to come crawling out of the alleyways towards us. The stench of sulfur and egg was overpowering. I felt helpless.

Livia aided me to my feet with a reach of her hand, and said, "We must get inside or we will be burned alive."

I countered, "And if we stay inside, we may get buried alive." "Come on."

We ran several more blocks past screaming women and children who, like us, didn't know whether to go inside or stay outside. The ash was now over four digitii deep and it was making my sandals feel like warm coals. I was coughing heavily from the combination of strenuous running and inhaling a variety of noxious particles. I took the piece of Livia's scarf off of my head and wrapped it over my nose and mouth. It didn't make it easy to breathe while running, but at least it helped with the coughing fits. People were taking things out of their houses and putting them in packs. Everyone was leaving. I asked if we should stop at our house to check on it, and Livia said no.

"It doesn't matter anymore. Just save Dania!" We hurried

on towards Aule's house. When we arrived, his cart and two horses were already parked in front of his villa and his wife was in the passenger seat holding our baby. He was putting the last of his belongings into the back of the cart. The horses were whinnying loudly and looked ready to bolt. Both he and his wife had pillows tied to their heads to guard against falling rocks. It made them look like sheepherders.

He saw us arriving, and said, "Oh thank the gods. We thought you were still in Herculaneum. The mountain will destroy it. But you are late. We need to go, NOW."

Livia took Dania, who was crying loudly, from Aule's wife and tried to calm the baby.

"Aule, where are you going?"

"To Nocera, if I can get there. We have relatives who can put us up. It is another half day's ride, even by cart. You should join us."

I looked skeptical. Nocera, or Nuceria as the Greeks who founded it had originally named it, was a long walk, but not that much farther away from the mountain than Pompeii. It lies mainly northeast rather than south. I looked at the pile of things that Aule and his wife had put in the back of his wagon, and I could not see any place where the two of us could ride. I considered that walk, which would be almost twice as far as Stabiae, with the constant threat of bombardment from the mountain, and I decided it was not a great option. I shook my head and thanked him.

"No, I think we are going to try to make it to Stabiae, as it is a shorter walk and hopefully is far enough south of the mountain to get away from this cursed ash. We will walk half of the night if need be, but we must get as far from Vesuvius as we can. Best of luck to you and your family in Nocera. I do not know when I will see you again. I'm afraid Pompeii is lost."

I looked around and saw the ash growing on all of the surfaces and even accumulating on the roofs. The air was getting incredibly hot, and breathing through my scarf was difficult.

"Goodbye, dear Aule, old friend. I hope we can meet in this life or the next." added Livia.

We hugged and then he hugged Livia and kissed Dania on the forehead. "It is a long walk on foot to Stabiae. If it will help you, you can use my boat. You should go to the marina. My fishing boat is docked there. It is not big, but it is big enough to hold the three of you. The winds are coming in from the sea, so you will not be able to sail out from the harbor, but there are oars in the boat, so you can use them to paddle the craft towards Stabiae. It should be faster than walking. You can use the sea water to keep from burning from this accursed pumice rock."

We thanked him again and he shooed his horses off at a fast pace down the via towards the Sarno gate. The two mares did not need much coaxing and his cart flew down the road.
We turned around and went back towards the shop and our villa. We were walking briskly and needed to get a few supplies before we left. I reached the back gate on Vicolo dell'Efebo and hurriedly swung the doors open. We entered the house, but it was stiflingly hot inside. Dania was crying loudly, and Livia could do nothing to settle her. She went upstairs to get some linens and a few things for the baby. I decided we needed a little food and some water. I turned on the spigot to allow the water to flow and it scalded my hand.

"Ahhh." I cried out in pain and pulled my hand back quickly. "What in Jupiter's beard is going on?"

The water was even hotter than the steam baths at the Stabiane bathhouse down the street, where slaves stoke warm fires underneath the water. We do not have heated water in our Pompeii house, nor does anyone else I know. I carefully put some of the hot water into a sheepskin flask canteen that I found in the house and filled it. I still managed to burn my hands and had to wrap them in the towel. I found some fruit and figs and put them into a bag with the water flask and put it over my shoulder. I heard Livia scream and I quickly ran up the stairs to see what the problem was.

"The walls and ceiling are scalding hot. They burned my hand!" she exclaimed.

"The water in the plumbing is also hot." I said. The upstairs room has a very low ceiling so I reached up and felt the roof.

I pulled my hand back quickly. "Goats beard! You're right. This ceiling is almost on fire. It must be from the ash on the roof. We must leave the house immediately. The roof will cave in soon or the whole place may catch on fire. It is not safe. We need to get outside."

Livia was crying and trying to decide what to salvage. She was looking in every room, but I finally stopped her.

"Livia! We have no time. We must leave for the marina immediately. We can take Aule's boat and soon be to Stabiae at the southern end of the bay."

She nodded at me; picked our daughter back up off of her pillow downstairs and we retreated out the door. It was only just early afternoon and less than an hour after the terrible explosion, but it looked like dusk or early evening. There was little light visible in the sky and ash, pumice and gravel were falling everywhere. I had to put the scarf back over my mouth and nose and instructed Livia to do the same for herself and Dania. We moved as fast as we could up the Via-dell'Abbondanza toward the Marina, but had only made a block or so when I heard one of my neighbors screaming. It was one of the Menando family. Livia looked at me as if we needed to keep moving, but I stopped anyway. I entered the massive villa through the front entrance way with Livia holding the baby following closely behind. Helena Menando was crying and waving frantically at me at the side of the house. The structure was on fire and one wall had fallen into a pile of bricks.

"It's Antonius!" She cried. "He is trapped under fallen timbers and rock. I can't lift them. I'm afraid he is going to die!"

I looked inside through the smoke and rubble, and slowly climbed my way over the fallen stone, mortar and heap of bricks. It was unbelievably hot and the air burnt my lungs. It was very hard to see and it looked like the roof had collapsed completely so that two whole floors above me were missing. I made it in only about eight cubits when I saw Antonius Menando lying on his stomach with several sheets of plaster and stone surrounding him. There was a large wooden beam across his back and I could barely make out his head. I lifted the beam with great difficulty and was only able to barely pull it to one side. He stirred a little and tried to roll over.

"Antonius! I can't hold this. I'm going to drop it. You must move your body out from under it. He only rolled over a few pedes, but it was enough for me to drop the wooden plank. A huge chunk of ceiling and roof collapsed on the other side of the room and flames were beginning to get much bigger. I was afraid we would be trapped. He seemed unable to move much, and was coughing and spitting up. I just grabbed him, and with as much strength as I could muster, threw him over my good (right) shoulder. We slowly made our way out the hole in the wall in front of us. I actually dropped him when I fell trying to climb over the pile of bricks. That was fortuitous, because it seemed to awaken him. He realized where he was and what was happening and scurried the rest of the way over the bricks, mortar and rock to the open air of this atrium. His wife Helena went immediately to his aid as he set down on the grass outside.

"Destroyed. Our home is destroyed!" he said as he looked at the remains in front of him.

"You are lucky to be alive. I could not reach you. Titus saved your life." Said Helena.

She looked up at me and blew me a kiss. "Can you help us?" "I need to get him to a healer."

It was Livia who answered. "Helena, there is no time to look for a healer. They are all busy with others. You need to leave Pompeii immediately if Antonius can walk. This city will be buried in ash soon and all buildings will be as yours is. We can only hope the gods will save us."

She handed me our daughter and hugged both of them. We left them sitting in their garden next to the ruins of their house and hurried further down the boulevard.

## CHAPTER 17: THE TRIP BY BOAT

We walked rapidly down the Via dell'Abbondanza, past the temple of Jupiter on our left, and noted that there were literally hundreds of people inside and outside and many more on the outer veranda trying to push their way into the sanctuary. One woman was sitting on her knees at the base of the steps, howling at the heavens. There was a prophet who was standing on a small perch decrying the evils of civilization and how the gods were punishing the wicked. People were yelling and children were crying everywhere. We pushed our way past this group and walked down the slick large cobblestones heading to the Marina gate. We passed the lone soldier I had seen all afternoon in Pompeii. He was standing at his position on the turret tower the right of the gate, but seemed lost and uncertain of what to do or where to go. He kept looking out at the sea with consternation and every once in a while would try to duck as another hot ember landed on or near him. I felt sorry for him having to stand up there and act brave while everyone else in the city hurried by.

The trip down to the Marina from the gate takes several minutes and is a steep downward climb along a twisting road that follows the contour of the hill to the water. I looked at

Livia and she was covered in ash. Her face and arms also had streaks of black soot from the smoke of the neighbor's house. We looked pitiful. It was very treacherous trying to make out the road on the way down to the docks. The ash was getting deeper and deeper. It should have been the sunny part of the day, but it was now almost as dark as night. Eventually we made our way down to the marina and noticed someone holding a torch on the marina landing. That light provided enough visibility to see at least a ways out into the gray of the ocean. There was a crowd of eight or so people on the dock looking out to sea. There were no boats anywhere in the docks. I went up to the group and asked about Aule's fishing boat.

A man I didn't recognize said, "Aule's boat? I don't know which one that was, but it is not here now. After the mountain exploded, people came here and jumped in whatever they could find. Some of the smaller boats had ten people inside. It was a free-for-all. People were behaving like animals. All of the boats were taken. It didn't matter who owned them."

He pointed to his wife who was sitting down beside him. She was bleeding from her forehead and held a bandage to her head. She was crying softly.

"They hit her with one of the oars. I think they will most likely be drowned at sea. There was not a sailor among them. They took my fishing boat before I could get here. I don't know what to do now."

"Titus, is that you?"

I looked to my right to find Gordianus and three of his servants standing over to one side of the dock. He said "Fine state of affairs. Even the equestrian classes can't leave. Do you own a boat? Perhaps I could purchase it." He held up a bag full of coins.

"Sorry, no."

I asked him why he didn't just go get his horse and ride out of town.

"Horse, hah. I tried. I went to the stable with my servants over thirty minutes ago. Someone had stolen my mount and my tack. I thought to come down here and buy passage on a ship, but they have all already left. I am too unhealthy to walk to Surrentum."

He paused a bit and then added, "I think we shall all die here."

He seemed to have given up. Someone from the other side of the dock said, "Look! There is a vessel heading this way. It has its sail up. It is coming for the dock."

We all looked in the direction that the man was pointing and sure enough, there, a quarter millarium off of the shore was a boat coming this way. It was not large but it did have a sail up and there appeared to be three people on board. Not much of a rescue party, but it brought hope to those few people left on the dock. When they got slightly closer, Livia grabbed my arm.

"Its Father and Mother! They have come for us!"

As they approached closer, I could make out Cassia, Leto, and Marius in the boat. They were moving at fair speed toward the dock, and people there started to crowd toward the front of the pier. One man said that the boat was much too small to take everyone and that he and his wife had waited the longest so he should be allowed to go with them. Gordianus held up a bag of coins that he was jingling, and he started yelling to Livia's father that he would pay for passage to Surrentum. People were crowding together and shoving one another. Three people got pushed into the water and one started swimming out toward the boat. It was chaos, and I could see no way that this was going to end without bloodshed. Livia kept yelling and waving at her family and they were waving back, but her father saw the trouble on the shore and turned the boat about. He dropped the sail and tried to determine what to do. He sat there floating forty cubits from the marina. If he came ashore, the boat would be overrun by frantic people. The water was too deep to wade all of the way out to where he was positioned, so it kept most of the group waiting anxiously on the docks.

"What will we do? The boat can't hold everyone!" asked Livia.

I said, "We can swim out to them. I'm sure not everyone here knows how to swim."

"But we can't swim with the baby!" she cried.

I was left with no options. I said, "I will take Dania with me. I will run south with her and meet you in Stabiae. Your foot is still twisted and you could not keep up. Better that you swim out to your father's boat and head for the south. I will meet you there with our daughter. You are a better swimmer than I anyway."

Livia handed me our baby and started toward the edge of the dock to jump in and swim out to the boat. The person who had only minutes earlier jumped in was now out trying to hang onto Marius' boat, but they were not allowing the person to climb in. Leto was threatening him and kept lifting his hands off of the bow so the man kept sinking back into the water. Marius and Cassia were trying to reason with the man and told him they were only here for their daughter's family, but he was frantic. As Livia stepped to the edge of the dock, Gordianus grabbed her by the neck.

He looked at me and then back out to the boat and yelled, "Boatman, Boatman! I have your daughter. I don't want to harm her, but we need passage. Now, I will pay you handsomely. You just move your boat in here and put me and my servants on board with your daughter and everything will be fine.

"Take us too!" yelled the man and the woman who had spoken earlier.

"Gordianus, please. Let my wife go. She means you no harm! We have always been good to you. We are your friends, not your enemy. Let her go."

He looked at me again, and his face was panicked. He had lost all reason and was doing whatever he thought he could to survive. Then Livia moved. She maneuvered her right leg behind his leg, and elbowed Gordianus as hard as she could in his overly large stomach. He screamed and let go, but not before both of them had entered the water with a large splash. He apparently couldn't swim and was bobbing up and down in the water, though it was only about six pedes deep, and he was taking in mouthfuls of water. His three slaves were doing what they could to try to give him a hand and bring him back to the dock. Livia had spent the first half of her life on board her father's fishing boat and could swim like a fish. It took her no time to reach the boat, as her father had already paddled it in a little closer to shore. Several of the others on the dock were now staring at Dania and me, and probably thinking that they might have more luck than Gordianus in extorting a ride. They were starting to surround me, when out of nowhere a dog came running down the hill and stood right beside me. He bared his teeth and let out a low growl at anyone who got within a few feet of me and the baby. Of course it was that crazy black and white dog, which had already saved my life at least once. But where in the world had he come from?

"Good Dog! Good Boy! That's my Hercules!" Bellowed a

voice from behind me. Crispus stepped up beside me and bent over out of breath. "It looks like you were in a bit of a spot."

"You are calling him Hercules?" I said grinning.

"He's from Herculaneum and he is a hero. It seemed to fit."

The dog growled again and bit at one of the men who had tried to lunge for the baby. Crispus pulled his gladius and pointed at the surrounding people and then at each one individually.

"I want each of you to leave the dock, NOW. Go immediately to Stabiae. You will be safe there."

Gordianus was being helped out of the water by his slaves and was wringing wet from his head to his sandals. He looked at Crispus and said, "Soldier, Septimus is a friend of mine, and he will hear of this. You will be in the ergastulum by the end of the day."

"There will be no amphitheatre, no arena, and no ergastulum by the end of the day. And the officers of the guard all have their hands full right now. Get you gone. All of you. Leave now or I will start separating your limbs from your body."

He brandished his sword and the crowd dispersed. As soon as they had cleared, Marius maneuvered his boat into the dock and I stepped on. I noticed that the man that had swam out to the boat was also aboard, so apparently Marius had changed his mind and let him join the crew.

Marius noticed me watching the man, and said, "I could not live with myself if I allowed another to die. The gods were good to us and allowed us to leave Herculaneum just in time. The city was ablaze as we pulled away."

"Is there room for Crispus?"

Crispus seemed surprised by the suggestion and looked back towards the city with trepidation.

Crispus looked at the boat with a doubtful glance, and said, "I don't know Titus. That boat looks pretty small for all of us. And I would go only if Hercules can come too."

Marius said, "This boat was made for three or perhaps four people and now we have seven, a baby and a dog." It will sit low in the water, but we will have to make it work. There are two more oars over there. We can use the extra paddles to try and go faster. Cassia, throw everything else overboard."

Crispus still seemed to hesitate, and said, "Maybe I should stay at the temple with Primus."

Livia encouraged him. "You will be able to meet up with the Stabiae guard and then go back to help the people of Pompeii."

Crispus considered that for a moment, and would probably have waited several minutes longer to make up his mind, but Hercules jumped into the boat and made up his master's mind for him. Crispus just shook his head, laughed, and jumped aboard with his dog.

"As soon as I get to Stabaie, I can join the rescue party and come immediately back. Primus will be glad to see me."

Thus it was that we took off in a heavily weighted boat with the sail down and four oars in the water. Leto and I sat paddling across from each other, and Crispus and the other man did the other paddling while Marius guided the stern and tried to help with the sail and rigging. Cassia was using a cup to bail water out of the hull which was splashing over the sides and Livia was holding the baby. We were crowded together like fish in a bucket.

Crispus told us that when he and Primus had arrived in town, they went to the forum to check in with the Prefect or the officers of the guard, but everyone had already gone. There were no officers to report to, and they hadn't seen any of the other guards of the wall.

"There were fires all over the city, and several roofs had collapsed from the heat and the weight of the pumice and ash. Primus decided to go to the temple to pray to the goddess for savior of the town. He really is a devout disciple of Venus since the event at the temple. I never had the heart to tell him it was a hoax. I didn't want to crush his beliefs. He's been acting much nicer the last two days!"

"I noticed that too."

"He could not really walk on his own, so I accompanied him to the grand temple in the forum. There were many people gathered when we got there, some of who were hurt, and many others who had burns from the fallen ash. Primus said he wanted to stay there and help the Pompeiians. They were happy to have a soldier around, because I think all of the others had already fled. He was enjoying playing the hero."

"Why didn't you stay there with Primus?" asked Livia.

"I wanted to, but I had a sense of duty. I'm a soldier, and I thought I should go to my commander and see what there was to do to help our citizens. I actually walked to the city gate, thinking I would see Septimus and be given orders. Primus was too injured to be of much use, except as a source of moral support, so he stayed."

"He wasn't walking very well on his own, when we left you."

He nodded in agreement. "While still at the temple, I was telling Primus that I needed to go and meet up with our unit. He kept urging me to leave the city. I think he knew that

most of the guards would not have stayed to help anyone, and he thought they probably fled with the city elders. We were having an argument about whether I should stay or go, and if I left, where I would head to, when Alycia came up to us. You know her; she's the servant at the wine bar. She said that she had talked to you and Livia, and that you were walking to Stabiae. Since I was planning on going to the wall anyway to try and find other guards, I thought I might catch you at the gate to say goodbye. When I was over at the wall by the marina gate, I saw Pentius up on the wall tower. He is a young soldier, much younger than me, and he was scared to death. He didn't know what to do and he flagged me down. I went up to him to ask what our orders were and to see where the officers had gone. He was the only soldier I had seen in the city, which was strange."

"Where did all of the soldiers go?" asked Cassia.

"I got much information from Pentius. Some of the soldiers apparently went to aid their families or to keep their homes from burning. Pentius said that the Prefect took several soldiers with him, as his personal guard. His mansion is down by the Sarno gate and the soldiers were used to haul some of his wealth and property through the Sarno gate out of town and out of the path of the mountain's fury. He was probably heading toward Nocera. Septimus and a few of the best soldiers of the wall were busy trying to put out fires. I wanted to help them, but Pentius told me that he had heard from one of the fleeing guards that Septimus and three others were caught in a building collapse and were all dead. He didn't know what to do since it was Septimus who had told him to man the Marina gate and watch for approaching rescue ships. He had spent an hour on that wall looking for boats from Micenum. Only one came, and we are on it."

"So you came down here to leave on the rescue ship?" asked Livia.

"No, I actually came down here because I thought there was a riot."

"I was about to leave Pentius and the wall for the city center and go back and sit with Primus together in the temple, when we saw the boat in the distance. From the height of the rampart, I also saw the commotion going on in the marina and decided to investigate. I didn't know that it was you, Titus, until we were close by. I told Pentius to leave his post and to do what he thought best. Since Septimus was dead and no longer in command, and there were no other boats coming, I relieved him of his watch and told him I would help coordinate the boat rescue so he could be with his family. As I approached the group of people, I saw it was you. You were being surrounded so I decided to help. Actually, I think Hercules was more helpful than I."

"Are you sorry you left your brother?" asked Livia.

"He would not have left the temple for anything, Livia. He told me when I left the temple that he would not be joining me anywhere, and that I should try to get out of Pompeii and away from the wrath of the mountain. He was happier just staying there playing the hero in the temple. Plus, I think he had his eye on Alycia."

He smiled briefly, but then shook his head and looked miserable. "I hope he'll remain safe. When I left the center of Pompeii, it was ablaze in several quarters and the ash was up to my knees."

Livia and Cassia both assured him that Primus was probably going to be fine. He smiled again.

All the while he spoke, he kept paddling and we kept making progress further south.

We paddled like that for another hour trying to stay within site of the shore. It was getting progressively darker. Several times we had to use our hands to put out small flames on the boat that were started by bits of flaming rock. The pumice and ash continued to fall and the ocean looked like milk. The air was thick with smoke and ash. The cries and screams from Pompeii were still audible across the water, although we were several millarium from the city walls. As it got closer to dusk, it was getting harder and harder to make out the shore. It was as dark as midnight after the sun went down, and the ash falling in the air seemed to have gotten worse in the previous minutes.

Marius looked on both sides of the boat and said, "Something is wrong. There is a current pulling us out to sea."

He was absolutely right. The water was being swept out towards the opening of the harbor to the open sea, and our boat with it. He raised the sail and turned the bow towards the shore. This slowed our progress, but we continued to move farther out away from land. This continued for several minutes. Suddenly, we heard something behind us.

"Great Gods! This happened yesterday in Herculaneum to the boat at the dock. Some of the smaller ships there were thrashed into pieces due to the huge waves. Everyone hold on!"

I was facing the stern of the boat with oars in hand when I saw it. There was a line of white behind us moving towards us very quickly. It was like a huge wall of surf heading our way. It hit the back of the boat with the force of a many horsed chariot. It lifted the bow of the boat up and then sideways before we were swamped. I was tossed into the sea amidst blackness everywhere.

I didn't know where I was in relationship to the shore or how deep the water was. I only tried to keep my head above water and hold onto the oar in my arms for support. The paddle at least kept me oriented on top of the water.

## CHAPTER 18: CAPSIZED AND WET

"Livia, can you hear me?" "Marius, Leto, Cassia, where are you?" I barely got out the words before I gulped a mouth of sea water.

I was up to my neck in the bay and completely disoriented. I could barely keep my head above water to speak. I didn't know which way the boat had gone. I could not see more than twenty cubits in front of me due to the heavy ash in the air. I heard someone yelling, but I didn't know what they were saying and I couldn't even see the boat. I lay on my back floating in the water on top of the oar for a few minutes and realized I was still being washed along by the surf. I couldn't see much and my eyes were burning with the saltwater. I heard crashing sounds and some distant screams in front of me. I heard a faint voice off in the distance, but after that I just had to concentrate on staying afloat. I was kicking my legs and moving my arms to stay above water, but it was tiring me way too quickly to survive. The water felt cold and the salt was burning the open flesh where I had been cut by the knife of Scaevolus. I didn't know if I could stay up, and if it hadn't been for the oar to lie across, I would have already sunk to the bottom. What about sea creatures? I imagined at any moment I could be eaten by sharks or whales or sea monsters. Even a legendary Kraken could come up from the deep and take a man alone in the water. It was even hard to breathe when my mouth was out of the water, due to the steady rain of ash and pumice in the air. At least the water kept the dust in the air from burning my skin. I was panicked and probably would have drowned if I had not seen a faint light in the distance that gave me hope that I was near the shore. I surmised that the light must have been Stabiae in the distance to the east. I flipped over on my back and tried to float as leisurely as I could on top of the oar, and oriented my head towards that light. I lay in the water with my arms outstretched and gently kicked my feet. I could not see any stars, but I saw flaming balls of light flying over my head at great heights. I guessed that must have been more of the mountain spewing its contents onto the surrounding countryside.

Over the next several minutes, I heard small thumps and sizzles as larger pieces of pumice hit the water. I was amazed that some of these pieces of rock actually floated on the water, smoking and crackling on the surface for several minutes before they went under. I marveled at how rocks could float. I was pretty sure no one would believe me if I ever lived to tell about it. The whole scene would have been fascinating had I not been struggling to stay above the water. I was sure I would drown in the waves, and I could not see much of anything in the darkness except the faint glow of the land in the distance. Occasionally I would flip over onto my stomach and swim for a bit, but I really wasn't sure I was going anywhere. There seemed to be a current moving against me, but the waves from behind were pushing me toward shore. After a few strokes, I would flip back over onto my back and rest. I was making very slow progress, but at least I wasn't drowning. After the better part of a half hour, I bobbed up and down to gauge the depth. I could actually feel the bottom touching my feet. I could not see the shore but I could hear the waves on the beach so I headed in that direction, alternating between bobbing in the water and swimming on my back. There actually was no beach. It was rock, but it was covered with pumice and silt from the air. There were grass and trees on the other side of the rocks but the water appeared to be covering a portion of the shore as if there was a very high tide that had partially flooded the bank. Water was slowly draining from the land back towards the beach. I called out again for Livia. No reply.

I crawled out onto the rocks and lay there for a few minutes to regain my strength. At length, I yelled at the top of my lungs for Livia.

I heard Leto first, faintly towards the southwest. Or at least I assumed it was the southwest, since the bay was oriented in that direction. "Titus? Is that you? "

I moved cautiously over the rocks toward his voice. I could see little in front of me and the going was treacherous in the dark. I called to him several times. I finally heard Livia call back to me.

"Oh Titus. Thank the gods. I thought you had drowned." She came crawling up to me. I grabbed her and hugged her and gave her a long kiss. "What of Dania. What has happened to our daughter? "

"She is fine. Cold, but fine. Come and I will tell you." She hugged me tightly and started crying heavily, then led me to where Leto was sitting with Dania in his arms.

"Where is everyone else?"

They both looked at me solemnly and shook their heads, and Livia cried even louder.

Leto handed our daughter over to Livia and said, "When the wave hit, most were tossed into the water. The boat turned sideways, but although it half-filled with water it stayed afloat. I held on to the gunnel with all of the strength I had in one arm, and to Livia with my other hand. We were able to stay in the boat when it righted. She never let go of your baby. My sister was heroic tonight."

Livia cried loudly and rocked Dania who was also crying now.

"The force of the wave drove us completely into the shore until we hit a tree on the beach."

He pointed inland towards the outline of several trees about a block away. "The wave was unlike anything I have ever experienced on the sea. It was not only tall, but it carried us far into the land, traveling many hundreds of cubits beyond where the surf always stops. Neptune must be displeased to show such force."

"There the boat was thrashed against the treeline and fell apart. It is in pieces. We made our way back down to the beach and have been waiting for a long time for anyone else to come ashore. We feared the worst. I'm really glad to see you, Titus."

"Likewise, Leto. My eternal thanks for saving my wife and daughter. I will forever be in your debt."

"Thank the gods for keeping the boat together until we hit the trees on shore. If it had broken apart or flipped completely over in the water, we would all have been lost."

We heard someone calling from the water about a hundred cubits farther south. Leto and I made our way towards the voice and kept calling back. It was Marius and he sounded hurt. We waded out into the water and helped him onto the sand.

He gasped for air several times and was holding his ribs. He was wet and shaking and his lips looked blue.

"Leto, Titus. Tell me of my family. Do they still live? Did I lose my granddaughter tonight?"

"No father. Against all odds, and by the grace of the gods of Olympus, Livia and Dania survived the swell and sit over there near the water, mending their wounds."

"Oh, thank Neptune and Venus. I feared they would perish. I hit the mast with great force when we were capsized and my bones are broken. I have great difficulty in each breath. Poor Crispus went into the water and he was wearing his armor. He had no chance and was sent directly to the bottom of the sea. He is with the gods now. I could not save him, but I saw him go under. I would not have made it if it wasn't for his stupid dog. It was swimming above where he went down for a minute or two and then headed for shore. I had no idea which way to swim and ended up following the dog."

"Did the dog drown then?" I asked.

"It is lying over there on the beach. It crawled out of the water ahead of me, but had no strength. It may have died."

I don't know why I suddenly felt so much regret for the dog, when I had seen so many people die in the past two days, but I had to go see to it. I ran over to a lump on short beach of sand. There lying on its side several pedes ahead was the black and white dog. As I got closer, I saw that it was still panting heavily but was not moving. I went over to it and patted it on the side. It was whimpering softly and it raised its head and acknowledged my presence. Its tongue was hanging out of its mouth and had sand all over it. The two men had followed me.

I turned to see Marius with his arm over his son's shoulder.

Had he not been held up by Leto, he would have collapsed on the sand.

"Where is Cassia?"

Leto looked at him and said, "We don't know. We haven't seen her yet. She may still be swimming here."

Marius looked panicked and started yelling out to sea in a hoarse voice for his wife.

"She is not a good swimmer." He said to himself.

I felt stupid worrying over the dog when we may have lost three people in the wreck. "Did you see what happened to the other man? I didn't even know his name."

"The fates were cruel to him." said Marius. "I should have never let him come aboard, but I couldn't just leave him there. In any case, I worry now only for my wife." He yelled again out to sea, but there was no answer.

We had no idea how far we were from Stabiae and it was now the full of night. The smoke had completely obliterated the starlight and not even the moon was visible. We could make out a light coming from Mt. Vesuvius off in the distance. The fires there were the only light around. We staggered over to where Livia was sitting with the baby, and she got up and held her father for a very long time. We waited for another two hours on the beach, but Cassia, Crispus and the stranger never came. No sounds were heard except the surf. I actually sat down on my side and closed my eyes and slept for a few minutes. I was exhausted, and as soon as the baby quit crying and fell asleep, my eyes closed before I even realized it. The air was a little cleaner than it had been earlier in the day, and at least we were not getting pelted with gravel and small burning rocks. I could take deep breaths without my chest hurting. I don't know how long I was asleep, but when I awoke, there was a tongue licking my nose and a big black and white shaggy face staring into my eyes. I screamed in alarm and sat up before I realized it was only the dog.

"Hercules. You truly were well named. It is good to see you up and around." I petted him. I sorely missed seeing Crispus around, and having the dog next to me somehow comforted me.

Marius had his head in his hands and was crying softly to himself. Livia was breast feeding Dania. I did not see Leto. I looked again at the mountain and wondered what could possibly come next. My home was probably destroyed; my entire town was even destroyed, as was the city of my wife's parents. Our livelihood was gone. We have nothing left. And lastly, one of my best friends is drowned and who I will never see again. I wondered how I was going to break the news to Primus, or if I even needed to. Either one of us, or both, might be dead by morning. I didn't know what was happening in Pompeii. I thought perhaps we should go back. I was wrong to try to move everyone. I cursed myself for making poor decisions that had caused others to die. We might have been safe if we had stayed in the temple of Venus with Alycia, Silvanus and Primus. It was cowardly to leave the city. I felt wretched.

I needed some food and water. Everything in the boat was now at the bottom of the sea. I lay on the beach and fretted over everything. A short time later, Leto appeared out of the darkness to our left. He sat down quietly beside me and looked at each of us in turn.

"We are only about two millarium from the marina of Stabiae to our south. In fact, the city walls are only half that distance beyond those trees. The city has suffered much damage, but it is not as badly hit as Pompeii or Herculaneum. The admiral Pliny has brought a rescue fleet from Misenum that has arrived in Stabiae's port, but alas, the winds have not changed and they are stuck there. There are not enough ships for passage of all of the inhabitants. Only the patrician class will be able to get away by that route. We can get food and drink in Stabiae, but it is dangerous to be within buildings for the roofs are hot and molten and even in Stabiae, so far from the mountain, they have been collapsing on to those inside. Some have said that Rome itself is destroyed, and others that all of the mountains in the known world are alive. I don't believe these people and think this is idle rumor and imagination. None yet know what is happening beyond Campania. Some of those from Pompeii say there is still danger in the mountain, but the flakes of ash and pumice seemed to have abated somewhat. The scientists and philosophers have all kinds of theories about what has happened, but the religious followers have their own views. In any case, it is still very dangerous out."

"What should we do?" I asked.

"We need to get some shelter, food and water for tonight. Let us be off to Stabiae. It is a short walk."

Marius said simply, "No."

"Father?" Both Livia and Leto looked at him as he sat there.

"I will wait for your mother. I have not given up hope, even if it is a false hope. In my mind, she is late, but not dead. I can sit here on this beach for another night and a day, but I will not give her up to the sea yet. And if she does not come, then I do not wish to go further. I have no home. I have no fishing boat, and now I may have lost my wife to the sea. Neptune, our great Poseidon of the Greeks, the god of oceans and the seas, can have me too if he has taken her. I would join Cassia in the halls of the underworld. Let the mountain do what it will."

"We will stay here with you." said Livia. "Yes." agreed Leto.

"No. You should not stay here. This is my task. I order you as my children to go with Titus. Dania is sick and needs a healer. Listen to the sounds coming from her chest. Make your way over the mountain to Surrentum. It is guarded from Vesuvius by its brother mountains, and I think it is far enough away that you will not be pelted by these flaming rocks and boulders from the sky. It is another full day's walk. Maybe more. I will not have my granddaughter put in danger for my own stubbornness and lack of will. My ribs are broken and I cannot walk anyway. Let me stay here and mend my body and soul. Surrentum is a blessed place among the gods. It was founded by Ulysses in the heroic age, and is the home of the sirens of legend. The gods would not destroy it. There you can seek refuge and start a new life. I will meet you there with your mother, or we'll both meet you in the underworld. Now go, or I will start swimming out to sea and drown myself in your presence."

He kissed both of them and then lay down, still clutching his chest with one arm. He was breathing with difficulty.

I could not bring myself to walk away, but Leto gained courage from his father's words and took Livia by the arm. Together the three of us moved slowly towards the trees. At first the dog stayed with Marius and kept putting his nose in the man's face to get him to come with us. After a minute, Hercules gave up and followed after us.

## CHAPTER 19: THE HOSPITALITY OF STABIAE

I carried Dania. I think Livia had no more strength physically or mentally. No one was talking, but at least no one was crying any longer. We reached a road, which was likely coming from Pompeii. There was a steady stream of people walking toward Stabaie. Most looked like the lowliest of peasants, but probably were made up of every class in Pompeii.

"This is where I learned all of what had occurred in Pompeii." said Leto. "There is a service area just inside the gate serving the refugees water and food. Everyone was talking about what had happened in the city."

"But we have no money." I replied.

"Neither does anyone else. There is great charity in times of tragedy. The city magistrate is providing this as a service to his brothers in Pompeii."

We moved through the northwestern gate to Stabiae with throngs of weary and downtrodden travelers coming from Pompeii. We were escorted by guards at the gate to a receiving area where we were greeted by city officials. They asked if we were hurt and told us they would provide food and shelter. We were shown to a building where there were large buckets of water outside and people with ladles and wooden cups giving out refreshment to parched refugees. Livia and I both greedily accepted the water and drank heartily. I was extremely thirsty from the combination of sea water I swallowed and the burning in my throat from inhaling the ash-laden air. When Livia asked for some more water to clean off her face, she was refused by the young woman with the ladle. Leto put a small bowl of water down for the dog, which lapped up almost the entire portion. I felt bad that we had no food for Hercules.

"Clean water for drinking is in short supply. Some of the aqueducts into town have collapsed and most of the others are clogged with almost a cubit layer of pumice and ash. The plumbing in the town is a mess, but as you know Stabiae has the finest spring in all of Campania. We are drawing as much water as we can out of the spring and providing for everyone as we may. However, to help conserve water, we are not allowing it for other purposes. You may still go to the bathhouse and rinse all of the ash off."

Livia thanked the woman and then gave some water to Dania. She was still coughing miserably.

"Is there a healer where I can take my baby?"

The woman pointed down the street and answered, "There are several who are tending to the wounded. Is your little girl hurt badly?"

"She has been coughing severely, even worse than the rest."

"They have some herbs there that should help." Said the woman, before offering some water to the person behind us.

She then handed all of us some fruit and some peppers to eat. We thanked her and walked toward the healers. We heard another boom off into the distance toward the mountain. We looked there and saw a new round of red and yellow flames in the distance.

Leto was becoming alarmed with the change in the mountain. He said, "Quickly. We must get inside somewhere. There may be more raining of rocks and debris from the skies."

Livia agreed but told Leto and I that we still needed to see the healers. We hurried over to a woman in a long gown who was applying bandages to a young man's arm.

"Do you have any herbs for my baby's cough?"

The woman nodded and pointed to a bench with several dried pieces of vegetation. "Put these in her mouth and let her chew on them."

Livia grabbed some and followed me down the block to look for shelter. The going was slow as over two pedes of ash and dust had covered the street, and it was like plowing through thick mud. All of the buildings had similar large deposits of gray ash and pumice on their roofs. Hercules had to jump up and down to make his way through the thick layers of ash. He suddenly stopped and let out a howl. As I was noticing this, we heard crashing off to our left somewhere. It sounded like another villa had collapsed. I began to worry about being trapped inside like Antonius Menando, but also was worried about being hit with debris. We began to hear lots of crashing noises and noted little flaming bits of gravel were now raining down everywhere. One hit me on the shoulder leaving a big welt right next to the spot where my wound was. I winced severely in pain and grabbed my shoulder. Livia came to me and asked if I was alright and looked again at my wound.

"It is not healing very well. It looks very red and swollen and needs attention. Maybe we should go back to the healer."

"No. I fear this city is going to be buried very soon and all of the roofs will collapse. We must flee to Surrentum."

"Not now. Let's wait. Let's get a bath and relax. All of this has been a hardship, especially for Dania. I fear she will not survive another long walk."

I was about to answer when we saw a bright, flaming projectile arch over our heads and land with an explosion in the center of town. We ducked and looked in the direction it landed. Within minutes a fire was visible. The dog was now barking continuously and looked at me with eyes that suggested he wanted to be somewhere else.

"Jupiter's beard!" said Leto. "That was a close one! How can heavy rocks fly like birds?"

"There are flaming rocks from the mountain again!" exclaimed Livia. "What shall we do? We will be crushed or burned. We have to go inside somewhere."

The ground began to shake violently and we could hear crashing sounds in the neighboring streets suggesting more buildings were collapsing.

Livia screamed. "Not again. Another earthquake. What else can the gods throw at us? We're doomed."

It was a several seconds later that the shaking finally stopped. I was incredibly scared that we would have a house fall on us. I stayed in the center of the street and turned to my wife.

"Livia, Leto, listen to me. Look at the depth of this ash. Feel its warmth on your legs. The fresh stuff is scalding hot, but even the deepest layers are all warm. Remember what we saw in Pompeii. The roofs were collapsing everywhere from the weight and the heat. Any more earthquakes and there won't be a building standing in Stabiae or Pompeii. The Menandos almost died that way, and Crispus heard that Septimus and several other soldiers had been trapped in a villa when the walls gave in. We are too close to the mountain. We need to reach

Surrentum at all cost, lest we be hit by one of the flaming balls or trapped forever under a heap of ash and bricks."

"I have never been to Surrentum. Is it a far walk?" she asked.

It was Leto who answered. "It is another fifteen millarium from here, but if we leave now, we can be there by midmorning. We have to traverse over the mountain pass to get there, but it is a good road. The longer we remain, the deeper the ash will become the slower our progress, and the longer it will be before we arrive. We have drunk water, we have eaten some fruit, and we have herbs for the baby. Let's get some more food and a flask of water and begin our journey. It will only be another five millarium or so past the city to get to Aequana. It is a mountain village about half way, and if we are weary we could stop there."

I looked at Leto and then at Livia, and said, "We should at least try to make it to Aequana."

They both shook their heads in agreement. Leto answered, "Anything is better than here."

With that we turned around and went back to the woman who had fed and watered us only a few minutes before.

"Another earthquake. It is all so terrible." She then suddenly recognized us and said, "You have returned too soon. Did you not find the healer?"

"Yes, thank you." said Livia. "We are leaving for Aequana immediately. Can you give us some provisions for the journey?"

"I have no fish or meat, but here is some more fruit and a few dried figs. I don't know how you will carry water."

A man to my right, said, "Here, take my leather flask. It is made from a sheep's bladder. It isn't very big, but it should sustain you until you get to your destination."

I thanked him profusely and the young woman filled the flask to the brim with three ladles of water, and corked it. I wrapped the leather strap around my neck and we started walking through the hilly streets of the town of Stabiae. The amount of ash was continuing to increase and the walking was difficult and slow. It was made even slower because Livia had been limping more severely since we were inside the city. The cobblestone streets were making her swollen ankle hurt even worse than it had last night. Hercules could barely keep his head above the pumice. I had blisters on my feet and lower legs from the heat of the ash we were wading through. Dania was coughing a little more severely now, so we covered her face with a linen to keep her from inhaling too much more of the foul vapors. My eyes were burning again.

We watched as people with pillows tied on their heads ran past us in all directions. We also saw several soldiers go by with water buckets, presumably to help with the fire in the center of town, which by now was burning brightly to our left. Several times I tripped when my feet hit a corner of the road or an object buried in the piles of ash on the street, but fortunately I never fell off of my feet. We continued to hear crying and screaming until we reached the Surrentum gate underneath the southern wall of the city. Unlike the northern gate of Stabiae, there were no travelers moving further south and the road looked dark and deserted at this time of night.

"What about Father?" asked Livia. "He won't know where we have gone. We must go back and get him so he knows to meet up with us in Aequana."

"I'll go." said Leto. "We can catch up on the way. There

is only one road. Don't wait for me. You must be far away from the mountain by tomorrow. I'll bring Father, if I have to drag him from the beach."

I wasn't sure he was going to be able to convince his father to come with us, but sending Leto to fetch him was the only way to get Livia to move. She was growing more and more concerned with Dania's chest cold.

"Go then. We'll catch up later tonight." I said.

The dog seemed torn between following us or following Leto, but in the end he went with Livia's brother, leaving us to head off on the road toward the highlands to the south. As we made our way along the road, we passed some impressive tombs to our right and left, the above-ground facades of the necropolis below the earth. There was obviously a lot of wealth in this town too.

"It was nice of the citizens of Stabiae to provide food, water and shelter for the Pompeiians."

Livia replied, "I have often heard of the generosity of this city, but yes, I thought that was a very nice gesture. Especially since it looks like they are battling the same forces of the gods that Pompeii faced."

"I wonder how our house has fared."

"I don't want to think about it. That ash is really deep, even here, and probably even more so in Pompeii and Herculaneum. I don't know how any of the roofs will be able to stand the weight." replied Livia.

"Or how they will withstand the fury of the fires and earthquakes twice daily." I added.

"Do you think Primus is OK?"

"I'm sure he is fine, and safe within the temple." I replied, but secretly I wasn't so sure. There was a glow coming from behind us that looked as if all of Pompeii was on fire.  I needed to change the subject or risk both of us falling into despondency.

## CHAPTER 20: THE MOUNTAIN ROAD TO AEQUANA

"It looks like the ash is much less deep here." The amount of pumice was only at about mid calf level, which was much less than on the north side of Stabiae. It was much easier to walk.

Livia looked down at her own legs, and said, "I hope that is a good sign. It does seem like there is much less ash in the air at the moment. Not as much falling from the sky." Suddenly, she stopped and started crying, and said, "Poor Crispus. Poor, poor Crispus. He had no chance in the boat. He must have sunk like an anchor. How are we going to tell Primus? He should have stayed with his brother in Pompeii."

"Crispus came on the boat because he wanted to, and he had the blessing of his brother. Everyone's fate is in the gods' hands. There will be many who will be missed tomorrow. There will be plenty of time later for mourning, for Crispus and all that perished today."

I took the baby from Livia's arms to give her a rest. We walked in silence for the next forty minutes. The road climbed steadily upwards. The night was as black as the caves of Herculaneum. We could hear a din of voices to the north in Stabiae, and could make out the city's outline from the fires still burning there, but we could not see any stars. Mt. Vesuvius was no longer visible and only a faint orange glow was present in the distance where Pompeii was located. It was very difficult to see anything on either side of the road, and I heard no birds or other signs of animal life. We saw a person in front of us sitting at the side of the road on one of the stone markers, and stopped to talk to him.

"Greetings, Stranger."

"Hello."

He looked us over and noticed the baby in my arms.

"It is not the night to be taking your baby for a walk. This is a dangerous road in the daytime. Tonight it could be deadly." He stood up and moved slowly toward us. "Where are you headed?"

I wasn't sure what to make of this man or his motives. I guessed he was just coming closer to talk, but something about his actions made me nervous. Livia set down the bag of fruit that we were carrying as I handed the baby to her, and turned to him with my hand outstretched in greeting. He did not shake my hand and in fact kept his hands behind him, which made me a little more suspicious. He eyed the bag on the ground greedily. I moved in front of Livia and motioned with my hand for her to fall behind me.

"We are going to Aequana. As far away from the mountain as we can."

"Anybody else with you?"

Now I was really suspicious of the man and his intentions. I exaggerated.

"My wife's brother and father-in-law are right behind us. They should be catching up to us anytime."

The man looked down the road and squinted. "I don't see anybody. You sure they are coming?"

Livia was now getting a bad vibe from the man, and it was she who spoke up. "Oh yes, they should be right along. They just had to pick up some more provisions."

"What do you do? Are you of the patrician or equestrian class?"

"No, but we're not slaves either. I'm a blacksmith. We are simple Plebians who have lost their home."

He looked again down at the bag on the ground next to my feet. I really did not like this man, and I was beginning to feel like a sheep in front of a wolf.

I said, "Well, we need to be on our way so we can make Aequana by midnight."

"Not so fast." The man pulled a knife from behind his back and pointed it at me. "What do you have in the bag there? Coins?"

Livia said quickly, "If you mean to rob us, you are going to be sorely disappointed. We have lost everything. All we own, our house, our shop, his tools, everything. You would be robbing the poorest of the poor."

"So you say." Was all the man replied as he looked at Livia, and simultaneously grabbed me by the left wrist. Unfortunately for both us, something snapped inside my head. I had had enough of the stress and duress of the last three days, and I could not sustain someone threatening my family again. I twisted my left wrist so that I grabbed the wrist of his hand that was wrapped on mine, and before he knew what had happened I had his arm bent completely backwards behind his body. While I was facing his back with his left arm doubled up to his shoulder blade, I grabbed his right elbow with my free arm and tripped him with my right leg. He fell forward onto his own blade. It cut him but did not go deeply. However, with his knife buried under his chest he could not pull it out to stab me. Instead, while I was lying on top of him on the pavement, I kept slamming his head into the stone pavement of the road. I was screaming, "I have had enough of this. Thieves. Murderers. Angry gods. Flaming mountains. Fires." Each time I said a word I shoved his head hard against the rocks.

It was Livia who stopped me. "Titus. Stop. Please." The man is not moving. You may have killed him."

I was shaking badly and I had tears in my eyes. I had completely lost it. She helped me up, and then we turned the man over. He was bleeding from his forehead but was conscious. At least I hadn't killed him. Yet, I took his knife and put it in my belt. He had a cut on his chest where the knife had pierced the skin when he fell. He opened his eyes and looked at me with fear and hatred.

"Why don't you just kill me? I'm a slave, and my master is dead anyway. I have nothing. Kill me."

"Mister, we don't want to kill you. My husband has just had a very bad two days, and you shouldn't have crossed someone at their wit's end. You are lucky he showed you mercy."

He only scowled at her and wiped his forehead of blood with his arm. He was sitting up but not standing.

I looked him over and said, "I'll keep your knife, Stranger, so you don't bother any other travelers. Go back to Stabiae. Maybe someone will take pity on you."

He staggered to his feet, looked at us again, and left back toward the north and Stabiae.

We picked up our bags and looked at each other, before turning towards Aequana. After a few minutes of walking, Livia looked at me again and asked, "What in the name of the holy goddess were you thinking? We had nothing for him to steal.

He would have left us alone. You could have been killed with those foolish heroics. Who attacks a man with a knife with only their bare hands?"

"I know. It was stupid. But I wasn't thinking. I was mad and I just lost all reason. I kept seeing Scaevolus in the man's face. I kept hearing Scaevolus in his voice, and I remembered that in the temple of Isis, he killed Tacitus without mercy, even though there was no reason to. I had a vision of poor Vibiana in the temple of Venus, and I imagined you and Dania lying here on the road just like Vibiana. I just lost it. I didn't care if he killed me or not. If you hadn't stopped me, I probably would have killed him in my rage. I don't know what has become of me in the past three days. I guess I have become an animal."

"You are no animal. You have done everything in your power to protect your wife and daughter. You have done more than anyone could ever expect of you and you have proven your bravery. You know your brother would be very proud of you."

We sat there for several minutes while I calmed down. I was sick to my stomach. I had never been in battle in my life and while I had grappled and practiced swordplay with my brother and friends growing up, until this week I have never even been in a real fight. I had nearly been killed in the cave of Herculaneum, and now I was unarmed, but willing to challenge a man with a knife. I thought of my brother in Britannia and wondered if he had undergone a similar metamorphosis when he first joined the legion. Perhaps I did have the courage and skill to fight against the Brigantes and march with the victorious Legion XX. I pulled the corner of my tunic away and looked at my shoulder wound. It was red and angry, but the sutures were still holding. It was still seeping some blood. I heard Dania coughing again and remembered we needed to get her to a healer before she developed pneumonia or something worse. I stood up and took the baby from Livia again, who had been feeding her while I sat daydreaming. She was used to my reminisces.

"Come on. It's time to be moving again. It must be after midnight and it is getting colder as we go up the mountain." I grabbed my arms with my hands and rubbed them.

"I am tired already and my feet hurt, but I don't want to stop on the mountainside." said Livia. "How far is the mountain pass?"

"I think it is less than an hour's walk from here, but as you can see the road goes steeply uphill."

In the distance behind us we heard a dog barking. "You don't think...?"

"Yes, it is Leto and Hercules, I'm sure. He must have found father and convinced him to come to Aequana." Her mood brightened considerably. "We should wait for him here."

I said "OK" and sat back down. It was about fifteen minutes later that a black and white dog with a bushy tail and red tongue came prancing up the road. He stopped in front of me and barked several times as his tail wagged feverishly in between licks to my face.

I bent down and looked at the dog and asked him if he knew where Leto was. All I got in answer was big wet tongue in my face as I held his head in my hands. Livia answered for him, as she could see someone in the distance. The ash was nearly gone in the air at this point, and despite the darkness, visibility was improving. From our position on the road well above the surrounding countryside, we could see Stabiae below us and even the lights of Pompeii in the distance. There was a faint glow of where Mt. Vesuvius was, but we could not make out the outline of the mountain.

"Oh great goddess. Thank you. Thank you. It is Father, he is with Leto and he's with…."

She stopped, started crying and handed me the baby. She sped off down the hill. I looked after her and into the dark to the north, and I could just make out three figures. Unbelievably, there was Marius, Leto …..and Cassia. Livia grabbed her mother and hugged her repeatedly. Both were crying. They soon walked up to Dania and me.

I smiled and said, "Cassia, you don't know how glad I am to see you…"

She smiled back at me and replied, "Hello Titus. You still look tired."

We both laughed and she took the baby out of my arms and gave her hug and a kiss. Dania only coughed.

"What happened?" asked Livia. "We thought you had drowned in the sea. We waited for hours, but Father never gave up. He waited even longer."

"Actually it was Leto who found me, or rather, I found him, in Stabiae as he was going back to the beach to get Marius."

"I am very weary. Come. Let me sit down and I will tell you the story."

We all moved off of the middle of the road towards a cliff face of the trail and leaned against it. It was a little chilled, even though it was late summer, but that felt good on the blisters on my legs and the wound on my shoulder.

Cassia began, "As you know I was sitting on the right side of the boat, right beside the stranger. I heard the sound of that horrendous wave just before it hit, and before Marius yelled a warning. I tried to grab onto the side of the boat and hold on, but we turned on our side and I was washed overboard. I think I hit my head, because I don't remember entering the water. It was the stranger who rescued me. He was a great swimmer and very strong, and I can remember him pulling my head out of the water and feeling him swim with one arm as his other arm was around me. I don't know for how long he did that, but it was many minutes. I finally told him that I could float on my own and that if he didn't let me go we would both probably drown. I am not the swimmer that Marius or Leto is, and my skills in the water are limited. I floated as best I could, mostly on my back. After what seemed like a half hour, I noticed that the stranger was gone. He vanished into the distance. I didn't know if he went under or not, but I called for him and got no reply. I didn't know what had happened to anyone else, and wasn't sure that the boat had not sunk to the bottom of the bay. I was frightened and in despair and ready to give up and die, when the gods intervened. As I laid on my back trying to float, all the time swallowing seawater and inhaling the horrid dust from the mountain, my hand touched something. It was an oar from the boat. I rolled over on top of it and just lay across it. I had no idea which way to go, so I just stayed flat over it and kicked leisurely with my legs. I was in the water for well over an hour when I heard the shore in front of me."

"But we didn't hear you or see you when you came ashore." I said.

"No, judging by where Marius was sitting on the beach when we went back to get him, the boat and your landings were just on the Northwest side of Stabiae, almost in the middle of the bay. I did not wash ashore anywhere near you. I hit the beach on the more southerly side of the bay, at least two millarium from where Marius sat. I had no way of knowing what had happened to anyone in our family. It was dark, and I was lost. I have never been to Stabiae. However, I saw the city lighted by fires and made my way carefully across rocks and through trees and finally reached the city wall. I followed it around until I reached a gate. I was cold and shivering from the water and my lips were blue. The citizens of Stabiae took pity on me, toweled me dry, and gave me some fresh linens to wear."

She lifted up her arms to show us her new wardrobe. "It's a little big."

"They offered me water and food. I asked everyone I met if they had seen any of you, but they were too overwhelmed with other refugees from Pompeii to recognize any individual. I started walking around Stabiae in the areas where they were helping stranded travelers and I was lucky enough to see Leto and that stupid stray dog of Crispus."

At that moment, she broke down and cried, and said, "Leto told me about Crispus as we were walking here. It is so terrible. He was so nice, and that boy helped saved you both on the mountain."

We all bowed our heads when we thought of Crispus and his fate on the boat. It was a few minutes before she could continue.

"Once I flagged down Leto in Stabiae, he and I hurried down to the beach and found your father still sitting there."

Marius smiled, and said, "I never gave up on her. I couldn't. I might as well die myself rather than live without her." They hugged tightly as Livia wiped her eyes. "The goddess gave me strength. I knew in my heart she would survive. I would have waited an entire day for her on that beach." He smiled brightly.

"But what of the stranger who helped you in the water?" asked Livia to her mother.

"I have not seen him, nor do I know if he still lives. Did anyone ever know his name?"

We all shook our heads negatively.

Cassia wiped away another tear and added, "This has been a terrible day for everyone. So many have lost their lives. Friends and strangers. So much kindness has been shown."

"Not by everyone. The ugliest of humanity have also shown their worst side today. Just before you arrived, a man tried to rob Livia and me with a knife."

"But you have no money." said Leto. "What did he expect to get? Were you hurt?"

I pulled the knife from my belt and showed it to him. "I'm not proud of it, but I took his knife and beat him senseless against the pavement. He didn't even get away with our food or flask of water. Something in me just went berserk, and he felt my wrath."

Leto looked back at me incredulously, and then said, "I wonder if that was the man that Hercules was barking at when he went by. The man didn't even stop to say hello, he just ran past us. The dog didn't like him very much and I was afraid Hercules would take his leg off."

Livia bent down to pet the dog and said, "We heard you barking, Hercules. You are a good judge of character."

Cassia chastised me for being rash and was glaring at me. "A man with a knife! You could have been killed! You would have left my daughter a widow. You should not be acting so hastily...so stupidly. My granddaughter needs a father. What in the name of Jupiter were you thinking?"

"I'll consider your advice thoughtfully, the next time someone pulls a knife on me."

"Ha." she said indignantly and turned around with her arms crossed.

I needed to change the subject, so I said, "Cassia said she was very tired, and so am I. We all spent a lot of energy this evening swimming to shore. It will be light soon and we will be crossing the pass over the mountain to Aequana. Perhaps we should stay here and rest or try to sleep for a couple of hours, so the light is better when we get over the mountain. I don't want anyone slipping off of the edge from fatigue."

Everyone agreed and sat back down. Dania was still coughing but at least it wasn't as loud. With the decreased pumice in the air, everyone was breathing a little easier, with the exception of Marius who was hurting badly from broken ribs. His breathing was still labored. We sat back against the cliff side and I went to sleep almost immediately.

## CHAPTER 21: BREATH OF THE GODS

I was awakened in the early morning hours by the movement of the ground. It was a pretty violent shaking and the whole mountain around us was rumbling. Marius yelled for everyone to get close to the Cliffside, in case of falling boulders from above. It only lasted for less than a minute, but it was enough for everyone to remain alarmed. The sun had not yet risen but it was light out with a magenta colored sky to the east. Visibility was surprisingly good from our vantage point. We were quite high, near the mountain pass and could look out on the bay to our left, the towns of Stabiae and Pompeii just to our right and Mt. Vesuvius in between them far off to the north. Smoke was still rising from its dome. There was also black smoke rising from both Pompeii and Stabiae, and there appeared to be a line of people on the road into Stabiae from the north. They were as small as ants from our vantage point and could not make out much more than just a line of dots. We saw it well before we heard it. Something was happening on the mountain. A thick boiling dark brown mass of dust was pouring down the side of the mountain towards the south. It looked like a huge wave of colored milk as it covered the ground and obscured everything in its path. It was moving incredibly fast, not like smoke rising from a candle, but more like water down a waterfall. We watched in horror as the cloud swallowed the area of Herculaneum around the base of the mountain and proceeded to Pompeii. Just before it reached there, we heard a deafening boom and an explosion the likes of which had never been heard in Campania. It was if the trumpets of the gods had all been blown at once. It hurt my ears and I covered them. Dania was crying loudly and everyone cowered in fear as they watched the massive rolling dark cloud approach, engulfing the tiny specks of people on the road. We very briefly heard some screams from Stabiae before everything grew incredibly quiet.

We had only a few seconds before the cloud covered the town and then seemed to roll over the beach below us and out onto the water. The cloud never reached us on the top of the mountain and instead clung to the area of the ground, reaching about two hundred pedes above the tree tops. We did feel a rush of hot wind hit our faces and everyone buried their eyes in their hands. We sat motionless for several minutes. The ground at the base of the mountain below and in front of us for several millarium was completely obscured by the dust cloud, which had yet to settle.

"Did you feel the heat in the wind?" asked Marius. "Surely that was the breath of the gods?"

"I would not have liked to be lower on the mountain. The heat of the wind was like my blacksmith's furnace. I think it would have burned my hands and face like a flame."

Leto looked pale, and said, "I still cannot see below that cloud. It is like an evil vapor that prevents one from gazing below. This is a bad omen. We should not return to Stabiae until this foul wind has dissipated. In fact, I think we should hurry to Aequana immediately, lest that cloud rise further up the mountain toward us."

We helped each other up, and Livia tried to quiet Dania, who was still fussing loudly. She finally handed the baby to her mother, who did what she could to make Dania feel better. I did not know what we had witnessed. I had never heard of anything like it in any of the old tales. It definitely came from the mountain, and I could only assume that it was some further wrath from the mountain god. I hoped that everyone in Pompeii and Stabiae were alright after that onslaught, but we could not see through the remnants of the dust cloud to see anything in the towns we had left. The sun was just coming up over the horizon. At least Apollo had not forsaken us. His chariot burned brightly in the morning air to the east. That gave me some comfort. Some of the gods may be taking their wrath out on Campania, but hopefully Apollo, Jupiter and the most powerful of the Olympians still counted us as their acolytes and allies.

We pushed up the hill for another twenty minutes before we passed a large reservoir which had several aqueducts arising from it heading down the mountain. Miraculously, they had not fallen in the earthquakes of the past few days, or the road would likely have been completely blocked. After another millarium, we finally crossed completely through the pass and onto the other side of the mountain. Here we no longer could see Stabiae or Pompeii but had a view of the vast sea in front and just ahead the large villas in the small village of Aequana.

There were no walls surrounding Aequana, and no gate. The villas that were present were generally large and extremely ornate, like those in Herculaneum. I did not know anyone who lived there, and had only passed through once when going to a job in Surrentum. I was hoping that we could find shelter for a short time until the mountain quieted (however no one had a guess how long that would be). We did not see a single person outside. There were less than fifty buildings here and only a few shops. They appeared to be closed. We knocked on several doors before someone finally answered.

"Go away. We don't take borders and I'm not buying anything." said a middle aged man in a fine tunic. He came to the door of the fourth villa we had tried. He was about to close his door, when Marius stopped him by holding the door open with his foot.

"We only would like you to answer some questions." said Marius. "We are travelers from Herculaneum and need to know where we might find shelter or work on this side of the mountain."

The man looked surprised, and replied, "Herculaneum? Then you are very lucky to be alive. The mountain has rained down chaos and ruin upon your city and several others. I have watched from my window starting yesterday and for most of the night. There has been fire and smoke from the depths of Vesuvius. Pluto has emptied the underworld and dealt his wrath on Campania. Even now, there is a deadly dark mist that blankets the valley. I think it has killed everyone it touched."

"Why won't anyone answer their doors to greet us?" asked Livia.

"This is a small enclave at the mountaintop. Many are only part time residents who summer here from Rome to escape the heat, and have already gone back to the capital city. Some are still here in their houses, but are afraid to come to the door in case you are beggars, or worse, thieves. It is still early in the morning, and many have had a terrifying night. Many believe this is the end of days, and are entrenched in their villas praying to the gods for forgiveness. None will provide you shelter here."

"How about in Surrentum?  Is there any place to sleep there?"

"If you have enough coin, there is always a place to sleep.  Surrentum was spared the fires that seem to have plagued Pompeii and Stabiae.  Here in Aequana, we still have had a little of the ash fall down from the sky.  "See the dust on the ground and on the roof of my villa?"  He picked up a pinch of pumice dust from the ground and showed it to us.

Marius laughed.  "This is a pittance of dust.  We waded through two cubits of this stuff near Stabiae, and some of it was glowing hot."

The man was intrigued, and looked at each of us in turn; examining the weathered clothes we were wearing and our haggard expressions.

"You walked from Herculaneum?" he asked, astonished.

I answered first, "My wife and I did. We have seen great horrors on our journey."

Leto answered next, "Three of us tried to sail from Herculaneum but a total of seven were capsized in the bay. We narrowly escaped with our lives to Stabiae and have walked since."

"My name is Claudius Antonius Aquilinus.  Forgive my rudeness.  There are many travelers on this road, and my neighbors and I have grown to ignore them over time. You have traveled far by boat or on foot, and obviously suffered much. Let me welcome your family into my home for a time and you can tell me what you have witnessed.  I would like to hear what is happening in the valley below.  I have seen much this night, but understood little of what was really happening."

We entered the elaborate two story villa and marveled at its opulence.  This was as grand a palace as that of Lucius in

Herculaneum, although it lacked the statuary and shelves full of artifacts. There was a beautiful mural on one wall depicting a nymph with a basket full of flowers and a dancing Pan beside her playing his flute. A giant multicolored mosaic covered the floor, almost from end to end. There was a grand staircase, which had marble and travertine covering the rail to the second floor. The corners of the room were also inlaid with marble insets in curvilinear patterns. The effect was striking, but nothing compared to the view out of his back porch, which appeared to be hanging over the mountainside overlooking the bay. We sat down in his triclinium and a servant brought us wine.

"Surrentum wine is the finest in the empire. Enjoy it as my guest."

We immediately drank the cups offered, and Marius told our host loudly that it indeed was the finest vintage he had ever tasted. The same servant followed with a plate of olives and some goat cheese.

After a few other pleasantries, Claudius pressed us to please give him the details of our journey.

We spent over an hour telling of everything we had seen since leaving Herculaneum. I didn't think it was necessary to go into our adventure with the Mithrans, so we began the story at the time after leaving Lucius' villa. We described what we saw on the road, our experience with the Menandos in Pompeii, and the harrowing events on the dock. When we came to the part about the wave and capsizing our boat, he asked each of us in turn to tell what had happened separately. When Livia finally explained how she and Dania had been

thrown upon the beach and the vessel crashed against a tree,

Claudius just sat amazed with his mouth open.

"Marius, your family is truly blessed by the gods. You each in turn have overcome tremendous hardships pitted against you, to survive and arrive at my door. I hope that a little of your luck and divine grace will rub off on me. Please stay the night in my house. My wife and I have ample room here, although you will have to stay in the servants' quarters."

"You are a most kind host, Claudius, and we gladly accept your generosity. We will clean up and be on our way tomorrow to Surrentum." answered Marius.

"Now tell me more of what you found in Stabiae?"

We told him of the generosity of its magistrate and the friendliness of the people there, and went into detail about the fires and the collapse of buildings from the earthquakes. He asked how high the ash and pumice had been and was astonished when Leto put his hand up to his mid thigh. He was most interested to hear about the terrible dark cloud that had engulfed part of the town earlier in the morning.

"Have you ever heard of such a thing? Even in the old legends?" asked Leto.

"No, but I am worried about the inhabitants of all of our towns. You said the wind reaching your face was very hot?"

"Like midday in the hottest part of the summer, and we were not anywhere near that dark cloud of vapors." answered Marius.

"It burned the skin and eyes, it was so hot." added Leto.

"It felt like the coals under a smithy's bellows."

Claudius looked at me and smiled. "Spoken like a blacksmith." I nodded.

"One or more of the gods has done great evil today, I fear." Claudius leaned back on his chair and looked outside. "It is clearer today. If the mountain does not spew rocks again, I should go into Stabiae tomorrow and see what has happened. Perhaps one of you would accompany me."

It was Leto who replied. "I would be happy to. My father has broken ribs and my mother has a bump on the head. They should proceed on to Surrentum."

"I would send for a healer for you, but I'm afraid they are all as busy as possible with the casualties in the valley. Perhaps you can find one in Surrentum. For now, rest and take comfort in my home. My wife has some talent at healing and may be of service."

At that instant, a beautiful woman with dark hair and eyes and an expensively woven robe came into the room from the stairwell.

"Ah. I see my wife has finally arisen from her sleep. Aelia, these are travelers from Pompeii. They will be staying with us until tomorrow morning."

The woman briefly showed her consternation with her husband, but immediately tried to put on a fake smile for the group. She was staring at our disheveled appearance and the dust and grime that covered our faces and arms. I could tell she thought we were too dirty to be entertaining in her living quarters. We introduced ourselves individually.

"I am sorry that I was not yet up when you arrived. I did not know we were having guests." She looked over at her husband who was trying to look away to keep from feeling the anger of her stare.

"The explosions and events of last night kept me awake until very late in the early morning hours. I only slept with the help of several glasses of wine." She looked at the pitcher of wine on the table as if she wanted another.

Cassia replied, "Mistress, I am sorry for imposing on

your hospitality. My family and I have been through great hardships this past evening, including fires, near drowning and almost being crushed by buildings and landslides. We are quite lucky to be alive. We are grateful for the shelter for the day in the servant's quarters while we try to mend our injuries. My granddaughter is sick from the journey and the protection of this house may yet save her life." She bowed low.

The statements from Livia seemed to soften the woman's attitude toward us. She looked over at the baby with pity in her eyes, and then looked back at Livia. "I am sorry that I have not been as gracious as I should have. My husband was right to offer you shelter. While here, feel free to roam the house or the grounds as you need to. I am no healer, but if there is anything I can do to help with your pains, I will try."

Cassia thanked her and Aelia sat down by her husband and we finished telling them of our journey. When we were done, Aelia suggested that we needed to bathe to get the ash off of all of us.

"There is a bathhouse only two doors down the street. My servants will take you there and you can refresh. It has not as yet been damaged by the quakes, although I don't know if there are any attendants working there today as they may have fled. The water may be a bit cold."

"You are most kind. I could really use a bath." said Livia.

We were escorted by the slaves of the house to the Aequana bathhouse down the street. The village was only two or three streets wide due to its position on the side of the hill. Although there weren't very many villas, they were all extravagant palaces that could only belong to the very wealthy. The black and white dog had been waiting patiently for us in the courtyard of Claudius' villa, and was overjoyed to see us again. He followed us down the street and waited again outside as we entered. The bathhouse was smaller than the one in Pompeii but it was very clean and highly marbled. As Aelia had suspected, there was no one working the bellows below the pools. I didn't know if Livia and Cassia were alone in the women's pool, but there was no one but Leto, Marius and I in the men's side. Marius's chest was completely black and blue. We found an amphora filled with oil, and each helped ladle the oil onto the other and to smooth it out with our hands. Leto was careful to work around his father's bruised ribs. We looked everywhere for a strigil or leather wipe to remove the oil, but we could only use the towels that were lying in the small changing room next to the suditarium. Marius tested the hot pool and found the water tepid, so we decided instead to go the larger pool in the courtyard with its mildly cool temperature. The number and variety of statues and bronzes that surrounded the notatio in the small courtyard were amazing. Virtually all of the Olympian gods and goddesses were represented. When we dipped into the water, there was a huge trail of black and grey grime that surrounded us in the water, and a thin coating of oil remained on the surface. We all laughed at how much dirt had stuck to our bodies, but I also marveled at how good the water felt. I was slightly embarrassed that we were fouling the Aequana pool, but considering what we had been through, I thought everyone would understand. There was some ash and pumice in the water anyway, despite the false roof over a portion of the courtyard protecting it from the elements above. It had likely been blown in by the winds from each side. The entire thermae appeared to be deserted. We stayed there for over an hour before we arrived back at the villa of Claudius and Aelia. Aelia had provided fresh linen tunics for us to wear, which we put on at the bathhouse. Mine was a little tight, as it belonged to one of the younger servants, but at least it was clean. Leto was also wearing one from the same servant, and his hung like a drape about him. We each made fun of the other.

It was late afternoon and while we were looking at the mountain from the porch, just before prandium, we saw another eruption of smoke and flame come from the mountain in the distance. Like earlier in the morning, we saw the explosion before we actually heard it. The force of it made the building rock on its foundations. Again a boiling dark cloud rolled down the mountain and toward Herculaneum and Pompeii, obscuring everything in its path. Marius warned us to go inside, but I stood transfixed as the cloud reached Pompeii before fizzling out and spreading towards the water. We could hear Hercules the dog howling at the top of his lungs in the front courtyard. I could just make out the outline of Stabiae far to the right in the shadow of the mountains that we were now residing on. The town was lucky to escape another exposure to the god's breath, as Marius called it. It did seem that the temperature of the air went up a little shortly after we saw the cloud, but I did not feel the hot wind, as we had on the other side of the mountain. I wondered what the hot wind felt like on the ground in the middle of that dark ominous cloud. I was pretty sure I didn't want to find out.

Aelia turned out to be a pretty competent healer herself, and helped rebandage my shoulder after applying a healing salve. She had an ample supply of herbs, and provided some to Livia to help with Dania's cough. Her herbs worked much better than those we had received in Stabiae. By late evening, Dania's cough seemed to have improved and my arm felt better. We ate heartily at the prandium meal, and had some more of the delicious wine from Surrentum. We could still see the flames of Mt. Vesuvius that night, but there did not seem to be as much ash in the air as visibility was pretty good and we could even make out the island of Capri off to our far left in the bay, which we had not seen since we arrived in Aequana.

Claudius finally asked each of us what we did for a living and upon hearing from Marius and Leto, said that there should be plenty of work for fishermen in Surrentum. He even offered to loan Marius some money to help build a new boat. As for me, he told me he had already inferred from my earlier comments that I was a blacksmith, but said there were not many horses in Surrentum, owing to the rocky terrain of the peninsula and lack of flat pasture. I did not know what I was going to do for a job once we reached our destination. I briefly mulled over the possibility of becoming a fisherman, but I quickly dismissed that notion. I was what I was.

Livia said, "Maybe they will need plumbing after all of these quakes. I'm sure many houses will need rebuilt. Especially if you go back to Stabiae."

"I thought you said you were a blacksmith?" asked Claudius.

I explained to him about my family's business and that I learned the craft of plumbum tubing from my father, Galleus.

"That is so amazing. Really, it is an incredible coincidence that you arrived at my door. I knew of your father." He smiled and pointed to one wall. "This house has Galleus plumbing. Actually most of the houses in Aequana have Galleus plumbing. Your father is a legend among the architects and homebuilders of our area. All of the villas in Aequana have cisterns on their roofs which supply the water for the houses. We do not have access to the aqueducts which supply Stabiae.

We have no one to fix them or to build the cistern pipework in new homes, since your father has died."

I had very rarely ventured south for work and never farther than Stabiae, so I was pretty surprised that my father had gone so far afield. When I thought further on it, I shouldn't have been amazed that he did so much work in Aequana. He was much more adventuresome than I, and never was that comfortable staying around the shop. His work often sent him on jobs for several weeks at a time in the countryside surrounding Campania, and even as far as Rome.

"I am very gratified that you know of my father and his work. Our family shop has continued to provide plumbing for the people of Pompeii even after his death, although I am not nearly so famous, or so skilled, as Galleus in the craft. I am afraid there will be no shop remaining, and no houses left in Pompeii to work on, after the events of the last few days. Perhaps Livia is right that there may be work in Surrentum or even Stabiae repairing the water supply."

"Once you are settled and find a place to stay in Surrentum, you send word for me. My neighbors and I will have work enough for you in Aequana for several months or more. We would love to have the son of Galleus plumb our homes here."

I did not know what to say, but I thanked him, and hoped that things would work out as he had foretold. I didn't have tools, but I supposed that was only a formality. I could get more tools if I had work waiting for me. I asked a few polite questions about the plumbing in his house and when he had met my father, but I was so preoccupied with the prospect of doing something other than becoming a fisherman, that I became distracted and completely lost track of the conversation for a few minutes. All kinds of thoughts were racing through my head at once and the future suddenly seemed wide open. Livia had to speak for me once when I failed to answer a question from Claudius. That embarrassment swept me back into the conversation. For several more minutes we talked of Surrentum and the people there. It sounded like a place I would enjoy living in.

I looked at Livia and she seemed to have relaxed. Dania had quit coughing and was sleeping soundly. My shoulder wasn't even hurting and it was no longer seeping blood. I was clean and comfortable. How rapidly things had turned around.

We sat quietly for several minutes, each person deep in thought. I walked out onto the veranda to reflect on recent events and to ponder my own fate. I silently questioned what the gods' purpose was in wreaking so much death and destruction the last few days. What greater purpose was served by the loss of so many people? Had their lives meant anything? I remembered the image of the bearded Zahret lying on the floor of the Temple of Isis. He expressed his eternal love for Vibiana and his comfort in knowing he would soon be with her forever in the afterlife. He was less bothered by his own death than he was for ensuring that she was prepared for the afterlife. It occurred to me again that it was Zahret who was responsible for my ultimate proof of innocence. It seemed ironic to me that in his death, he had been responsible for saving my life and the life of my wife. Perhaps that was enough to give his entire life purpose. Or perhaps, having another person to deeply love and care for was enough to give his death purpose. I looked through the door into the living space at Livia and smiled as she held our daughter in her arms. In that moment I realized that I too would give my life to save my wife and daughter. I thought back to the horrible evening when I found Vibiana in the temple vestibule. I considered how senseless her death had been. Then it occurred to me -- had she survived the attack from Scaevolus, it is quite possible she might have died in the mountain's ravage of Pompeii. I shuttered as I thought of how few could have survived the heated blast that we had called "the breath of the gods." Would I have died in Pompeii too, if she had not sent the message for me, and started in motion the sequence of events that led to our adventure in Herculaneum? I wondered.

My thoughts came back to the Mithran dagger and the medallion. The Egyptian priests had said the medallion had great healing powers and had belonged to Isis herself, but Blandus and Lucius had both thought that the objects were instead from the far east and had came to our land via the Persian. I didn't know what the truth was, but I didn't believe either article were objects of healing. The medallion had been associated with nothing but death since Palindus had brought it back from his exile in Egypt. Many of those dead were victims of the dagger itself. Palindus had died on the trip to Campania with the medallion in his possession, while Zahret had owned it only briefly and was stabbed to death. Vibiana had worn the medallion and was murdered. Scaevolus had taken it from Vibiana and was also now dead by the sword. Crispus had carried the medallion for only a half day, and he had drowned in the bay. Lucius had purchased both medallion and dagger, and unless through some miracle he had escaped, he now lay buried in ash at the base of Mt. Vesuvius. The medallion seemed to be cursed by the gods, and I actually felt relieved that it now lay hidden in Herculaneum for eternity. I realized I was very glad that Vibiana had never given me the medallion to examine in detail, and that Livia and I had only briefly seen or touched it. I remembered Livia holding it for only a few minutes back at her parent's house. I felt a rush of fear and foreboding knowing we had even been in the presence of the medallion. I relaxed when I realized that we had had several opportunities for death in the past few days and had survived all of them. I figured the curse of the medallion must not have passed onto either of us.

I should have been angry at Vibiana for getting my family involved in the cursed web of events surrounding the medallion and companion dagger, but I knew she would never have meant me any harm. I pitied her fate, and when I considered the tragedies of the past week, I realized her summons to me on that afternoon may actually have helped save my family. I don't know what would have happened had I still been working in my shop when the mountain erupted. Would we have stayed and become trapped in our home? We probably would not have had the chance encounter by boat with Livia's parents. That was both fortuitous and disastrous. My thoughts went immediately to the twins, Primus and Crispus, and I could feel tears welling up. They had each saved my life, and now Crispus was dead and Primus almost assuredly dead as well. I don't see how anyone in Pompeii could have survived the hot wind of the mountain. The entire town was sure to be buried in ash and rocks, even if it had not burned to the ground. I felt guilty when I considered that my family had survived while many of my friends had not. I understood what Odysseus had experienced when he survived his great ordeals and vanquished his enemies in the age of heroes, only to lament the death of innocent friends and family. The fates could be cruel.

I reflected back on the last few days and realized how dependent humans are on each other for their own survival. I wondered if the gods had a hand in directing our fate, or whether they simply watched in amusement and bewilderment as we played like game pieces on a board as they set events in motion. Rather than divine intervention, I wondered if instead, it could have been pure luck that accounted for our survival. Even before the mountain blew up, each decision we made, and each event that transpired had altered our destiny in some way. I could attribute our successful journey to chance encounters with a host of individuals over the last few days. With or without meaning to, each of these interactions had set me on a course that had ultimately resulted in my standing on a veranda in a villa in Aequana, while the city of my home burned in flame. Even the vile Scaevolus had played a part in my survival. Those deadly encounters with the murderer had bestowed upon me resolute courage. I pondered whether the gods had given me that strength, and if so, which one I should credit for that heavenly gift of courage. I said a quiet but brief prayer of thanks to Jupiter, Venus and Vulcan each in turn. That new found sense of bravery had empowered me to survive near-drowning, face down an attacker and had pushed me continuously onward in order to save my family from ruin, while others cowered in their homes. This feeling of confidence in the face of adversity, and the sense of accomplishment and perseverance must be what it felt like to be a soldier in battle.

I wondered what Gallianus would say when we would meet again. I think I agree with Livia, when she said he would be proud of me. I still didn't know how I would react if I had to face the barbarian hordes from Britannia coming at me with weapons raised. However, I was no longer in awe of my brother's ability to stare down fear and act with valor. For the first time in my life, I felt like I was his equal. I hoped my father was proud of me too, peering up at my family from Pluto's halls.

After a few more hours, the entire group sat down with Claudius and Aelia and we enjoyed our evening prandium meal. The talk around the table was lively and we were all kept in good spirits. The mountain seemed to have quieted itself. There were no further explosions that evening and the rain of ash and pumice seemed to have ended. For the first time in three nights, I slept soundly, with Livia next to me, and our baby on a pillow nearby. When I would awake the next day, I hoped to start the trek to Surrentum, to begin a new life. Perhaps in a week or month or a year, I could return to Pompeii and see what had befallen my home, friends and fellows. I did not know what the future would bring to me or my family, but I knew I would never again be the same person that I was only four days ago. I had found something inside myself that I never guessed was there.

Ken Frazier

*Glossary:*

Aedile – low level bureaucrat in Roman society working in government administration

Amphitheatre - The giant stadium complex where gladiatorial bouts were staged in Pompeii. A very large building, but somewhat less impressive than the similar coliseum in Rome.

Balteus – thick belt of a roman soldier, can handle the weight of a sword

Cella – main chamber of a temple, usually where the statue of the deity is placed. May be in front of the sanctuary or inner sanctum

Cenae or Coena– This was dinner and the main meal of the day in the ancient Roman world. It started around 3 or 4 PM and could last several hours if guests were attending. Wealthy Romans ate this meal reclined on soft couches or triclinium, but poorer families ate at more typical tables with chairs or stools.

Cinculum – thin belt of a roman soldier; has attached pteruges.

Cubit – length of measure equal to about 1½ feet or about 45 cm

Delubrum – the actual building, not the sacred section of a temple. This is the term most Pompeiians would use for talking about the structure of their temple, somewhat like

Christians might talk about a rectory or "chapel" rather than their "church."

Denarii – silver coins; 25 denarii are equal to one gold aureus coin

Digitii – a unit of measure in the ancient Roman world, equal to about 2 cm. An uncia is about an inch or 2.5 cm,

Dupondii – bronze coins; 2 dupondii are equal to a sestertius, another bronze coin;  4 sestertii are equivalent to a silver coin, the denarii

Duovir – one of two senior magistrates of a Roman colony, elected annually, who preside over the Decurion council of the town. Often report directly to a senior magistrate or governer.

Effete - Prostitutes in the ancient roman world were made up of several classes. The effete class served a very distinguished clientele and were able to charge the most money. There were generally only a small number of these in a village or town and were held in generally high regard. Prostitutes of the plebeian class were less expensive, catered to the masses and were well treated as well.  Most of the prostitutes in a given city were of the slave class and had meager surroundings, poor furnishings and their wages went largely to their owners.  They were not shunned or made illegal, as in present day, but did not share the advantages of working women in the higher classes.

Fratres and patres- literally the fathers and brothers of Mithra; these are what the cult followers called each other, which may have eventually led to catholic priests similarly being called brothers.

Frentarii and triarii - are types of elite soldiers within the Roman legions, who could be citizens or foreign mercenaries, but who had tactical skill and were each used in specific ways in battle.

Frigidarium – cold pool in the bathhouse complex

Gladius – is the bronze sword used commonly by the Roman legions. It has a short straight blade and comes to a sharp point. The grip is bordered by a round or square metal pommel which can be used as a blunt instrument like a hammer.

Hobby horse - a type of short, well muscled, strong-backed horse with thick necks that were derived from the Turkmene breed of horses in Persia. They were favored by the Romans for their pacing gait, and were raced in carriages in the coliseum and hippodrome.

Hospitium – There were no inns or hotels in Pompeii or Rome, but citizens travelling on vacation could stay in each other's villas on a rotating basis. This was the ancient equivalent of time sharing or house sitting and these vacation rentals were called Hospitia.

Lorica Segmentata – This type of armor can be made of metal or leather and composes the chest piece and shoulder pauldrons for the Roman soldier. It is made in overlapping strips or segments of either metal or leather, and extends down almost to the navel.

Klinia- couch which had two or three separate sections and usually surrounded a table. People reclined on these while dining.

Macellum – market place in ancient Pompeii located on the northeast side of the forum across from the great temple.

Millarium is 5000 pedes, or about a mile

Notatio - A large swimming pool within the bathhouse complex, often located in the courtyard.

Palaestra – A public gymnasium in the Roman world, particularly for boxing and wrestling, but also for other physical sports.

Pallium – dress robe, usually of white, worn over a toga for formal occasions by patrician romans.

Pannonia -- modern day Hungary: The ancient fortress of Aquinicum is at the site of Obuda or modern day Budapest.

Pes (plural = pedes) a length of measure that is equal to approximately one foot or about 30 cm. A cubit or cubitus is 1 ½ pedes or 45 cm.

Plumbum – in modern parlance, this is known as lead, but the atomic symbol still refers to its ancient name, Pb. The white layer on the inside of Pompeii's lead pipes is calcium buildup, which actually protected its citizens from lead poisoning.

Prandium - a lunch or late brunch often eaten around mid-day

Pteruges – strips of leather that hang vertically from the belt of a roman soldier and over his tunic.

Quadroportico de teatre: This was the Pompeii square which was adjacent to the entertainment complex (which included the Teatro grande and teatro picolo, two theaters in ancient Pompeii that were the stages for plays, concerts and occasional gladiatorial bouts). The quadroportico was an open atrium surrounded by colonnaded porticos on 4 sides which gave it its name.

Sestertii – bronze coins, worth more than dupondii but less than denarii

Strigil – instrument for scraping oil from the skin prior to bathing

Sudarium – hot pool for bathing or soaking in the bathhouse complex

Tessera – individual cube shaped marble or stone tiles that make up a mosaic when applied together

Thermae – bathhouse complex where both men and women in the Roman world would gather and bathe

Triclinium – dining area in a roman household, usually with a table and surrounded by three banqueting couches (klinia)

Vestibule – entrance hallway to a temple

Via- is an avenue in Pompeii, often 2 lanes to allow for 2 horse cart passage.

Vicolo- is a smaller street and a single lane. It may accommodate one way cart traffic.

Titus of Pompeii

# ABOUT THE AUTHOR

Dr. Ken Frazier is an internationally recognized pathologist and toxicologist with a passion for history and science. He has authored over seventy articles for scientific journals on topics related to human and veterinary medicine. He travels extensively and is a fencing and swordfighting enthusiast.

Made in the USA
Middletown, DE
22 May 2015